"Between Hello and Goodbye"

The Soundtrack To My Life trilogy
Book two

Jody Clark

DEDICATION

For all my family & friends.
Especially Erica and Owen for their endless support and encouragement!

ACKNOWLEDGMENTS

Thanks to Fairlee Anderson for the cover design.
Thanks to Corey Cain Photography for the cover postcard photo.
Thanks to Owen Clark for the cover concept.

Although the characters, dialogue, and scenes are loosely based on
the author's experiences, make no doubt about it —
this book is a work of fiction!

I'm sure there were many times I probably took my summers at
York Beach for granted, but looking back on it now, I am so very
fortunate to have grown up in such a beautiful place!

For Tony, Jason, Tim, Ian, and all the *summer friends* who have come
in & out of my life over the years.
No matter how long or short the friendships—
you've all left a handprint on my life!

1

"WAITING FOR MY REAL LIFE TO BEGIN" – Colin Hay

With the *Empty Beach* I brought you back to the summer of 1995, but with this book, I'm fast-forwarding to the summer of 1999. Looking back, most of my summers just seemed to blur and fade into one another, but 1999 was definitely a stand-alone summer.

I suppose a lot of things have stayed the same since 1995. The beach was still the beach, and the heart of its season still ran from Memorial Day through Labor Day with Columbus Day marking the official end to most of the beach businesses.

The Fun-O-Rama was still a noisy haven for families and teeny boppers alike. To be honest, I hadn't stepped foot in there in two full summers. I could only assume the foosball table was still the hub for boys trying to impress the cute summer chicks.

The Goldenrod was still the salt water taffy king of southern Maine, maybe even all of New England. And yes, the tourists still flocked like taffy zombies and pressed their faces into the front window to watch it being made.

In '99, Pizza by Paras was still the spot for a great slice of pepperoni pizza and a tune on the jukebox.

And then there was York's Wild Kingdom and Amusement Park, which was also completely and totally the same. Well, so I've heard anyway. I hadn't stepped foot in there since the infamous Elise date back in '95. My lack of patronage to the amusement park had less to do with Elise and more to do with not really having a good reason to go there anymore. If my friends and I wanted amusements, we either hit Canobie Lake Park in Salem, New Hampshire or Fun Town (Splashtown) USA up in Saco, Maine.

Ever since the summer of '95 ended, I pretty much put the entire Short Sands area in my rear view mirror. Once again, this had less to do with Elise and more to do with several other factors.

1. By the time 1999 rolled around, I was knocking on the door of turning 30 years old.

2. By the time 1999 arrived, almost every one of my summer friends had moved on and moved away, and the ones that were still around were married with kids. So, the idea of spending the summer hitting the beach or foosballing it at the Fun-O-Rama were long since gone.

3. I felt like I had outgrown the novelty of Short Sands; maybe even York Beach in general.

Because most of my friends had moved away, I rarely went out on the town anymore. I'm not sure if they were still doing quarter night at the Aqua Lounge, or nickel night at Captain

Nicks, but either way, I was getting too old for that scene. (I did mention I was almost the big three zero, right?) Going out drinking four or five nights a week was definitely a younger man's game. And speaking of games, by the time the summer of '99 rolled around, even the beach basketball courts had been relegated to shoot-around status only. Besides the occasional one-on-one battle with Doug, I hadn't played a full court game down there in years. I did mention I was pounding on the door of turning thirty, right?

After the 1995 summer season was over, I never again worked at Murphy's restaurant. The next three summers leading up to 1999, I ran a popular beach store up on Long Sands Beach called The Oceanside Store.

Anyway, this story really got started on July 13, 1999. I was in my car parked up at the Nubble Lighthouse, and before your mind gets too far in the gutter, I was there by myself. It was in the morning, so even if I was there with a female, I'm sure nothing too racy would have been happening.

As usual, the parking lot was packed, and also as usual, I was one of the only cars there with Maine plates. It had been a long time since I'd been up there, but for whatever reason that day, I needed some lighthouse-thinking-time.

As the waves crashed into the rocks, and as the Smashing Pumpkin's *Adore* CD played on my radio, I had a very intense internal (at times external) conversation with myself. It went something along the lines of this:

When you're twelve, you can't wait to turn thirteen, a teenager. I remember the word itself, "teenager," conjured up feelings of… well, I'm not really sure what it conjured up, but I do remember how I couldn't wait to be one. Maybe it had to do with having more freedom, or the fact that you get your driver's license as a teenager.

Of course, soon after you become a teen, you then start looking forward to turning eighteen, because in your head, eighteen equals adulthood. No more high school… no more rules… adulthood!

Although, if you still live with your parents and don't have any real bills then the whole eighteen/adulthood thing doesn't mean jack shit. It's at that point your attention immediately switches to the next huge milestone—the big twenty-one!!!

The excitement and anticipation for twenty-one far outweighed the previous age-milestones. It's not like you hadn't drank yet, but there's nothing like the taste of your first legal beer.

Fun fact: my first legal beer was at a bar in Kittery called Norton's, which was a great live local band venue. I believe the bands that were playing that night were Fly Spinach Fly and Thanks to Gravity.

From that point on, your twenties go by just like that. The once aspired-to feeling of adulthood begins to take shape and rear its ugly head. Real responsibilities… consequences for your actions… they are all on full display.

A lot of times, we find ourselves working jobs we hate, and getting paid far too little and drinking far too much. Then there's the drunken stupors, one night stands, love gained then lost, and yes, the more than occasional broken heart. Not to mention, that giant group of friends that once surrounded you is now down to a handful at best.

I think a lot of us (or maybe just me) have this timetable in our heads; of when we'll get married, when we'll have kids, and what we'll be when we grow up, and more importantly, what we'll be like when we get there.

The next thing you know, you're kicking down the door of turning thirty. Thirty: the first milestone-age we do NOT want to reach. You start to examine your accomplishments, or in my case, lack thereof. Almost every box on my timetable list still remained unchecked.

As I sat there in my car that day, I realized I would be turning the dreaded thirty in exactly six months. What the fuck age can I look forward to now? Sixty-five? Retirement? AARP eligibility? It felt like from here on out, that dark cloud that had been following me, just kept getting bigger and darker. It was one ominous mother fucking cloud for sure.

Anyway, that was the conversation I had with myself up at the Nubble that day. I probably could have stayed up there longer and continued to wallow underneath my imaginary black cloud, but I had a coffee date with Jane to get to. Yup, the infamous Jane Wheeler; the girl who always found her way back into my life and back into my heart.

Just to refresh your memory: Jane and I met back in the summer of 1990, and although we immediately hit it off, and although there was an obvious sexual spark, we never acted on it until the final night of summer. After that, each of us went our separate ways with both of us assuming the other thought it was a no-feelings-attached-one-night-stand.

By the time our true feelings were revealed, it was a year later and Jane was in a relationship with some dude named Brandon. Their relationship didn't last long, but from that point on, our timing would always be off.

Our friendship remained strong. Our sexual attraction remained obvious, but for whatever reason, our timing was always, always off. It was usually a case of me being single but she was not, or vice versa. And then, of course, there was her job. I think her job and her lifestyle were the main reasons we never got together.

If you remember from *The Empty Beach* book, in the summer of '95, Jane took a job in London for some small-time record company. Her job was to follow some of their bands around as their official photographer. Her pictures were used for promotional type shit, I guess.

In the summer of 1997 that all changed. The record company disbanded, and she ending up back in York Beach at her parents' summer house. Things also changed regarding our seven year stretch of *bad timing*.

By July of '97, things between us finally clicked and fell into place. It only took a few weeks for us to be considered an item... a thing... a real couple. Technically, I guess it took seven years and three weeks, but either way, it was perfect.

I think that by us remaining close friends over the years really helped. The speedbumps that naturally arise for new couples were non-existent for us. Like I said, it was perfect. Perfect communication, perfect sex, perfect time together, and worth mentioning twice—perfect sex.

After all of those years of saying *if only*, it finally paid off and came to fruition, and the end result was even better and happier than I could have imagined. I was smart enough not to reveal this to Jane too soon, but there wasn't a doubt in my mind that she was the one. The one!

Labor Day came and Labor Day went. The tourists were here and then they were gone. But unlike most Septembers, I wasn't left with just an empty beach. Well, I guess I was... but I had Jane there to share it with. September of 1997 turned out to be the best September ever!

Then October happened.

An old contact and friend that Jane had met over the years, reached out to her and offered her a job. It was for some travel magazine. Not like Maine travel or U.S. travel—it was a world travel magazine.

When this happened, Jane was in the process of moving in with me. From the moment she told me about the offer, I knew this was her dream job. I'd like to tell you I did the admirable thing and told her to take it, but I didn't. I was selfish. I had waited far too long for our timing to be right, and I had no intention of letting a job offer take that away.

To be fair, she did ask me for my honest feelings towards the job offer. So, I was honest. And selfish. Selfishly honest.

What if the job doesn't work out? What if we never get the timing right again?

These are some of the things I pointed out to her. Ultimately, it was Jane's choice, and she chose to forego the job offer and stay in York and continue our relationship. I repeat, this was *her* choice. I did not force her to stay.

She stayed because she wanted us to work just as much as I did. I knew she loved me, but I guess I also knew how much she really wanted that job. I should have done the unselfish thing and let her go, and by *let her go*, I don't mean *allowed* her to go, I mean let her go from my heart. But I didn't, and our relationship and friendship would pay dearly for that a couple of months later.

2

"SHE GOES ON" – Crowded House

When I was done talking to myself up at the Nubble, I drove up the beach towards the harbor. My nerves started to get the best of me. This would be the first time Jane and I saw each other since it all ended nineteen months earlier. We had talked and written letters over the past few months, but this would be our first face to face.

There's a line in the movie *Cocktail* with Tom Cruise which states, "Everything ends badly, otherwise it would never end." I'm not so much of a cynic to think this is always the case, but it did ring true in many of my relationships, and Jane was no exception.

By the time that summer of '99 rolled around, Jane and I were in a better place than the previous nineteen months, but make no doubt about it, when it ended in 1997, it ended badly.

I'm sure it's the same for girls, but for us guys, it would be much easier if the girls who broke our hearts turned out to be fat, ugly slobs with bad body odor.

Unfortunately, this would not be the case. Jane looked the same, better actually. Oh, and she smelled fucking amazing too. I had plenty of time to take in her scent, for our embrace lasted longer than the embraces of most old friends.

I met Jane at the local hotspot, Rick's All-Season Restaurant down in York Village. By the time we got our coffees, my nerves had completely subsided. Like always, it was as if no time had passed between us. We were laughing and talking just like old times. That summer of '99 was the ninth summer Jane and I had known each other, and we rarely ever had awkward or uncomfortable moments. I always fuckin' loved that! Don't get me wrong, there was still a little weirdness having a platonic face to face with someone who you used to have sex with— lots of sex with.

Back when we dated in the summer of '97, there were many times I thought my dick was going to fall off we were having so much sex… great sex. I was utterly confident if there was ever a police line-up for boobs, I could pick hers out in a second! Okay, so maybe there was a tad bit of awkwardness sitting across from her drinking coffee, but mostly it was comfortable; comfortably awkward, if you will.

As the summer rain continued to fall outside, we continued to laugh and talk over coffee. It was so great to see her again, but I have to admit, the disintegration of our relationship nineteen months earlier, still hung in the air. It wasn't prevalent, but it was still there.

So, what happened to us back in '97? How did it end?

Well, like I said, Jane turned down the job offer and moved in with me as planned, and for a while things were good. After the Oceanside Store closed for the season, Doug got me a job in the kitchen at the bar he worked at in Portsmouth.

I think that's when it started going downhill for us. Not because of my job, but because Jane was forced to look for a job around here. To my knowledge, that was the first winter Jane had actually remained in the York area. I think the more she saw what was available for work around here, the more she regretted not taking her dream job.

I saw this weighing on her, but I did nothing about it. Nothing. I basically stuck my head in the sand and pretended all was perfect. I told myself she would eventually get past this.

She didn't.

She ended up taking some shitty waitressing job, and a few days after Thanksgiving, she finally hit her breaking point. She sat me down and we had *the talk*. She let me know in no uncertain terms that she loved me, but... (there's always a fucking but, isn't there?)

The gist of her talk were things I knew all too well. The small seaside town of York, Maine (especially in the winter) just didn't cut it for someone needing to spread their wings, and neither did working at a dead-end waitressing job.

This time, I didn't try to convince her otherwise. I knew she needed to fly away. So, as we had *the talk*, I just sat there, politely nodding and supportively smiling, all the while my heart was breaking. If this was how our relationship ended, it would have sucked, but eventually, I would have dealt with it.

But this wasn't how it ended.

After our talk, Jane contacted her friend, only to find out the job offer was filled and officially off the table. Over the next few weeks, her disappointment turned into bitterness... bitterness towards us... towards me.

I shit you not when I tell you, Jane and I never fought or argued. Up to that point, we had our disagreements but even that was minimal. Over the next few weeks, the weather wasn't the only thing that grew colder. She shut down and shut me out, and whenever I tried to talk to her or tried to cheer her up, she would lash out at me.

You know the saying, *never go to bed angry*? Well, if that was the case, we would have never gone to bed for three weeks.

On Dec. 19, 1997, Jane moved out and Jane moved on. She went to live with some old college friends in NYC. She eventually landed a photography job that allowed her to travel. It was relegated to U.S. travel and not the world, but she loved it, and why wouldn't she, she was no longer stuck here in fuckin' Maine... York fuckin' Maine.

In time, we started talking again. At first, it was strictly letters, but eventually, it worked its way up to phone calls. So the fact that we were sitting face to face laughing and talking again, was huge. It certainly wasn't where our relationship was two years earlier, but after all that had transpired, I would take it.

"I'm sorry I haven't seen you since I got into town. I've had so much family shit to catch up on, ya know? Four days in town is never enough time to see everybody." she said.

"It's okay, I understand." I said. "How are your parents doing? I see them sitting on the porch sometimes when I drive by."

"Ah yes. They love sitting on the porch people watching. You should totally stop in and see them. They would love that. You were always one of their favorites."

Is it me, or does it kind of suck when your ex tells you that her parents love you? I suppose it's better than them hating my guts, but I would have gladly traded all of that for *her* to still love me.

"So how's your new job?" she asked.

"Um, different, that's for sure, but in a good way. It's a lot more relaxed than the beach store or the restaurant biz."

"I still can't believe Doug has his very own bar," she laughed. "I mean, he always told us he would, but—"

(More on Doug's new biz venture later)

"He also told us he was going to quit his job and train to be a Nascar driver," I pointed out.

Jane laughed. "Oh my God, I totally remember that! That was like the first summer I met you guys, I think. He couldn't even beat me on the go-carts at York's Wild Kingdom."

"He couldn't beat anyone there," I said. "He was awful."

"What made him want to be a race car driver again?" she asked.

"I think part of it was because the idiot held the high score on Pole Position at the Fun-O-Rama, but the bigger part was Doug seeing the movie *Days of Thunder* at the York Beach Cinema."

"Ah yes," she laughed, "I forgot Doug was a big Tom Cruise fanatic."

"Don't even get me started about *Top Gun*," I said, shaking my head.

We finished our coffees and I paid the bill.

"When are you leaving?" I asked.

"I fly out of Boston tomorrow morning."

"Where to this time?"

"Chicago for a few weeks and then I'm not sure," she said.

There were definitely times I envied her lifestyle and all of her adventures. There's something liberating about not knowing where you would be in a few weeks.

I smiled and shook my head at her. "You're like a hummingbird. You're constantly moving and fluttering your wings but never stay in one place for too long."

She returned my smile and grasped my hand, and said, "Who knows, maybe one day."

That my friends, was my life in a nutshell; always waiting for one day. Whether it was Jane, some other girl, or my career, it always seemed like I was waiting for my real life to begin.

"You should swing by the bar tonight. Doug and I will be there until close."

"I have a dinner thing with my parents and cousins, but I think my wings could flutter their way in for a drink or three," she smiled.

As I walked her to her car, she asked, "How are things going with that Felicia girl?"

"Eh, it is what it is," I shrugged.

"Sounds like my dating motto as well."

From day one, Jane and I have always been able to say anything to each other. Whether it was about a girl I was interested in or a guy she was into. Don't get me wrong, sexual details were off the table. She never revealed that stuff, nor did I want to know. My imagination did very well to cover those images, thank you very much!

Although, knowing my vivid imagination, I probably exaggerated what really transpired with Jane and other guys. I mean, there was no way she could really be having the Best Sex Ever with every guy, right? Right??

Due to Jane's travel schedule and her free-spirited nature, the longest relationship she had since me was only five weeks, which was two and a half weeks longer than mine. That would be Felicia. More on her in a bit.

I will say this about Jane, usually the biggest fear for me with girls I'm interested in is for them to have eyes for another guy. That was always secondary with Jane. I was always more worried about her having eyes for the next big career or travel opportunity.

We pulled out of Rick's parking lot and went our separate ways. Again. I felt a little sad, but mostly relieved. Our face to face went better, much better than I expected. I crossed my fingers that Jane would make an appearance at the bar that night.

3

"CONFETTI" – Lemonheads

Okay, back to my two and a half week romance with Felicia. I met her exactly six months earlier… January 13, 1999… my birthday. Like most recent birthdays, I wanted nothing to do with celebrating it, and like most recent birthdays, Doug was ALL about celebrating it.

When I woke up that fateful birthday morning, Doug had let himself in and proceeded to steal all of my Depression Session mixes. Major douchebag move! He was bound and determined to make that day about celebrating and drinking (not necessarily in that order). It didn't really take much for Doug to find a reason to celebrate and drink. Let's just say, Flag Day last year was out of control.

I knew his heart was in the right place, so I reluctantly joined in on celebrating my twenty-ninth day of birth. Besides, I kind of owed him one for bailing on New Year's Eve. We were supposed to go down to Boston and ring in the New Year at one of the big clubs on Landsdowne Street, but I was in a little funk and didn't really feel like going out.

In my experience, New Year's Eve was always an overrated night and was never as fun as anticipated. That being said, I did regret not going out that night. Ever since I heard the classic Prince song – "1999," I'd been waiting to one day party like it was actually 1999.

Because I bailed on him, Doug ended up at some lame house party over in Kittery instead of Boston. He never forgave me for that, so when he told me he was taking me out for my birthday, I couldn't really refuse.

Our celebration took us into Portsmouth and we made our way from bar to bar; from the Gaslight to the Brewery to the State Street Saloon and everywhere in between.

Don't tell Doug this, but the night was actually pretty fun. We ran into a lot of old friends, including a couple of co-workers from back in my DJ days at Goodnight Ogunquit. Big Mo was manning the door at one of the bars, and behind the bar was bartender extraordinaire, Siobhan O'Hare.

One of the early highlights that night was watching Doug trying to get Siobhan's digits. She rejected him not once, but four times. Do you know that saying, *it takes nine no's to get one yes*? Well, Doug was thoroughly testing that theory out.

Another highlight was when Doug challenged Big Mo to an arm wrestling match. There was a reason he was called Big Mo. He stood nearly a foot taller than Doug and weighed as much as both of us combined. Big Mo was used to Doug's drunken antics and laughed off his silly challenge. His laughter turned into a huge smile when Doug threw down a fifty spot.

Fun Fact: This would go down in the Guinness World Book of records as "The easiest bet ever won" and also as "The dumbest bet ever made."

Even though Doug did his best imitation of Sylvester Stallone from the movie *Over the Top*, he was no match for Big Mo, who nearly put Doug's hand through the table. Doug laughed it off and gave Mo a big *I love you, man* hug, but Doug's hand was seriously crushed.

At one point, he had to ask Siobhan for a towel full of ice for his hand. And yes, he used that opportunity to ask her out again. I think his exact words were, "Can you think of anything better than having wild hot sex on a cold winter's night?"

She then handed him a second towel of ice.

"What's that for? You already gave me one," he said, motioning to the towel of ice on his hand.

"I know," she smiled. "But I'm thinking your blue balls are gonna need this one tonight."

Score one for the bartender extraordinaire.

To this day, however, Doug swears that if he would have just changed his phrasing from "having wild hot sex" to "making sweet love" that she would have said yes. And he wonders why we call him an idiot.

Sorry, I'm getting off topic here, so I'll cut to the chase. At some point that night, Doug and I met two girls, Felicia and Kristen. Felicia and I immediately hit it off. We had so many things in common, like movies, and music, and… well, I guess that was it, but it felt like an amazing connection.

Doug and Kristen also had things in common, like wanting one-night-stand-sex. In less than thirty minutes, they hailed a cab and were headed back to her place.

Not to be outdone, I also had sex that night, but it wasn't until after Felicia and I had talked and laughed well into the night. It started out as kissing and *stuff* in her car, but by the time we got back to my place, it had graduated to sex… and *stuff*.

She wasn't the first sex I had since Jane and I broke up, but she was the first one that I felt something more for. Neither of us had to work the next day, so we stayed in my apartment all day listening to great tunes and watching cheesy 80's movies. Happy birthday to me!

It took a couple of weeks for us to put a label on things, but when we did, the label read: "exclusive relationship". By then, Jane and I were talking again, and it kind of felt good to tell her about Felicia. Not that I was trying to rub it in her face, not at all.

One of Doug's theories is: "You can't totally get over someone until you find someone else." Actually, his precise wording might have been, "The best way to get over someone is to bang someone else." Whether it was dating Felicia, or banging her, I definitely felt like I was finally getting over Jane.

Unfortunately for me, two and a half weeks later, the exclusive relationship label completely wore off. Felicia decided exclusivity wasn't for her, and long story short, I spent the next six months trying to change her mind and win her back. Trust me, I'm well aware of the patheticness of that, and I'm also aware that patheticness is not a word.

4

"NOTHING LASTS FOR LONG" – The Samples

After I left my coffee date with Jane, I decided to head back to my apartment to take care of a few important things. And by important things, I mean I had to check my answering machine to see if Felicia called. I know I said earlier "it is what it is," but constantly checking my answering machine was part of that motto.

After I left Murphy's restaurant back in '95, I moved out of Doug's place and landed a sweet winter rental directly on the beach. My apartment was located up on Long Sands Beach across the street from the bath house. My landlord also owned the Oceanside Store directly next to my apartment.

One thing led to another, and not only did my winter rental become a year round rental, but they offered me the opportunity to run their store during the summers. It was more of a beach store than a full-on restaurant. The food was strictly take-out. It was definitely a different dynamic than I was used to, but the whole thing was a welcomed change.

Doug was a good roommate, but I thoroughly enjoyed living on my own. It was also nice getting away from the Short Sands scene. Like I said earlier, our days of shooting hoops, hitting the Fun-O-Rama, and scouring the beach for summer chicks had long since run its course (for me, not Doug).

On the rare occasion when a few of us got together, it was always in downtown Portsmouth. The bars and restaurants there provided more of an adult scene than that of the beach.

For a couple years, I got back into DJing at a club in Portsmouth, but even that ran its course. The key to being a good DJ is to be able to keep up and adapt with the changing times and musical trends. What can I say, I like what I like. If you're forced to play shit you hate, the gig gets old very fast. The "Macarena"??? Pfft, no gracias!

So, considering Jane was in the process of leaving town (again), and considering there were zero messages on my machine (again), and considering it was a cloudy, drizzly day outside, it would probably have been the perfect day to crank up some of my Depression Session mixes and crawl back into bed, but I didn't. I decided to head into work a little early.

Oh, by the way, that summer of '99, I was no longer working at the Oceanside Store. After three summers working there ('96-'98), I decided to take another job offer. I decided to head back down to good ol' Short Sands. I know, I know, I just got finished telling you how much I was DONE with that area. The only reason I decided to head back down there and work is... well, I got sweet-talked into it.

No, I was not going back to Murphy's restaurant. It was a completely different crew from when I was last there, and as far as I knew, Todd was still leasing the place from Mrs.

Murphy. Sadly, Mr. Murphy passed away back in February from a heart attack. I was in Florida at the time visiting my dad, so I wasn't able to attend his funeral. I'd been meaning to stop in and see Todd but something always came up. That's actually not true. I had plenty of opportunities to pop in, but ever since my final summer working there, I felt weird about going back. And now, knowing that old man Murphy had passed away, I just figured it'd be too eerie to go visit.

What was this place I got sweet-talked into working? It was a new bar in Short Sands called Here Hey Hoohahs. It was located where the Golden Fortune Cookie used to be. Mr. Wong called it quits at the end of '98, and he and his wife went back to China to be closer to their families. Personally, I think he decided to follow Sting around on his world tour.

As much as I'd like to explain the origin of the name Here Hey Hoohahs, I'm not sure I understood it myself. Who would come up with such a silly name for a bar? You guessed it—one of my long-time friends, Doug Andrews.

Just like he predicted all those years ago, Doug indeed, now owned his own bar. Apparently, one of his uncles came into some money, and when Doug heard that Mr. Wong was leaving, he put his long-time plan into motion. His uncle loaned him the start-up money, but he is not a business partner. That position was offered to me, but I politely turned Doug down. Owning a bar was always his dream, not mine. Don't get me wrong. I was flattered that he offered me to be his partner, but I basically turned it down for two reasons.

1. I didn't have any money to bring to the table, and even though Doug had no problem with that, it still didn't feel right to me.

2. The bigger reason was I couldn't see myself co-owning a bar for the foreseeable future. I didn't want him to make me a

partner only to see me walk away a year later. I still didn't know what I wanted to do with my friggin' life, and I didn't want to feel guilty for ending the partnership a year or so in.

I was however, definitely due for a change, and the thought of a non-restaurant job was very appealing, and I knew, at the very least, with Doug as my boss, I would constantly be amused and entertained… slightly annoyed, but entertained.

Again, as far as the bar's name is concerned, I'll let Doug tackle that explanation later. If you read *The Empty Beach*, you'll remember that the Golden Fortune Cookie was a cozy, but small space. Seeing as Doug wasn't going to serve food, we knocked out the wall that separated the restaurant from the kitchen. We gutted the kitchen and utilized its space. Eventually, Doug was hoping to get some live bands in there.

I have to admit, it was pretty fun spending the winter helping him renovate the place, and I actually loved how it turned out. He wanted a beach-themed sports bar with great background music. Every corner of the bar had a speaker, which was held inside lobster traps. Driftwood frames held pictures of classic Boston sports stars. It might sound tacky, but it came out very cool.

Besides bartending, Doug put me in charge of his bookkeeping, but the real selling point for me deciding to work for him that summer was being in charge of all things music. You have to remember, back in '99 we were still years away from satellite radio or Pandora. That being the case, I was more than happy to make a shit-ton of mix CDs for the business.

That's right, technology had allowed me to graduate from tapes to CDs. It was a much easier and faster process, but still, there's something not-as-cool or nostalgic about holding a mix CD versus a mixtape. That in a nutshell was probably why I was always the last of my friends to embrace technology. I was the last one to switch from tape deck to CD, I was the last one to get a computer, and in the future, I would be one of the last ones to get a cell phone.

I will say, that particular summer of '99, I did discover the absolute best technological advance ever for DJs and mixtape/CD makers like myself. It was a company called Napster. Back in my DJ days, I was spending 20 to 30 bucks a week on a handful of new songs, but with this thing called Napster, I was able to download those same songs for free! I would have downloaded even more, but I had a super-slow dial-up and half the time my downloads would timeout because of the slow connection.

Like all good things in life, Napster was short-lived and came to an end a couple years later, but not before my music collection grew by about 5,000 songs. If the music police are reading this right now, this is the part of the book that is 100% fiction, so don't even think about suing me for royalty infringement!

Anyway, back to Here Hey Hoohahs. Seeing as the place no longer served food, we opened from early afternoon through 1 AM. This would have been the perfect job back in my early twenties; sleep in late, still get to hit the beach for a bit, then go to work. But considering that I was almost thirty, and practically over the hill, I found myself waking up early with zero desire to hit the beach at all.

As you can tell, I was totally over the whole summer York beach scene. If I didn't have such a reasonable monthly rent situation, I would gladly have moved out of town.

When I got to work that day, it was still a little before opening. Doug was already there, beer in hand, sitting at the bar watching *Sportscenter*.

"Hey bro, you're here early. I thought you were in later this afternoon?" he said.

"Yea, but I didn't feel like sitting around my apartment all day."

"Did you see the game last night?" he asked, pointing to the highlights on the TV. "Pedro had fifteen fucking strikeouts. I'm telling ya, this is their year!"

"I caught some of it," I said. "I think I dozed off in the fifth inning."

Doug shook his head and said, "I'm not sure what's worse, the fact that you fell asleep during a Pedro start, or that you stayed home on your night off."

"What can I say, that's what happens when you're almost thirty… as in six months away… exactly six months today."

"Oh for fuck's sake! We're not doing this the rest of the year, are we?"

I just shrugged, knowing full-well there was a good possibility I would indeed be doing this the rest of the year.

"Please tell me this doesn't have to do with Felicia?"

Again, I shrugged. "I haven't even heard from her in weeks," I said. "The last time we talked, though, she did say we should get together soon."

"Really?" exclaimed Doug. "I bet that means she wants to get back together with you."

For a millisecond I almost bought in, but then I remembered who I was talking to.

"Why do you always feel the need to bust my balls about this?"

"Why do you always feel the need to go after the wrong type of girls?" he replied.

"Do you really think you're the one to judge the right type of girls?" I said.

"Yes. Yes I do. By my calculations, in the last ten years, you have gone after the wrong type of girl 54% of the time. If this were baseball, batting .460 would put you in the Hall of Fame. But in the game of relationships, that only gets you in the Hall of Shame."

"Oh God, why did I come in early today?"

"The question you should really be asking yourself is, why are you still hung up on someone who was never right for you in the first place? And you should also be asking yourself, why are you so depressed about turning thirty? We're only as old as we act."

"So that must make you thirteen or fourteen?" said a voice from behind us.

We both turned and saw Taylor Hart entering the bar. Taylor was one of the bartenders here, and because Doug did all of the hiring, she was twenty-one years old and super-hot. She was also extremely feisty and equally as sarcastic as Doug. It made for a very entertaining shift, that's for sure.

"So what's the big topic of conversation today?" she asked.

"We were just celebrating Josh's birthday," said Doug.

"Today is your birthday?"

Before I could answer, Doug blurted out, "It's his HALF birthday. He's twenty-nine and a HALF, to be exact. He seems to think in six months it'll all be downhill."

"Aww, come on Josh, thirty isn't that old. Besides, we're only as old as we feel," she said.

"I know," I said. "You're probably right."

"Oh, I see how it goes," said Doug. "When she says it, you buy into it, but when I say it, you file it away as bullshit."

"That must be one huge file cabinet you have there, Josh," she smiled, and then headed behind the bar.

"The sad thing is, you actually think you're funny," replied Doug to Taylor.

"She kind of is," I said, giving her a high five.

Without missing a beat, Doug said to me, "Why don't you take the night off. That way you can wait by the phone all night for Felicia to call and tell you she wants you back."

"Ohh, Josh, you're not still trying to get back with that girl, are you?" asked Taylor.

Apparently, my look said it all.

Taylor sighed and said, "This is where we part ways, my friend. I have to side with Doug on this one. You can do so much better than her."

"And speaking of the 54%," laughed Doug, "Is Jane still in town?"

I didn't dignify his percentage comment.

"She's leaving tomorrow," I said. "We actually met out for breakfast earlier."

"I'm just kidding with you, bro. I've always liked Jane. She's definitely not one of the 54%. I actually thought you two made a good couple… as brief as it was."

"Thanks," I said. "And who knows, maybe one day the timing will finally be right."

Doug burst out laughing.

"What's so funny?" I asked.

"Dude, you spend half your time trying to win back Felicia and the other half hoping that one day Jane will come back to York permanently. Oh, and the other half whining about turning thirty."

"And you wonder why I never trust your math?" I said.

Taylor and I shook our heads as Doug looked on, clueless.

"Whatever, dude. My theory is: you need to live in the here and now and not in the then or what might be."

Out of the corner of my eye, I saw Taylor nodding in agreement. I knew right then and there, I should never have brought up the half birthday thing. The only thing left to do was join Doug up at the bar for a beer and hope his sarcasm would take aim somewhere different… to someone different. Luckily, it only took two sips of my beer for this to happen. Doug turned his attention to Taylor, who was prepping the bar.

"So, did you end up going home with that loser who was hitting on you last night? He was practically feeling you up from across the bar."

"Jealous?" smiled Taylor.

"Yea, right."

"And what about you?" she fired back. "Who was that little skank-ho you kept buying beers for?"

"She's not a skank-ho. She was nice," he said.

"Oh yea? What was her name?"

Taylor new exactly where to land her punches. Doug was staggered. I almost repeated her question back to him, but I decided to simply remain a spectator. It was a rare occasion for Doug to become speechless, but it was blatantly obvious that he had no clue what the girl's name was.

Doug fumbled around a moment, but all he could muster was telling Taylor to get back to work. Before she headed out back, Doug flailed a last-ditch punch at her.

"Oh yea… what was the name of that shmuck who was eye-fucking you across—"

Before he even got the words "the bar" out, Taylor replied, "Charles."

As Taylor began to walk off, we smirked and gave each other a virtual high five. It was official, Doug Andrews was down for the count.

When Taylor was out of sight, all that could be heard was Doug mumbling something about Charles in Charge not being allowed in his bar anymore.

I should have just finished my beer and let well enough alone. After all, you never kick a man when he's down, right? But there's no rule about poking him a little, is there?

"So, did you end up hooking up with that chick... you know, the one you can't remember her name?" I asked.

"No! I found out at the end of the night she had a boyfriend."

"Ahh. So how many free drinks did you give her before you found out?"

Doug was too beat up to put up a fight.

"Six," he sighed.

"You bought her six drinks and she wasn't drunk enough to forget about her boyfriend?"

Doug dropped his head in shame then quietly said, "Apparently, only two of the drinks were for her. The other four were for her boyfriend." Again, he sighed.

I knew he was down and defeated, but I couldn't help but laugh.

"You didn't know he was her boyfriend?" I asked through my laughter.

"No!" he said defensively. "I thought he was her brother or something."

"Live and learn, my friend," I said as I patted him on the back.

"Fuckin' skank-ho," he mumbled, and then pounded the rest of his beer.

I held off my real laughter until I reached the back room with Taylor.

"Is he gonna be alright, or what?" she laughed.

"Yea, he'll be just fine. As soon as the first cute girl walks into the bar today… single or otherwise."

"He does bounce back awful quickly, doesn't he?" she said.

"That he does, Taylor. That he does."

I grabbed a couple of cases of Sam Adams, but before I headed back to the bar, I turned to Taylor.

"Charles, huh?"

"What?" she asked.

"The name of the dude that's been hitting on you? Or as Doug put it, the dude who was eye-fucking you across the bar?"

"Ohhhh, him," laughed Taylor. "Nothing really came of it."

"Ahh, so you guys didn't…" I gave her the universal fist gesture for having sex. (Btw, you totally just did the gesture after reading this, didn't you?)

"Nah. We fooled around a bit after work, but that was it," smiled Taylor. "And between you and me, his name isn't Charles. I just made that up because I couldn't remember his real name."

"Oh God," I laughed. "You and Doug are like two peas in a pod."

She smiled and said, "Remember, just between us."

"Yea, yea, yea," I said as I carried the cases of beer back into the bar.

***

Seeing as it was a rainy Saturday, the bar was extra busy. I mean, what else is there to do in a beach town when you can't go to the beach? Drink! It was just the three of us working, so the night went by pretty fast.

To my pleasant surprise, Jane indeed made a final appearance. After she and Doug exchanged their typical jabs at one another, Jane gave him a big hug and congratulated him on his bar. Doug hooked her up with a drink or three, and we all reminisced about the good old days. Jane went through her list of old summer friends, and we gave her a *where are they now* update.

Due to a busy bar and our trip down memory lane, the time flew by, and before I knew it, Jane was on her way out. She gave Doug a hug goodbye then asked if she could have a word with me before she left.

I walked her out to her car in the Shorts Sands parking lot. The rain had subsided and a cool mist filled the foggy night.

"I just wanted to tell you how great it was to see you today, Josh. I miss our conversations, and I do miss this place a lot."

Just not enough to stick around, I thought to myself.

It was as if she read my mind. She grabbed my hand and said, "I'm sorry for how things ended between us. And I'm sorry for blaming you and holding it against you."

"I'm sorry too," I quietly spoke. "I should have encouraged you to take the job from day one."

"You need to know that I absolutely loved our relationship," she said, clutching my hand tighter. "None of this was anybody's fault. It's just that—"

"It's just that this little beach town isn't big enough for you and your dreams. I guess I always knew that," I said.

"What can I say," she smiled, "rumor has it, I'm like a hummingbird."

We arrived at her car and as she pulled me in for a hug, she whispered in my ear, "Despite what you might think, Josh, this beach holds a very special place in my heart… as do you. I will always come back here to see you."

And I will always fucking be here, I thought as she got into her car and drove off.

Usually, saying goodbye to someone, especially Jane, left me utterly depressed, but on that particular occasion, it felt more cathartic than sad. Don't get me wrong, when I got home from work that night, I definitely popped in a Depression Session mix (Volume 5) and thought about Jane. And yes, I also might have checked my answering machine to see if Felicia called (she didn't).

I probably shouldn't make it a habit of mentioning Jane and Felicia in the same sentence. Felicia wasn't even close to Jane's league when it came to my emotions, but Jane and I were done, and I needed to start rebuilding somewhere. So even though Jane and I had a wonderful reunion, and even though a flood of emotions came out, I was still kind of hoping that Felicia would come to her senses and restart our relationship.

5

"THE BOY WITH THE THORN IN HIS SIDE" – The Smiths

I awoke the next morning to a quiet knocking on my door. It was the kind of knocking that when you open your eyes you wonder if the knocking was real or just a dream. I sat up in bed and listened. A moment later, I heard it again; a soft rapping sound on my front door.

I knew it wasn't Doug. His hand had no clue what soft rapping was, and even though Doug knew where my spare key was, he would much rather perform a drum solo on my door than knock softly.

Thinking it might be my landlord's wife, I threw on a tee and sweats. As I moved towards the door, the knocking remained soft and sparse. For a second, for just one quick second, I thought I might be Jane stopping in for one last goodbye before heading to Boston. The thought was fleeting as I looked at the clock: 9:30 AM. I remembered Jane said she was leaving York around 6 AM.

Who the hell could it be then, I thought? I know what you're thinking; just answer the fucking door and find out! Enough overthinking everything!

When I finally opened the door, there was no one there. Check that. There was no one there at eye level. When I lowered my sleepy eyes downward, I was slightly shocked to find a girl… a cute girl… a cute three-foot tall girl, who looked awfully familiar.

As I looked curiously down at her, she covered her mouth and giggled. She then looked over to her right. It wasn't until I peered around the corner that it hit me. It was Kayla! Pete and Michelle's daughter.

Sure enough, standing off to her right with big grins were Pete and Michelle. The last time I saw them was for a day back at Christmas.

How did I not recognize one of my best friend's little girl, you ask? First of all, I had only seen Pete a handful of times since they moved to Florida, and one of those times was their wedding. His job kept him very, very busy so their trips home were usually just at Christmas.

Second, this was 1999—pre-Facebook, so the only time you saw pictures of your friends or their kids was when they opened up their wallet and showed you in person.

"Holy shit! What are you guys—"

"Language!" scolded Pete as his eyes motioned to Kayla.

"Oh, sorry," I said, smiling at Kayla.

"She's getting big, huh?" asked Michelle.

I nodded. "I barely recognized her."

Pete peered into my apartment and said, "I'm assuming we're not interrupting anything, are we?"

"No," I said, and then took offense. "Wait, why would you assume that? I could have someone in there."

"I thought you were done with the summer girls," smiled Pete.

"I am. But I could have my girlfriend in there with me."

"You have a girlfriend?" asked Michelle.

"Well... no, but..."

They both laughed then moved in for hugs. We moved our little reunion into my apartment.

"Did I miss a message or something? I didn't know you guys were coming into town," I asked as I cleared a place for them to sit on the couch.

Pete continued to stand, but Michelle sat down with Kayla joining her on her lap.

"We figured we'd surprise you," said Pete.

"How long are you guys here for?"

They looked at each other and smiled.

"We have a few loose ends to tie up back in Florida, but it looks like we're back for good," said Pete, continuing to smile.

"Are you shitting me?" I asked.

"Dude! Language!" Pete said, motioning again to Kayla.

Scolded twice for cussing in five minutes? Yup, Pete was officially in *Dad-mode*. Doug was going to love this. If I got scolded for just saying the word shit, surely Doug would get a time out or something.

"Wow, you're really moving back here?" I asked. "Wait. You didn't lose your job, did you?"

"Quite the opposite," said Michelle. "Go ahead, honey, tell him."

"My company has been expanding lately. We have a handful locations throughout the country, and our latest spot is right here in Maine... up in Portland."

"Tell him the best part," Michelle excitedly interrupted.

"They want me to head-up the Portland office," he said modestly. "We'll be staying with my parents for now, but—"

"But if all goes well, we'll be closing on a house off of Mountain Road," interrupted Michelle.

Here are the top four things that were going through my mind at that moment:

1. I was excited to have one of my best friends back in town. Like, very excited.

2. I was slightly jealous that Pete was doing so well at his job, and here I was working for Doug—still trying to figure out what I really wanted to do.

3. Closing on a house? Again, I was jealous they were buying a real house, and here I was living in a basement apartment.

4. Did their daughter just pick her nose and wipe it on my couch? Yes, yes she did.

When I used the word jealous, I didn't mean it negatively towards them, not at all. There were people I had known in my life who had everything handed to them and they never had to work for what they got, but Pete was not one of them. Pete was a hard worker and deserved everything he had. Both of them did.

So, even though Pete earned his success at his job, I kinda sorta couldn't really tell you what he did exactly. I don't think Doug could either. It had something to do with computers. IT maybe? Marketing maybe? I have no idea.

Yes, we've asked him a couple of times to explain it, but we still don't have a clue. Once someone has worked at a job for four years or so, it's a little embarrassing to ask them what they do again. Whatever it is though, he's good at his job. Good enough to be put in charge of the Portland division.

"So when did you guys get in town?" I asked.

"Late last night," answered Pete.

"Have you told Doug yet?"

"Not yet. We figured he'd still be sleeping."

"Either that, or still have a bimbo from last night with him in bed," laughed Michelle.

Why did they assume I would be awake… and bimbo free? I was slightly insulted.

We talked for another twenty minutes, and before they headed out, Pete suggested Doug and I meet him down at the courts to shoot around like old times. It had been a long time since I shot a basketball, but I happily agreed to a reunion shoot-around.

6

"EVERYTHING COUNTS" – Depeche Mode

I suggested to Doug that we hit the courts before work, but I didn't tell him about Pete being there. I figured I'd give him the same surprise as I had. Doug was beside himself with excitement when he learned that Pete and Michelle were home for good.

When we arrived at the beach courts, there was a full court game being played on the main court, so we took one of the vacant side hoops. I was never a big fan of the side baskets, mostly because they were always missing their nets. What's fun about shooting at a netless rim? When you launch an 18-footer you want to hear that beautiful swish sound as the net rip-curls. Without the net, it would be like bowling a strike but having the pins make no sound as they fall. Or the analogy Doug would use: It'd be like having wild sex but neither of you can make a sound.

Pete and Doug's first shots clanged badly off the rim, while my shot may or may not have been an air ball. It had clearly been awhile since any of us had played. Pete's next shot missed even worse than the previous one.

"How long has it been?" I asked.

"Honestly, I think the last time I played was the last summer living here in York. When was that... '95?" said Pete.

"Don't they have courts in Florida?" I asked.

"Well yea, but I'm always too busy with work or with the family."

"Ah yes," said Doug, "too busy doing your little husbandy chores, huh? I bet if you had a dollar for every time you said the phrase *yes dear,* you'd be a billionaire."

"No," Pete quickly replied. He then smiled and said, "A millionaire maybe."

"See! See!" boasted Doug. "I know what I'm talking about. Yet another reason why I'm never getting married, and never mind having a kid too! Jesus, between your job, and your *yes dears*, and watching cartoons, and reading Dr. fuckin' Seuss books, you must not have any life at all."

"Eh, the marriage thing isn't as bad as you think," replied Pete. "It's nice to have someone to come home to... someone to talk to... someone to wake up with."

By the look on Doug's face, it was as if Pete was speaking a foreign language.

"First of all," began Doug, "talking in a relationship is overrated. Second, it's really not that hard to find someone to wake up with."

"Someone who you actually remember their name in the morning," I pointed out.

Doug shot me a look, shrugged then said, "If you're into that sorta thing, I guess."

Each of us finally got on track and hit three shots in a row.

"I will say this, Doug, you're not wrong about me not having a life," said Pete. "Don't get me wrong, I love my marriage and being a Dad, but between that and putting in all those long hours at work, I have zero time for myself."

Doug picked up his dribble and gave Pete a serious look and asked, "So, how often are you... ya know...?"

"How often am I having sex with Michelle?" asked Pete.

"Fuck no!" snapped Doug. "I just assumed that would be nonexistent by now. I meant how often are you whacking it?"

"Our sex life isn't nonexistent," answered Pete, less than confidently. "Besides, it's the quality not the quantity."

"What's your ratio?" asked Doug.

"My ratio?"

"Yea, your ratio of masturbation to sex," Doug said matter-of-factly.

Leave it to Doug to go there. Of course, I had to admit, I was a little curious about the whole marriage, sex, masturbation ratio myself.

Pete tried to ignore the question and attempted to grab the ball from Doug. Doug put it behind his back and awaited Pete's answer.

"Give me the fuckin' ball," Pete said as he tried to snatch it from behind Doug.

Doug quickly passed it to me. I think Pete expected me to take his side and pass him the ball, but like I said, I was curious about the ratio. When it became apparent that he was caught in a monkey-in-the-middle situation, Pete shot us a look that was usually reserved for his three-year-old.

"And to think, I almost missed being back here with you two idiots," said Pete.

"Ratio," repeated Doug.

Pete let out a long, resigned sigh and said, "Fine. But it stays just between us!"

"Of course," smiled Doug. "What's said at the courts, stays at the courts."

"You guys really want a stupid masturbation-to-sex ratio?" asked Pete.

Both of us nodded.

Pete shook his head in bemused disgust then finally answered.

"I don't know... 6-to-1? Maybe 7-to-1."

"Holy shit!" exclaimed Doug. "You guys are still having sex three times a week?"

"What?" said Pete, completely confused.

I stepped in and asked Doug, "If that were the case, Doug, a 7-to-1 ratio would mean he's masturbating twenty-one times a week."

"Yea, exactly," said Doug. "I was expecting a way higher ratio. Masturbating three times a day is the norm."

"There's no fuckin' way you're whacking off three times a day," said Pete. I nodded in agreement.

"Yea, maybe you're right," hesitated Doug. "Yesterday was only one and a half times."

Neither Pete nor I questioned what would constitute a half.

"Although," pondered Doug, "last Wednesday was five times, so I guess it all averages out. Yup, definitely three times a day."

Once again, Doug left us speechless. By now, the full court game had ended and there were just a handful of guys left shooting around. It's hard to believe, but back in the day, there would have been a bunch of teams waiting for *next*. It's not like the popularity of basketball was waning, but I guess people just had better things to do with their time.

Anyway, as Pete and I were still mulling over Doug's masturbatory revelation, one of the guys on the main court asked if we wanted to do a four on four.

We all knew we were fairly out of shape, and definitely out of practice, but now that the three of us were back together, there was no way we were turning down a challenge. One of the main reasons I stopped coming down here and playing games was mostly due to my friends all moving away. It's always more fun playing with (or against) your friends.

Also, the older I've gotten, the idea of fighting the beach traffic and feeding quarters into the parking meters had kind of lost its appeal. Bottom line, real life and real responsibilities tend to take precedence. But like I said, now that the three of us were back together down here, we felt a renewed sense of nostalgia and youth. It was like we were in our early twenties again.

We took to the main court and prepared to turn back the clock ten years. There were five of them and three of us, so one of them volunteered to be on our team. We introduced ourselves, and as expected, all but one of them was from Massachusetts. Everyone's ages ranged from seventeen to forty. Naturally, they gave us the forty year old, which made us "Team Old Dudes."

Luckily for us, their skills ranged from average to suck-ass. There was no one waiting for next game, so we decided to play to twenty-one, straight up. We easily won 21 to 10 and were never in jeopardy of losing, but the true story line was what transpired throughout the game.

I truly missed playing full court games with my friends, and I missed the adrenaline of competition, but what I absolutely, positively DIDN'T miss was the annoying and obnoxious behavior of the players. Coming down here all these years, we've had to deal with many, many classic and cliché basketball court characters. That particular game was a perfect snapshot of these characters and behaviors.

Take for instance, the guy who joined our team: He suffered from the classic case of "Coach" syndrome. Every dribble, pass, or shot we took, he would give his "coaching advice" to us.

Things like: "Less dribbling, more ball movement." Or "Make at least three passes before we take a shot." Or "Box out better, boys. No rebounds, no rings." Or "Ohh, that was a tough shot, ya might want to move your range in, buddy."

He was the type of guy who had a comment on every shot we missed, but whenever he missed a shot (which was often), he would cover it up by telling us we had to rebound better.

"Will you shut the fuck up and just play!"

Those were Pete's exact words.

"None of us here are going pro, so we don't need to be coached up by someone who obviously never made it as a player themselves!"

Out of all of my friends, Pete was always the level-headed and practical one, but get him mad on the basketball court and he had a temper like no other.

Pete's words pissed him off, but I think "The Coach" realized that we were *all* annoyed with him, so he played the rest of the game without a peep. There was the occasional eye roll when we did something "wrong" but other than that, he kept his mouth shut.

Pete's temper was just warming up, however. Not only could you always count on him getting into a verbal confrontation down at the courts, but it wasn't a real game until it turned physical.

It was never an all-out fist fight. Usually, he'd just throw a purposeful elbow or maybe a forearm shiver. But seeing as it had been a long time since he'd been down at the courts, I think he had a lot of pent up court-anger. Not to mention, the poor guy's masturbation-to-sex ratio was 7-to-1.

That day's incident involved the guy (kid) who was guarding Pete. I'm not sure what set Pete off the most, but whatever it was, it resulted in Pete throwing him into the backstop fence with his hand around the kid's throat. Doug and I pulled him off of the kid, all the while Pete was yelling how he was going to "end him".

Pete was definitely a hot-head, but to be fair, the little punk had it coming. The kid suffered from another classic court behavior: "All talk, no game syndrome." Let's examine this further, shall we?

First of all, his look: hat on sideways, a Kobe Bryant jersey on (oversized), and his baggy shorts (oversized) hung down to his ankles, revealing more boxers and ass crack than I cared to see.

Every time he touched the ball, he would start dribbling between his legs once or twelve times for no apparent reason except to show off to the few girls watching on the grass. He would then motion to his team for isolation and begin trash-talking to Pete.

"You really don't think you can guard me, old man, do you? Ya better double or triple team me, bitches."

After his seventeenth between-the-legs dribble, he would do the same predictable move: He would drive to the right, spin move to the left, take a wild off-balance shot, and miss... badly.

Embarrassed by his brick, he would always yell out, "Foul!" Actually, his exact words were, "Yo, I got fuckin' hacked!"

This continued the whole game, and with each time, Pete's temper grew more. The "Coach" might have been annoying, but this little punk was fuckin' obnoxious. It got to the point where Pete would just stand still with his hands straight up in the air and watch this little hip-hop-reject flail his body into him and yell, "Hacked!"

On the fifth "hacked," Pete lost his shit.

"You wanna see hacked? I'll fuckin' show you hacked!"

That's when Pete's hand made its way around the kid's throat, pinning the kid into the fence. Not only did Pete utter the phrase "I will end you," but he also managed to give the kid some fashion advice by telling him, "Pull your fuckin' shorts up, ya fuckin' hip-hop punk!"

Anyway, these are just a couple of the classic types of characters one might come across down at the courts. As annoying as "The Coach" was, and as obnoxious as "Hip Hop" was, I'm afraid Doug got stuck guarding the worst of the court characters; not worse because the guy was rude or loud-mouthed. As a matter of fact, the guy Doug guarded was a super-nice guy and barely said two words during the game. Let's just say, this guy was a *tough* guy to guard.

Doug was always bragging how he's an animal on defense, so naturally, we chose Doug to guard their biggest player, and by biggest, I mean most rotund... overly husky, if you will. Simply put; man boobs type of guy. That in itself would have been perfectly fine, except he also had a couple few more... body issues?

After the game, we grabbed our Gatorades, which we bought over at the Bread-n-Butter, and we sat and drank... and breathed heavily. The small strip of grass where we sat separated the basketball court from the road.

I noticed two very cute bikini-clad girls walking down the sidewalk in our direction. Pete and I assumed Doug would be preparing for the runaway ball trick, but we were wrong. As a matter of fact, Doug didn't even notice them walking by. Apparently, he was still traumatized by his experience guarding Mr. Man Boobs.

Okay, I might have left out a few other details about the guy. After a long, dead silence, Mount Saint Doug finally erupted.

"I can't fuckin' believe you guys made me guard that guy! I always get stuck with those types!"

"He was their best low post scorer," said Pete.

"And you always claim to be an animal on defense," I added.

"Oh don't give me that shit!" he snapped. "You didn't stick me with him because he was their best player, and you know it!"

Pete smirked and said, "He did have a little sweating problem, didn't he?"

"And it didn't help that we were shirts and they were skins," I said.

"A *little* sweating problem?" yelled Doug. "Every time he backed into me, it was like I was on a God damn slip-n-slide!"

If this guy's only issue was an overly active sweat gland then Doug wouldn't be so worked up, but he might have had another "condition."

"Every time he boxed me out, I got a face-full of sweat-dripping hair!"

"Yea, he did have a lot of hair on his back," I said.

"Ya think?" Doug sarcastically said. "It was like I was guarding Teen Wolf for Christ sake!"

If a sweaty, hairy-bodied guy was the extent of it then maybe Doug's rant would have ended, but, well… it wasn't.

"Seriously, why do I always get stuck guarding the sweaty, hairy guy with bacne (back-acne)?"

Pete and I both knew the bacne was the worst of the whole deal, yet Pete tried again to undersell the issue.

"Yea, he did have a slight acne problem."

"Slight?" yelled Doug. "I spotted seven different zit constellations on his back throughout the game."

Pete and I couldn't decide if we were disgusted or amused.

"At one point, he backed into my mouth and my front tooth popped the Big Dipper."

Our decision was made—disgusted.

When Doug finally calmed down, the nostalgia of the beach courts began to seep into our minds. We sat there and exchanged story after story of all the crazy characters we had come across down at the courts. Doug had a long list of sweaty, overweight, acne-plagued guys, who he had to guard over the years. Pete had an even longer list of fights he had gotten into.

"I bet we woulda won by even more if Scott was on our team today," said Pete.

Doug and I both nodded and awaited the inevitable question from Pete.

"Has anyone seen Scott around?" asked Pete.

"Nope," replied Doug. "Not since his wedding last year."

I was determined to keep my thoughts to myself until Doug forced my hand by saying, "You really should have gone to the wedding, dude."

I waited for Pete to nod in agreement then I let them have it.

"Are you fuckin' kidding me?" I said. "The only reason we were invited was because Doug and I ran into him at the store and he felt guilted into inviting us."

Neither one of us had seen or hung out with Scott in a while, so our run-in with him at the store was awkward at best. What made it turn from awkward to pathetic was when Scott said, and I quote, "Oh, by the way, I'm getting married next weekend if you guys wanna come."

What the hell kind of wedding invitation is that? An invitation by default, that's what kind of invitation it was.

Considering it was a last minute notice, Pete wasn't able to make it up from Florida, and considering it was a bullshit invitation, I refused to go. Doug ended up going. I think he hoped by showing up, it might rekindle Scott's friendship with us, or at the very least, it might get Scott to explain why he slowly distanced himself from us in the first place. Neither one would be the case.

They both knew I had a right to be upset. The last time all four of us hung out together was four years ago back in '95. Well, technically, it was early 1996 at Pete's wedding. But even then, Scott seemed distant.

After that, he just faded away. He didn't move away, he simply just faded out of our lives. None of us could explain it.

It would have been easy to blame this on his new girlfriend at the time, and now, new wife, Lauren, but deep down, we knew this wasn't about her. We really liked her, and from all accounts, she liked us as well.

The Scott situation was just another thing that played into my mood and philosophy in that summer of 1999. You might say, '99 was my "woe is me" summer. I wasn't any closer to finding my calling in life, and I certainly wasn't any closer to finding my true love. The only thing I was closer to was the big three zero. More than anything that summer, as if you couldn't already tell, my attitude on life had gone to shit.

Some (most) would say that I've always been a hopeless romantic, but personally, I've always considered myself more of a *hopeful* romantic.

Did I used to be the king of giving girls mixtapes? Yes.

Do I have 17 volumes of Depression Session mixes? Yes, yes I do.

Do I enjoy listening to them while sitting in a darkened candlelit room? Well, I don't know about *enjoy*, but I do find it cathartic. Despite all of that, I've always bounced back in search of a brand new day... a brand new love. But sadly, by the time the summer of '99 came, I was completely beaten down by life and I was jaded as fuck!

Don't get me wrong, I was very excited that Pete and Michelle were moving back home, and it really did feel great being back down at the courts with my best friends... even if Scott wasn't there.

As we continued to sit on the grass, our reminiscing moved from basketball games to the beach in general.

"God, I missed this place," said Pete, looking around. "A lot of memories down here."

Doug and I nodded in agreement as Pete continued.

"Remember when we'd come down here and play ball from sun up to sundown?"

"Or we'd hit the beach all day hitting on the Fun Float girls," I added. "No worries... no responsibilities."

"The only worries were if we were gonna get laid that night," said Doug.

Again, the three of us nodded.

I looked down the road at the Sands Motel and smiled.

"I remember one night, I snuck into the laundry room with some chick at the Sands, and we had sex all over the clean linens. Well, they started off clean, anyway."

Pete smiled then revealed his own recollection.

"I once had sex on one of the lifeguard stands."

"So. Who didn't?" said Doug. "There were many a late night that I also had sex on a lifeguard stand."

Pete smiled widely and said, "But mine was during the day… while I was lifeguarding."

"No way," I said.

"I swear," laughed Pete. "It was a cold, foggy day, and Michelle and I were working the stand at the end of the beach. There was absolutely no one around. Let's just say, the seagulls got quite the show."

"How professional of you two," I said. "I can see the headline in the *York Weekly* now: 'Kid drowning—Lifeguard fucking'."

Before I could say another word, Doug chimed in with, "Oh yea, I can top that. I once had sex in the playground over there."

Doug pointed over to the large fenced in playground, which separated the courts from the actual beach.

"During the day or at night?" asked Pete.

"Late at night," replied Doug.

"Was she underage or legal?" I asked with a smirk.

"No, she wasn't underage, you idiot. At least I don't think she was."

"Sex on a playground late at night? What's the big deal about that?" I asked.

"Yea, what's the big deal about that?" echoed Pete. "We've all done that."

"We did it on the merry-go-round," boasted Doug.

Pete and I looked curiously at Doug. We still had no clue what the big deal was.

"Uhhh, hello?" snickered Doug. "It just so happened that the girl I was banging was named Mary. Get it? Mary go round?" Doug began laughing harder. "Fuckin' funny, huh?"

At the same time, Pete and I uttered, "You're such a dumbass."

"It's not my fault you guys don't have a sense of humor."

We all stood up and started to head out. Pete made his way to his car.

"I'm gonna head home to check on the fam," said Pete.

"Why don't you get your mom to babysit tonight and you and Michelle can come by the bar?" said Doug.

"That's a definite possibility," said Pete. "Maybe I'll give Scott a call and see if he wants to meet us there."

"I'll make sure not to hold my breath," laughed Doug.

"Well, I'll give it my best shot," said Pete, getting into his car.

I kept my comments to myself. I knew there was no chance in hell that Scott would show up. Doug opened his new bar four months ago, and Scott still hadn't shown his face in there to congratulate him, and he only lives 3.2 frickin' miles away!

7

"GREEN EYES" – Coldplay

Later that night, myself, Taylor, and Dawn, handled behind the bar. Dawn was another one of Doug's bartenders. She was a quiet girl in her mid-twenties and was much less sarcastic than Taylor, and much more normal than our other two bartenders, Hillary and Steph (AKA - the tie dye twins)(AKA - the granola girls)(AKA - the non-deodorant deadheads).

Doug was across the room schmoozing with a table of girls. Young girls. I swear, the guy thinks he's still twenty-one. We watched as the three girls laughed at one of Doug's many animated stories. If this was a few years ago, I'd probably be right there with him, but like I said, I'd retired from that sort of thing. Nothing good was going to come from flirting with summer girls. Especially ones who are nearly ten years our junior.

Doug motioned to Taylor to get the girls another round.

"He is trying to make a profit in this business, isn't he?" I mumbled to Taylor.

"No, he's just trying to get laid," she smiled. "Too bad he doesn't stand a chance with any of them."

"You don't think?" I asked as I watched them laugh louder at Doug's antics. "They seem kinda into him. Especially the brunette with the UMass sweatshirt on. She keeps touching his arm every time she laughs."

Taylor shook her head and laughed at me. "You guys are thirty years old and you still can't tell the difference between an *I want to have sex with you* arm grab, and an *I just want more free drinks* arm grab?"

Before I challenged her on her theory, I made sure to point out I was only twenty-nine and a half, not thirty! Not yet.

"I don't know, Taylor, she seems pretty into him. Ten bucks says he at least gets her digits," I said.

Taylor countered with, "Twenty bucks says not only does he not get her digits, but she uses the excuse that she has a boyfriend."

At that point, Doug made his way over to collect their next round. Before I agreed to the bet, I needed to read Doug's confidence level.

"Ya got this?" I asked, looking in the direction of the brunette.

"Oh I got this," he said.

I sensed an 8.9 on the confidence scale, so as he walked off, I cemented the bet with Taylor. I spent the next half an hour serving drinks all the while keeping a close eye on my investment.

Yes, Doug could be a complete dumbass, but I had the utmost faith that he could pick up this little college chick. Over the years, I had seen him use the cheesiest and stupidest lines on girls; the type of lines that are laughable because they're so stupid. But I tell you what, 66% of the time they actually worked. Of course, 11% of the time, it ended with a drink getting thrown at him or a slap across his face.

"Hey," said Taylor, "I'm gonna go grab some more ice. You wanna take her drink order?"

Until Taylor pointed her out, I didn't even notice the cute blonde sitting by herself at the end of the bar. I was too busy observing Doug in action.

I know I just referred to her as a cute blonde, but trust me, the last thing on my mind that night was cute... or blonde. And certainly the last thing on my mind was to pull a Doug and start flirting with her.

"Hey, how's it going?" I asked. "Are you meeting someone? Can I get you a drink?"

"Um, no," she quietly said. "I mean, no to meeting someone, but yes, I'd love something to drink."

As I stood there waiting, it took her a moment to realize she hadn't actually specified her drink order.

"Oh gosh, I'm sorry," she said. "I suppose you want to know my order? I swear I'm not as ditzy as I seem."

"Eh, it's okay. You don't seem that ditzy," I smiled. "But if I had to guess, I'd say you're a red wine drinker?"

She scrunched up her nose in disgust. "Beer. The colder the better," she said.

"Yea, that was my second guess," I said. "Although, I'm not gonna venture a guess which kind."

She glanced up at the many beer bottles on the shelf and then over at the beer taps.

"I tell you what," she said, "usually I'm just a simple Budweiser girl, but why don't you give me something that screams Maine."

I pondered a second then cracked open a blueberry ale. She smiled widely as she read the label. She took a giant swig, and her smile quickly transformed into a look of disgust.

"Umm, maybe something that doesn't scream so loud," she said, trying to get the taste out of her mouth.

I laughed and then poured her a draft and slid it down to her. She took a sip, and the smile of satisfaction returned to her face.

"Now that I like," she said. "What is it?"

"Bud Light," I smiled.

Her face flushed with embarrassment, and as I removed the blueberry ale from in front of her, she quietly said, "I'll pay for that one."

"Nah. You're all set... with both drinks. The first drink is free to new out-of-towners."

No, we don't give free first drinks to new out-of-towners. And yes, I did it because she seemed nice and, well... pretty God damn adorable. But NO, I still had no intentions of flirting with this young and apparent summer girl. I was simply being polite and hospitable.

"Aw, thanks," she said. "Is it that obvious that I'm an out-of-towner?"

"Well, considering 89% of our customers are out-of-towners, I would say it was an educated guess. So where are you from?"

"Iowa," she said.

"Iowa?" my voice raised. "As in *Field of Dreams*? Kevin Costner? Shoeless Joe Jackson?"

She looked at me like I was crazy. Apparently, my enthusiasm for all things *Field of Dreams* overwhelmed her a tad bit.

"Umm, yea, I live about thirty minutes from the field," she said.

"Shut up! That is so cool!"

She laughed. "If you say so. To be honest though, I've never been to the field... or the town... or seen the movie."

"What?" I said shocked. "That should be required for all Iowans. It's like if you live in Maine, you have to go to the L.L. Bean store at least once. Personally, I think the *Field of Dreams* field might be cooler than the Bean."

Again, she looked at me as if I was off my rocker.

"Wow. From Iowa, huh? I've met a lot of people here from a lot of different states but never anyone from Iowa."

"Trust me, it's really not that big of a deal," she said.

"Agree to disagree," I smiled. "So what brings you all the way to Maine?"

"My college roommate and I decided after we graduated that we would take a big two week vacation here to Maine. Sort of a reward, I guess."

"Ah, just graduated, huh? A youngin'."

"Why, how old are you?" she asked.

"Older. Much older," I said.

She gave me a look of disbelief, but before she could comment, I said, "Wait. Did you just say you chose Maine as your reward for graduating?"

"Uh huh," she smiled.

"Why not Hawaii? Or the Caribbean? Or Europe? Or... anywhere besides Maine?"

"Wow," she laughed. "I hope you're not planning on joining the Maine tourism committee?"

"I'm serious," I said. "You had the whole world to choose from and you picked Maine?"

She took a sip of her beer and blushed slightly. "Do you want the truth?"

"Well, yea," I said. "Because I can list at least 127 places I'd vacation at besides this place!"

After she shot me an incredulous look, she said, "When I was in sixth grade, we all had to pick a state and do a detailed report on it. Technically, we didn't pick it ourselves, it was the luck of the draw."

I looked blankly at her and said, "Are you telling me you chose to spend your hard-earned savings on Maine because of a silly report you did when you were in the sixth grade?"

"Well… yea," she smiled. "Up until that point, I didn't know a thing about Maine, but I totally got into it. I think it was the lighthouses and the rocky coast that really drew me in. In case you don't know, Iowa has neither."

Again, I just stared blankly at her and smiled.

"Make fun of me if you will, but I got an A+ on it! Did you know that York was the first chartered city in the country? 1641!" she said proudly.

This caused me to laugh and say, "Is that why you chose York?"

"Ha ha. No. We had to do a presentation in class, and one of my poster boards was a giant picture of the Nubble Lighthouse. Constructed in 1879, by the way."

I continued to laugh and shake my head at her.

"After I did the report, I totally became infatuated with lighthouses. The next thing I knew, my room was filled with lighthouse knick-knacks and calendars and all that kinda stuff. I know it sounds silly, but ever since then, I've had my mind set on visiting Maine!"

"Ah, I see," I said. "So what made you choose York Beach?"

"The York part was kind of random. When I went to the travel agency, they recommended York, Ogunquit, Kennebunkport, or Old Orchard Beach. I chose York!"

"And why wouldn't you," I sarcastically said, "Rumor has it that York was the first chartered city in America."

"Ha ha. Go ahead, make fun of the country girl."

"I'm just kidding. It still blows my mind you picked Maine over the rest of the world, but to each his own. So what did you go to school for?" I asked.

"Nursing."

"Nice. That's a very commendable profession. Do you have a job lined up yet?"

"Actually I do. I landed a job in our local hospital starting in mid-August."

"Wow. That was quick. Good for you."

"I actually got super lucky. My friend had an inside connection so we both got positions offered to us."

I looked around and asked, "Where's your friend now?"

She gave me a slight frown and said, "One of the positions opened up earlier than planned, and she was offered it a few days ago. She couldn't really turn it down."

"Aw, that sucks," I said.

I paused a second and then it hit me. There was no one sitting with her.

"Wait, wait, wait," I said. "You didn't come here on vacation by yourself, did you?"

Embarrassed, she slowly nodded.

"You didn't have any friends who would come with you?"

I immediately felt bad. What if she didn't have any friends? But what kind of girl, especially a cute, blonde, and green-eyed one doesn't have friends? Before I could debate with myself just how many friends she had, she spoke.

"I didn't find out she couldn't come until the day before our flight. At that point, it was pretty hard finding someone at the last minute. To be honest, I don't really have that many close friends anymore. I come from a small town and most of my friends have either moved on to bigger and better places or they're all knocked up. The few people I did ask didn't really want to spend their money or vacation time in Maine. Sorry, no offense."

"None taken," I said. "I wouldn't spend my money on a vacation here either!" I laughed. "I still don't get why you chose Maine."

She paused a moment then smiled and said, "And I don't get your infatuation with a silly baseball field in the middle of a cornfield, but you said yourself you would love to go there."

Shit, she had me there, but I still didn't get why anyone would make Maine their destination. Especially with the whole world to choose from.

"We thought about postponing our trip, but—"

"You'd never get your money back this late in the game," I said.

She nodded in agreement then said, "Yea, it was way too late for that, so I decided to come here anyway... by myself."

"Wow. Personally, I wouldn't even go to the movies by myself, never mind vacation," I said.

I hoped she didn't take that as a put down. I was actually impressed by her.

She shrugged and said, "I've been trying to be more independent in my life. That was actually one of my New Year's resolutions this past year."

As I watched her drink her beer, I really hoped my comments didn't make her feel bad. Truth be told, if Doug backed out on me at the last minute on a vacation, I would really have to scramble to find someone to go with. I was truly impressed by her independence.

"Hey, for the record, at this point in my life, I can count my friends on one hand," I said. "Less than one hand actually. I think it's great that you came anyway."

She gave me a warm, appreciative smile. Out of the corner of my eye, I spotted Pete and Michelle enter the bar. They gave me a wave and made their way to a table in the back.

"I'm Anna, by the way."

I turned my attention back to the green-eyed girl.

"I'm Josh. Nice to meet you, Anna."

Just then, Doug barged in and sat next to Anna.

"Hey, you said I get to flirt with the next girl who sat here." And with a big, dumb smile, Doug looked at Anna and then to me and said, "Sooo, who's your new friend?"

Hesitantly, I replied, "Doug, this is Anna. Anna, Doug."

Anna politely smiled at him. Doug stared curiously at her.

"You're not from around here, are you?"

"She's from Iowa," I pointed out.

"No shit? As in the Field of frickin' Dreams?" he asked excitedly.

Anna looked at us and simply shook her head and smiled.

"Well, I don't mean to interrupt," he said, "but Pete and Michelle just got here. Let's go drink!"

"Um, you're kinda paying me to be working right now, aren't you?" I said.

"And now I'm paying you to drink with us!"

This was definitely one of the perks of working for your best friend.

"Besides," continued Doug, "it's pretty slow tonight. Taylor and Dawn can handle it. Right, Taylor?"

"That's why you pay me the big bucks," said Taylor.

"See? Come on, let's go drink!"

"Alright, alright. I'll be right over."

Doug nodded and headed over to Pete and Michelle.

"You should probably go join your friends," Anna politely said. "And thanks again for the drinks."

"Not a problem. If you need anything else, Taylor will take care of you, and if I don't see you again, have a good vacation."

"Thanks," she smiled.

For the first time, I noticed something unique about her smile. It was... kind of crooked. Not in a weird, deformed sort of way. Not at all, actually. It was kind of endearing, adorable even, but don't let my observations fool you though. I still had no intentions or desires to flirt with her. None.

I made my way over to my friends. This wasn't the first time we had all hung out since they moved away. They had been back home a handful of times, mostly for the holiday seasons.

After about fifteen minutes of reminiscing, it hit me. I was so distracted earlier with Anna that I lost track of what happened with Doug and the UMass chick.

"Hey Doug, what happened to the girls you were sitting with?"

"Eh, they went over to the Union Bluff to meet up with some friends."

"What happened with UMass girl?" I asked. "She looked like she was into you."

Doug huffed. "Yea, that's what I thought too."

"Did you get her digits," I asked hopefully.

"I tried, but she said she had a boyfriend."

And just like that, I lost twenty bucks. My main man let me down.

"Maybe in the future, you should find out their relationship status *before* you give them free drinks," I pointed out.

"Yea… I know," he sighed.

"Glad to see nothing has changed around here," laughed Michelle.

Truer words were never spoken. It really was great having Pete and Michelle back home. It was like we picked up where we all left off four summers ago. Although, this time our topics of conversation varied slightly from when we all did this back in '95. I'm not saying it was a bad thing, but Pete and Michelle's topics tended to now revolve heavily around their three-year-old daughter.

They rambled on about all the cute things she had ever said or done. They also talked about the many adventures Pete had in diaper changing.

Please, please, please don't get me wrong! I love that Pete and Michelle are so happy, and I love that they have a beautiful daughter. I really do! But to two single guys, hearing cute, little toddler stories out at a bar was a bit on the boring side.

When I looked over at Doug, I knew he was about thirteen seconds away from flipping the conversation in the most opposite and inappropriate way possible. I could tell just by the way he was staring at his empty shot glass that there were some random and disturbing thoughts forming in his head.

In 3…2…1…

"Hey, how many sessions do you think it would take to fill this shot glass?"

When Doug said the word sessions he gave the *hand* gesture for masturbation. And just like that, the conversation went from talking about Elmo giggling on Sesame Street to Doug gizzing in a shot glass. Michelle was first to comment.

"That's nasty, Doug!"

"Seriously, dude!" added Pete, "Do you stay up at night coming up with this shit?"

Doug pondered then said, "Yea, usually. But this one just came to me now."

"You need some serious, serious help," I said.

"What? Are you telling me you guys have never thought about that before?"

"Doug," I said, "we're telling you that nobody on planet earth has ever thought about that before."

"Really? Hmm, what can I say," he shrugged, "I guess I'm a trailblazer then."

As disgusting as his question was (and it was disgusting) we couldn't help but ponder it and do the mental computations on it. Pete was the first to break the ice.

"I'd say you'd have to whack off at least a dozen times."

"No way," I said. "Eight at the most."

By now, Doug had the shot glass in his hand and was carefully examining it. Finally, he spoke.

"I think I could fill it in five whacks."

Michelle was now less disgusted and more amused.

"Well, there you guys go," she said. "You should turn this into a bar contest. Instead of guessing how many jelly beans are in a jar, they'll have to guess how many 'sessions' it'll take for Doug to fill the glass."

We all laughed. I then informed Doug that she was only kidding about the contest idea.

Pete smirked and said, "I'm not sure how many it would take, but going by what you told us at the courts earlier, it would only take you a day to fill it."

I laughed and added, "Yea, no shit, there, Mr. Masturbation Marathon Man."

"Hey, hey!" snapped Doug. "What ever happened to our guy code? What's said at the courts, stays at the courts! Or should I tell Michelle about your ratio?"

"What ratio?" she asked.

Pete immediately remembered the masturbation-to-sex ratio question from earlier.

"Ummm, it's nothing. Just silly guy talk," Pete uneasily said. "Besides, Doug is right, what is said at the courts, stays at the courts. You know, guy code and shit."

Michelle just shook her head at us. She was well-versed in our inane guy banter.

Again, Doug examined the shot glass.

"I definitely could fill this in a day," he boasted.

"Pfft," scoffed Michelle. "You'd be shooting blanks before it was half full."

"What? There is NO WAY I'd be shooting blanks!" Doug said, way, way too loudly.

All eyes in the surrounding tables looked directly over at us, but Doug's boisterousness continued.

"I don't know who you've been talking to, but Doug Andrews does NOT shoot blanks! Want me to prove it?" Doug said, standing up.

"Relax," laughed Michelle. "Sit down and put your gun back in your holster, there, Billy the Kid."

It took a second, but Doug eventually joined us in our laughter. Yup, it was just like old times. It didn't take Doug long to turn his attention to Anna, who was still sitting up at the bar talking to Taylor.

"So what's the deal with you and blondie over there?"

"There's no deal. No deal at all. We were just talking," I said convincingly.

"Who is she here on vacation with?" asked Doug.

"Actually, no one. Her friend got a big job offer and had to bail the day before they were supposed to leave."

"So she's here all alone?" questioned Pete.

Michelle chimed in, "For the summer?"

"That's perfect for you, man!" Doug said, slapping my back.

All six of their eyes were looking a little too excited towards me.

"Oh, no, no, no," I said. "One – she's only here for two weeks, *not* the summer! Two – I don't *do* summer romances or flings anymore! Three – She's only like twenty-two or something."

"Too old or too young?" smiled Doug.

"We should invite her over," said Michelle.

"That's a winning idea," exclaimed Doug.

"That is definitely NOT a winning idea," I said. "I'm sure she doesn't want to—"

That's as much of the sentence I could utter before Doug yelled across the bar.

"Hey, Iowa girl! Come on over!"

As I looked over at Anna, I felt my body slump lower in my chair. It was obvious that she was a little embarrassed by Doug's booming request.

Taylor approached Anna, and I'm assuming she informed her that she better come on over before Doug got any louder or more obnoxious. Anna got off her stool and hesitantly made her way over to our table.

"No talk of fluids and shots glasses. Got it?" I said, firmly to Doug.

He completely ignored me as he stood up and gave Anna his chair next to me. That should have been my first clue that I was being set up.

"Have a seat right next to Josh," he said, pulling out the chair for her.

"I really don't want to interrupt," she politely said.

"Trust me," said Michelle, "their conversations are worth interrupting. Especially his!" she said, pointing at Doug.

"Hey, are you gonna control your wife or what?" he joked to Pete. "Oh, that's right. You're a little too whipped for that."

I interrupted Doug's banter and provided introductions. After everyone shook hands, Pete commented.

"So, you're from Iowa, huh?"

"Only thirty minutes from the *Field of Dreams*," I pointed out.

"No shit?" he exclaimed. "Very cool!"

Anna looked at the three of us guys and just shook her head.

"It's a guy thing," Michelle said, joining Anna in shaking her head.

As the Beastie Boys blared out over the speakers, Anna commented on the sights and sounds of the bar.

"This is a really cool little bar," she said.

"Why thank you," accepted Doug.

"And I love the music that you play."

"You can thank Josh for that one. He's in charge of all things music here."

"You two own this place?" she asked.

"Doug does. I just work for him," I said.

"Not for lack of trying to get him to be partners with me," he said.

"Well, if I ever quit my job, I'll be partners with you, bro," said Pete.

"That's what I'm talking about," said Doug as he gave Pete a fist bump.

I was hoping this wasn't going to turn into an inquisition on why I didn't want to be partners. Luckily, it didn't. Doug raised his drink in the air and offered a toast.

"A toast! To old friends, new friends, and great fuckin' tunes!"

We all clinked our drinks. It was at that point that Doug noticed Michelle was drinking water.

"Have you been drinking water this whole time?" he asked. Michelle nodded.

"What's up with that?" I asked. "You used to be able to drink me under the table."

"Oh, I'm sure I still can," she said. "but don't you guys know alcohol is bad for a baby?"

There was dead silence for a moment as she shared a smile with Pete and they held hands.

"Why didn't you say something earlier?" I said.

"We were waiting for the right moment," said Michelle.

"I almost told you guys down at the courts," said Pete, smiling.

It was at this point, Doug finally caught on.

"Holy shit! You're pregnant, aren't you?"

"Nothing gets by you, huh?" said Michelle.

We all laughed, and this time I was the one who raised a glass in the air.

"A toast. To Pete and Michelle and baby number two."

I was happy for my friends, of course I was, but hearing the news of them buying a new house and now on kid number two, I couldn't help but feel old. I knew it was my own fault for creating that stupid timetable in my head, but in times like these, I just felt like I was WAY behind in the game.

The dialogue over the next twenty-five minutes revolved around baby names. We heard both of their top three names… for a girl and for a boy.

We also had to listen to Doug make his plea why he would make the perfect godfather. We also had to listen to him doing imitations from *The Godfather* movies.

After the baby and godfather talk subsided, Anna turned to Doug and asked, "What's the story behind the name of your bar?"

"Yea," echoed Michelle. "What's that all about?"

"The name actually came to me years ago when we used to hang out at the bars. So picture this… we're all sitting here, and Scott enters the bar. He starts scanning around looking for us. We yell, 'Over HERE'! He comes over and we all say, 'HEY!!!' And then we all drink and laugh all night, or in other words, we have a bunch of 'HOOHAHS' all night. Pretty fuckin' clever, huh?"

We all just stared blankly at Doug.

"You were drunk when you thought of this, right?" asked Michelle.

"Oh, totally shitfaced," smiled Doug.

Michelle laughed and raised her water and said, "A toast… to Here Hey Hoohahs!"

"Now you're talking!" exclaimed Doug as we all clinked glasses.

A few minutes later, Doug turned his attention to Anna and said, "So, Iowa girl, Josh tells us you're here by yourself because you have no friends?"

"I never said that!" I snapped. "What I said was, your friend had to cancel right before you left, and you couldn't find anyone in such short notice… so you came anyway… alone. Right?"

Anna smiled and nodded. "The truth is," she said, "I really don't have very many close friends. Certainly not many who

I'd want to spend two weeks on vacation with. I even got desperate enough to ask my mother to come with me."

"Jesus! She turned you down too?" laughed Doug.

Anna blushed a bit and said, "Yea, something like that. Actually, she would have loved to come, but she has a pretty strict boss and there was no way she could have gotten two weeks off, especially last minute. And like I was telling Josh earlier, my New Year's resolution was to be more independent. I guess it doesn't get any more independent than coming here alone."

"I think that's great!" said Michelle. "I would love to get away… just by myself. No offense, honey," she said, turning to Pete.

"None taken," he said, putting his arm around her. "A little vacation alone does sound good."

As she held his hand, Doug shook his head in disgust and blurted out, "Reason number two hundred why I'm never getting married!"

"There's nothing wrong with each us of wanting to get away for a little me time once in a while. It's perfectly healthy in a marriage," said Michelle.

Doug continued shaking his head at them. "Yet another perk of being single, I get all the *me* time I want!"

I couldn't resist, "Of course, Doug's me time consists of a bottle of lotion, a box of tissues, and the Spice channel on."

Doug just sat there with a proud look on his face as everyone laughed.

"That wasn't really the *me* time I was referring to," said Michelle. "There's more to it than just that."

The look on Doug's face was as if someone just told him the world was flat. "Like what?" he asked.

"For starters," began Michelle, "an uninterrupted bath with a good book…"

Pete chimed in with, "A reclining chair, a cold beer, and the game on… also uninterrupted."

Doug couldn't believe what he was hearing.

"Wow. You guys are worse off than I thought."

Doug got up and headed to the bar for another drink. When he returned, he glanced over at me and said, "And what are you doing bringing up tissues and lotion? You're the one who told me no masturbation talk around the innocent, little Iowa girl."

Before I had a chance to respond, Anna quietly said, "I'm not that innocent."

As all of our eyes looked at her, Doug relished in the moment and said, "Okay, Iowa girl, give us your best masturbation story."

Her face immediately turned a bright red, and we all shook our heads at Doug. The guy positively didn't have a clue what a filter was.

"Ignore him, sweetie," said Michelle. "You don't have to answer any of his idiotic questions."

Doug and Michelle proceeded to have a playful stare down, and just when we thought the moment had passed, Anna shocked the shit out of us. She didn't reveal a personal masturbation story, but rather a disgusting, yet comical one that she had heard.

She told us about a fraternity out in Iowa and one of their hazing rituals. Pete, Michelle, and I were disgusted yet amused. Doug, on the other hand, was completely intrigued and mesmerized.

"So wait, let me get this straight," he said. "All of the pledges had to stand around in a circle and whack off?"

"Ahh, the infamous circle jerk," laughed Pete.

"Actually, what they had to do was referred to as the 'limp biscuit,' Anna pointed out.

Over the next few minutes, we all sat in shock as Anna pointed out the difference between the two. Apparently, the "limp biscuit" involved a cracker to be placed in the middle of the circle and... ummm...

"Wait a fuckin' second!" yelled Doug. "Are you telling me that they all had to whack off onto a cracker? And the last one to cum had to eat the cracker?"

Anna smiled and nodded. We were all grossed out but couldn't help but laugh.

"I've actually heard about that," said Michelle, "but I always thought it was just one of those college myths."

"So that's where the band Limp Bizkit got its name, huh?" said Pete.

"No wonder why they suck so badly," I said.

I had to admit, I was disgusted yet impressed with Anna's story. It takes a rare breed to join in on our strange conversations. Iowa girl seemed to fit right in.

Just when we thought the topic was over, Doug blurted out, "Wait! What kind of cracker was it?"

Our eyes slowly and curiously made their way over to Doug.

"Really?" said Michelle.

"What?" he said. "Weren't you guys wondering that yourselves?"

He continued to stare at Anna, awaiting an answer.

"Ummm, I'm not really sure. A Ritz maybe?" she shrugged.

Pete then followed with, "It might have started off a Ritz, but it ended up a Saltine!"

We all burst out laughing. It really was good having them back home. Michelle switched gears and turned to Anna.

"So, Anna, have you done any sightseeing yet?"

"Not really. I just got in town late afternoon yesterday, and it was raining pretty hard. I did lay out on the beach today and I took a nice walk on the long beach."

"Long Sands," corrected Doug.

"And this afternoon, I did a little browsing in the shops down at the other beach."

"That would be Short Sands," Doug pointed out, a little more snidely.

"Oh, yea, Short Sands," smiled Anna. "I spent a lot of time in that Goldenrod store. They have the best taffy, and did you know they make it right there for you to see?"

"Shut the fuck up!" exclaimed Doug. "You're kidding? We should all go down there right now and press our faces in the window and watch!"

Doug's seriousness quickly faded into laughter.

"I'm just playing with ya, Iowa girl," he said.

"That was a total tourist thing to say, huh?" she said.

"Yup!" smiled Doug. "But we'll give you a pass on that one."

"I really want to go see the Nubble Lighthouse," said Anna.

"You should have Josh show you around the area," suggested Michelle.

"Yea, he would love to play tour guide," added Pete.

And just like that, Pete and Michelle had overstayed their welcome. It was time to ship them back to Florida.

"I'll even cover your shift tomorrow night," smiled Doug. "That'll give you the whole day to show her around."

It was evident that I was in the midst of a conspiracy. My idiot friends were lamely trying to play matchmakers. Don't get me wrong, Anna seemed like a sweet girl, and there was definitely an attraction there, but at that point in my life, I was

100% burnt out on the summer-girl thing. 110% actually. And not to mention, in the back of my mind, I still kind of had aspirations of getting back together with Felicia.

I gave my friends a slight glare and then looked at Anna. I could tell my hesitation made her feel a bit uncomfortable.

"It's okay," she quietly said. "You don't have to show me around. I'm sure you're busy."

"Well, I'm not that busy," I said. "I suppose I could show you around a little bit tomorrow, if you wanted?"

For the record, I was simply being a nice guy. I had zero intentions of making this a romantic thing. Zero.

"Really? You don't mind?" she asked.

"Of course he doesn't mind," Doug answered for me. "He would love to."

"Yea, he would love to," echoed Michelle.

Seeing as my friends were doing all the talking for me, I just sat back and drank my beer. Anna headed out soon after, but the rest of us stayed through closing. The three of us guys had more than our share of alcohol, so Michelle became our designated driver.

Doug ended up crashing at my place. It was nearly 2 AM when we entered my apartment. Considering the late hour and how much we had to drink, all I wanted to do was sleep. All Doug wanted to do was talk… and talk… and play music… loudly.

While Doug fumbled through my CD collection, I noticed the red light on my answering machine was blinking twice. As tempted as I was, I knew I couldn't check the messages with Doug there. Giving his drunkenness, the shit storm would have been unbearable. Doug settled on "Sodajerk" by Buffalo Tom, and popped it in and cranked it up.

"Dude, turn it down! My landlord is upstairs. Jesus!"

"Sorry, man," he said as he (kind of) turned it down. "I just love this song though. Such a fucking summer song, huh?"

I nodded in agreement and then turned it down a few more notches.

"Oh shit," exclaimed Doug. "We totally should have asked Pete to do a walkabout tonight. It's been forever since we've all done one together."

It had been a long time; years, in fact.

"Well, now that they're moving back, we'll have plenty of chances," I said.

"Pffft, fat chance with kid number two on the way! And there's no fuckin' way I'm doing a late night walkabout while Pete pushes a stroller, especially those double-seated bad boys. It would take up the whole fuckin' sidewalk. Or worse, Pete wearing one of those ridiculous baby-hammock-sling thingys. It's like we'd be taking a walkabout with a God damn kangaroo, for Christ sake!"

Although the imagery was quite amusing, Doug was right, this scenario would put a major crimp on our walkabouts. I can see it now; a late night walkabout with two kids in tow and our beer backpack replaced with an oversized diaper bag. I somehow pictured Doug drinking beer out of sippy cups and going on about some stupid masturbation story. Yup, times were a changing.

"You and I should do one right now!" urged Doug.

"No, no we shouldn't. I'm exhausted, dude. And besides, someone volunteered me to play tour guide bright and early tomorrow."

"Oh come on! You need some fun in your life. You've been a fuddy duddy for far too long."

I don't think I'd ever been called a fuddy duddy before, but I didn't like it. I didn't like it at all. I knew better than to attempt to argue the finer points of fuddy duddyness with Doug, especially this late at night and with our alcohol levels being what they were.

I motioned to the pile of dirty clothes on my couch and said, "You can just throw them on the chair. I'll go get you a blanket."

When I came back into the room, Doug was hesitantly removing my dirty clothes from the couch.

"None of these socks are your nutrags, are they?" he asked suspiciously.

"No! I don't use socks for nutrags, you idiot!"

"You should. They're way better than just using tissues," he said matter-of-factly.

I had no response. It was 2:12 AM and I wasn't about to start a debate on what was the best type of nutrag to use. I simply gave Doug my typical *you're a dumbass* look, tossed him the blanket, then headed into my room. A second later, I reentered my living room and preventively removed my pile of clothes… especially my socks.

8

"ALL YOUR FAVORITE BANDS" – Dawes

Doug did get me thinking about our walkabouts. I really did miss them, especially when it was the four of us: Doug, Pete, Scott, and myself. And even though Pete was back in town, I knew the chances of getting Scott to hang out with us, never mind doing a walkabout, was slim to none.

As I lay in bed, I flashbacked to some of our more classic walkabout conversations. The first one that came to mind was the summer of 1992. It was my second summer as the Sunday night DJ at Goodnight Ogunquit in York. That particular night was absolutely packed, and by the time we all got home it was nearly 3 AM. But being young, wide awake, and drunk, we all decided on a walkabout up and down Long Sands.

"Holy shit!" said Pete. "Did you guys see the rack on that chick Doug was hitting on tonight? Tits Ahoy!"

"You ain't kidding," said Scott. "Those were some huge fun bags."

I nodded and said, "I thought she was going to knock herself out with them when I played House of Pain's 'Jump Around.'"

"Whatever happened to her anyway? She looked like she was into you?" asked Scott.

Doug scoffed, "She was into me all right. Into me for three Long Island Iced Teas before confessing that she had a boyfriend back in Mass that she loved and could never cheat on."

We all looked at each other then offered Doug our condolences.

"Ouch," said Pete. "So what did you do?"

Doug hung his head in shame and mumbled, "I bought her another drink."

We all laughed. Not at Doug, but at the whole *buy drinks for a girl all night only to find out she has a boyfriend* situation. At one point or another, we had all been there.

Scott spoke first. "It's not our fault, bro. It's like they all have these super-evil woman powers over us."

I chimed in with, "Yup, they flip their hair that certain way, smile a cute smile—"

"And the next thing we know we're paying for their drinks," finished Pete.

"As soon as we see miniskirts and belly shirts, we're defenseless," Scott said as we approached the bathhouse at the center of the beach.

Our responses must have cheered Doug up because he got all excited and joined right in.

"Yea, you guys are right! They have super-evil woman powers over us! We see miniskirts and belly shirts and it's like we're hypnotized and can't help but buy them drinks all fuckin' night."

Doug didn't stop there, he continued his excited drunken babbling.

"They think they can show some cleavage, bat their eyelashes in that certain way, run their long painted nails through their hair… and the next thing you know, you're back at her place and she's having you walk around wearing her lingerie…"

At this point, Scott, Pete, and I stopped walking and stared at Doug. He feebly attempted to save himself by saying, "Umm, that happened to my cousin once. Pfft, the stupid mother fucker."

We laughed and continued our walkabout. A few minutes later, Scott posed one of his famous questions. Doug was definitely known for not having a filter on his thoughts, but Scott was known for playing into this with these random and out-of-the-blue stupid questions.

Case in point:

"Hey guys, what if a spaceship landed on the beach and this alien says to you that the only way to save our world from total destruction is for you to have sex with it. Would you do it?"

I looked at Pete and then back to Scott and said, "Where the hell do you come up with this shit?"

"Seriously," added Pete. "I think you've been watching too many *X Files*, dude."

"Is the alien a male or female?" asked Doug, much too seriously.

"We'll say it's a female," answered Scott.

And just like that, Scott had Doug hooked on his every word.

"Does she have boobs?" asked Doug.

"Three of them, but they're covered in a green, toxic, pus-filled slime."

"Really?" said Doug, taken aback. "Does she have a vagina? I mean, how else am I gonna have sex with her, right?"

By now, there was no point in Pete or me saying a word. It was obvious that Scott's scenario had Doug intrigued beyond belief.

"Yea, the alien chick has a vagina, but it's not between her legs. It's on the top of her head, and it's all scaly with giant tentacles coming out of it. And the smell..."

"Bad?" asked Doug, completely enthralled into Scott's disturbing alien scene.

"Awful!" laughed Scott.

We all joined in with laughter. The alien scenario was one of the many inane questions asked on our walkabouts throughout the years. As we continued down the sidewalk along the beach, the conversation switched to which local bar had the hottest chicks. Was it Goodnight Ogunquit? The Lobster Pound? Bogarts? The Aqua Lounge?

Before we could come up with a consensus winner, Doug interrupted and declared, "I'd do it!"

"Do what?" we all asked.

"I'd bang that alien chick!"

No wonder why he was so quiet in the last few minutes, he was still debating the stupid alien question.

We all gave Doug *a look*.

"Now, before you judge me, just hear me out. I have a theory," he said.

That's right, even back then, Doug had theories.

"So, one time when I was like seventeen or something, I was wicked shit-faced, and I ended up having sex with this ugly girl... like seriously fugly. I swear her bush was so hairy that I had to use a machete to get through it. Kinda like when I was back in 'Nam…"

"Oh God, Doug, just tell your fuckin' story already!" I said.

"I am!" Anyway, above the equator she smelled great… like, stripper great."

With that, Doug closed his eyes and took a deep sniff, smiled, then opened his eyes and continued.

"But below her equator was a different story. It was bad. Disgustingly bad. Like, low tide bad."

Coincidentally, it was low tide as he spoke, and we all couldn't help but inhale a whiff and cringe in disgust at Doug's imagery.

"And you still had sex with her?" asked Pete.

"I told you already, I was wicked shit-faced! And besides, she kept telling me I reminded her of Tom Cruise in *Top Gun*."

Obviously, *she* must have been shit-faced as well, I thought.

"All night she kept calling me Maverick," he proudly declared. "That was his name in the—"

"We fuckin' know his name in the movie, dipshit," laughed Pete.

"What is your point to all of this, Doug?" I said. "Please tell me you have some resemblance of a point?"

"Yea, what does this have to do with my alien question?" asked Scott.

"My point is, as hairy and disgustingly bad as she smelled, I still had sex with her, and I did it for nothing. If I bang this alien chick, I'd be saving the whole world. I'd be a frickin' hero! And we all know heroes get the hot chicks, right? Right?"

Pete and Scott smiled widely.

Scott gave Doug a high five and exclaimed, "Fuckin' A!"

Pete followed with a high five and a, "Fuckin' right!"

All that was left was for me to finish up with a high five and a, "Fuckin' Maverick!"

Not all of our walkabouts were that graphic or immature (84%), but for whatever reason, that was the one that popped into my mind that night as I lay in my bed. It was probably because I had been watching the *X Files* earlier in the day.

Now that Pete was back, I knew that Doug had high hopes to start our walkabouts up again, but... but to be honest, I knew it'd never be the same again.

Sadly, our walkabouts weren't the only thing that crossed my mind before I dozed off that night. You guessed it—the answering machine. My curiosity was killing me, so I decided to stay awake until the coast was clear.

Fortunately, I only had to wait three and a half minutes. That's when I heard the obnoxiously loud, house-shaking rumble of Doug's snoring. The more drinks he had in him, the higher the number on the snoring Richter scale.

As soon as I felt my bed rumbling and shaking, I quickly jumped up and headed for the living room. I took a deep breath and hit play. No, I didn't bother turning the volume down. If you've ever heard Doug's snoring, you'd understand why I actually turned *up* the volume.

Unfortunately, my disappointment was immediate. The first message was from my mother (no offense, Ma). Of course, it took her twenty-five seconds to realize she was talking to a machine and not to me. By the time she actually started to leave a message, the machine beeped and cut her off. I loudly sighed, knowing full well who the second message on the machine was from.

9

"POSSIBILITY DAYS" – Counting Crows

The next morning, as promised, I showed up at Anna's little cottage. It was a pothole-ridden dirt road, which was tucked away and hidden enough that it wasn't a well-traveled road for cars. We used to traverse it many a night on our walkabouts. I had a good idea which cottage was hers, and it was confirmed when I saw the rental car.

Now, to be clear, even though I was pressured into this little sightseeing day, I wasn't dreading it. Also to be clear, I wasn't completely psyched either. Anna seemed nice enough and definitely cute enough, but as you'll hear many times throughout this book, in the summer of '99, I was NOT looking to get involved with anyone, especially a two week summer girl… from Iowa.

I barely put my car in park, when she exited the cottage with a giant smile on her face. She wore shorts, a tank top, sunglasses, and had a large backpack in tow. Seeing as this wasn't a date, and seeing as I wasn't trying to impress or romance her, I didn't feel the need to get out and open her door for her.

That being said, I also didn't want to be ungentlemanly, so I chose the safe middle ground. I pushed her door open from the inside.

"Awwww, thanks," she said as she got in and put her backpack on the floor in front of her.

Hmmm, the fact that she said 'Awwww'(with 4 w's), indicated that not only did she notice my gesture, but that she was touched by it. I hope she didn't read into it too much and think that I was romanticizing her. I didn't want that at all. I probably should have let her open her own door!

"I thought you might forget about me," she said.

"Nah. A promise is a promise."

"Did you see the sunrise this morning?" she asked excitedly.

"Umm, I'm afraid I missed it… again. You were really up that early?" I asked.

"Yup. I drove up to the long beach… I mean, Long Sands," she corrected herself with a smile. "Don't tell Doug I said that," she laughed.

"Yea, he takes that stuff a little too personally," I said. "He's kind of a local snob in that way. I guess most of us locals are."

"I'm sure you guys get sick of idiot tourists like me."

"Relax, you're not in the idiot tourist category. Not yet," I smiled.

"I have to admit, I was hesitant about coming here by myself, but after seeing the sunrise over the ocean and hearing the waves wash over the sand, I am so glad I came. And the salt air! Did you smell that this morning?"

"I must have missed that one too," I said, putting the car in reverse.

"Thanks so much for today," she said.

"Uhhh, we haven't even done anything yet."

"I know, but I'm sure it'll be fun."

Cute, funny, *and* appreciative?? I should have known right then and there that I was in for it.

"Do you think we can go up to the lighthouse today?" she asked.

"Well I wouldn't be much of a tour guide if we didn't. I'm surprised you didn't go up there to watch the sunrise."

"I wanted to, but... I didn't know how to get there, and I didn't want to get lost."

Normally, Doug and I would have had a field day with her statement, but I saved my "typical tourist" comment, and continued driving up the bumpy dirt road.

"You can put your bag in the backseat, if you want?"

"Oh thanks," she said, lifting it between the seats and into the back.

"What do you have in there anyway?"

"Suntan lotion, Chapstick, my purse, my camera, and a sweatshirt... I heard the weather in Maine can change just like that.

"Yea, I did hear there was a chance of snow flurries later today," I said.

She fell for it for almost three seconds before giving me a glare.

"Ha ha. You're trying to get me to reach idiot tourist status, aren't you?"

I gave her a playful shrug and said, "What else ya got in there?"

"A towel, in case we go swimming, a change of clothes..."

"A change of clothes? You do realize this isn't an overnight trip, right?"

"Yes, I know," she smirked, "but I've kinda been known to spill stuff on myself. Food, drinks... it's not pretty. I just wanted to be prepared, that's all."

"Ahh, gotcha," I said. "Is that it?"

She thought for a second then said, "I also brought a book. And no, not because I thought you'd be boring. I just always carry a book with me. Just a habit, I guess."

"I see. You just want to be prepared for anything, right?"

"That's right," she nodded. "Oh, and I brought some CDs. Do you wanna listen to one?"

Normally, I was pretty territorial when it came to a stranger (or anyone) playing music in my car... or my apartment, but I decided to make an exception for her. No, not because she was cute and sweet, but because my curiosity was piqued in regards to her musical taste.

"Just so you know," I said, "I get full veto power."

She saluted me then handed me a CD. I gave it a quick look-over before inserting it. It was titled *Anna's Mix* (with a heart over the i). Definitely a rookie title, I thought. Rather than give her a tutorial on the art of mix-CD-making, I decided to just bite my tongue. That being said, if her mix was filled with shitty songs, all bets were off, and I would let her have it!

"This isn't full of those stupid boy bands, is it? Or some of that jug band, country-lovin' cornfield music, is it?"

"Cornfield music? Just put it in already. Geez," she said, rolling her eyes.

Hesitantly, I put it in and was pleasantly shocked when the Counting Crows came on.

"Tour guide approved?" she asked.

"So far."

84

Her mix ended up being full of 90's alternative rock (Verve, Offspring, Foo Fighters, Veruca Salt, etc), and although there were a few bands I didn't really like (Sublime, Green Day, Creed, Oasis), for the most part, I approved.

Technically, I liked Oasis' music, but after the Providence, Rhode Island incident, I, along with Scott and Doug despised the Gallagher brothers. What was this incident I speak of? Oh, I'll tell you!

All three of us excitedly drove two hours down to Providence to see Oasis at the very cool and intimate Strand Theater. They performed a handful songs before storming off stage and ending the show (No money back)! All of this because someone in the crowd threw a shoe on stage. It didn't really seem like a vicious throw, but it was enough to make the Gallagher brothers swear at the crowd and storm off. The fuckers!

Knowing Anna's excitement, I decided to make the Nubble Lighthouse our first stop. As usual, it was packed with picture-taking tourists, so Anna fit right in. I don't think the smile left her face the entire time we were there; the whole day, as a matter of fact.

Again, this was 1999, so we were still a few years away from cell phone cameras, and even digital cameras were still a few years from being a big deal. Anna had an old school camera with real film and everything. With the amount of pictures she took on that day alone, it must have cost her a small fortune to get developed.

Her smile nearly jumped off her face when I asked her if she wanted me to take some pictures of her and the lighthouse. I took picture after picture of her jumping from rock to craggy rock. On a few pictures, I even caught the spray of the waves over her shoulder.

The picture taking was definitely a touristy thing to do, but seeing her child-like excitement, I didn't feel all that awkward. Besides, it wasn't like she was taking pictures of me, and it certainly wasn't like we were asking strangers to take a picture of us together. I mean, why would we? It wasn't a date! It was just me playing tour guide to a sweet girl from Iowa. A girl I would probably never see again after today.

We ended up staying there for nearly two hours. As a matter of fact, that might be the longest time I've ever spent there. Well, except for girls I had sexual relations with. Actually, even then, I was never there very long :)

Our next stop was going to be exploring the shops and whatnot of the Short Sands area, but seeing as she had already done a little bit of that on her own, and seeing as it was a mad house down there that day, I decided to keep to more of the landscape-type scenery. After seeing her excitement at the lighthouse area, I figured she would love the Cliff Walk down in the harbor.

I know what you're thinking, didn't I take Elise there on our infamous first (only) date? Yes, yes I did. But that night with Elise wasn't the only time I had been on the Cliff Walk with a girl. I say that not to brag or sound like a player, but with all the summer girls who had come in and out of my life over the years, it was inevitable that more than a few of them would enjoy the Cliff Walk. And no, not all of these girls were hookups or whatever. Not at all. Elise was the perfect example of that.

Actually, I had only been there once since that night with Elise four years earlier. The Elise-night was definitely my most memorable, but after the way it all ended, I did my best to put it out of my mind. To be honest, I did my best to put the entire

Elise experience out of my head. I was more than a little embarrassed by my silly pursuit of her that summer.

Since that fateful summer of '95, I had obviously pursued, flirted, and even dated other summer girls, but I never allowed myself to get as overeager and as stupid as I did with Elise.

Anyway, the bottom line is, it didn't feel that weird taking Anna to the Cliff Walk, and like I said earlier, it wasn't like I was trying to make this a romantic moment.

Anna absolutely loved the walk, as was reflected by the many, many pictures she took. There wasn't a cloud in the sky, which made the ocean below us look swimming pool blue. The glimmer off the water was blinding to the eyes. It really was a beautiful location. It wasn't even noon yet, and she had already thanked me over a dozen times. It was quite endearing.

Although we kept our conversations to small talk, they seemed to flow easily, very easily actually. If you had to play tour guide to a complete stranger, then Anna Jensen was the perfect candidate.

From the Cliff Walk, I decided to drive her down the coast into Kittery. Kittery is the southernmost town in Maine, and while it's not the crazy tourist destination like York, it still had plenty of scenic spots.

We stopped at the old Frisbee's Market and grabbed some drinks and sandwiches and made our way over to Fort Foster. The fort was active from 1901-1946, and along with the pier, it provided many amazing views out to the ocean.

It had probably been ten plus years since I had been there. We used to go there all the time when I was a little kid. I relayed the stories to Anna of how my cousins and I used to run around playing army. Back then, the whole fort was open to the public. The dark underground bunkers provided perfect hiding spots for kids. The eerie darkness mixed with the urban legends of ghosts, provided the perfect place for kids to run around and be scared shitless. Good times.

"My dad is big on history, and he used to take us to a lot of the forts in our area," she said. "Most were from the Wild West days."

"Cool," I said. "I've always loved old forts too. I'll have to check some of them out when I go see the Field of Dreams one day."

"You're really infatuated with that silly baseball field, aren't you?"

"I'm telling ya, you need to see the movie. I bet your dad loves it. It's kind of a guy movie."

"Actually, my dad was never really into sports. He would much rather watch the History Channel or classic Western movies."

Anna went on to tell me about her parents divorcing when she was ten. Her dad and stepmother now live five hours away from her in Omaha. I could tell how sad she was when she mentioned how little she saw him. At that point, I mentioned my parents had divorced when I was eight.

We both went back and forth regarding our experiences with divorce. I hadn't talked about stuff like that since the Jane days. It felt a little strange, yet comfortably strange. Anna went on to talk about a lot of things with me. She was never long-winded or boring, and her extensive conversations never fell into the babbling category. It was nice having someone else carry the conversation.

Anna was an open book and appeared eager to let me into her world. I was polite and engaged when needed, but I wasn't as eager to open up my book to her. It wasn't personal, it was just a case of not wanting to get too private, especially to someone who would be gone tomorrow or next week or whenever.

In case I haven't made it clear to you guys yet, the summer of 1999, I was officially retired from wearing my heart on my sleeve. That being said, Anna and I had a fun time together, and even though I had been to these locations hundreds of times, it was nice seeing them again through her eyes.

While at Fort Foster, we walked the path along the ocean's edge. When she wasn't raving about how beautiful it was, she was snapping picture after picture. We walked onto the pier and I pointed out another lighthouse (Whaleback) to her.

Her excitement over forts and lighthouses (especially lighthouses) got me to thinking. *If* this was a girl I was interested in, I would have filed away that info, and I would have planned an amazing future date; a date consisting of the ultimate fort and lighthouse excursion up the coast of Maine. But as of that moment, Anna was not a love interest. She was just a girl passing through the revolving door known as York Beach.

After our non-romantic picnic, Anna somehow got us involved in a giant game of Wiffle ball, which was being played on the grass field by the fort. There were about a dozen kids ranging from six to twelve-ish.

"Hey, do you mind if we play too?" she politely asked.

Considering that we were the only two adults, the kids assumed we were both good players, so they split us up. Let's just say, the kids learned a valuable lesson about assuming.

To put it politely, Anna wasn't very good. To put it bluntly, she was awful. She struck out three times on nine pitches, and four of them were either ten feet outside or ten feet over her head. Some of the kids felt bad for her. Well, not the kids on her team, but most on mine did.

I'll give her credit, I've never seen someone strike out three times yet still continue to laugh and smile about it. If that was me, I would have thrown the skinny yellow bat into the damn ocean, and the kids would have learned a few new swear words.

After our game (we won 18 to 11), she said to me, "See, I told you I sucked at sports."

I was going to ask her if that was the case then why did she ask to play in the first place, but I didn't because it was obvious she did it just to have fun and be social.

Before we headed out, Anna took a few more pictures of the fort, the ocean, the lighthouse… pretty much everything surrounding us. We took a short drive down the road to another old Kittery fort (Fort McClary). It was a smaller fort with much smaller grounds, but that didn't seem to curb Anna's enthusiasm one bit. It was late afternoon when we finally left the Kittery area.

"Thank you so much for today," she said. "I had such a great time."

The way she worded it, provided me with the perfect opportunity to call it a day with this tour guide gig. When the day started, I planned on being home by five with my ass loungin' on my couch, a beer in one hand and the remote in the other. That's what I originally planned, but something strange happened throughout the day —I actually enjoyed myself.

Anna provided the perfect relief from that black cloud known as my life at the time. I was enjoying myself so much, I suggested we drive up and explore the town of Ogunquit. Ogunquit is the beach town just north of York. It's considered a bit more upscale and more quaint than York Beach.

"You really don't have to," she said. "I'm sure you're getting bored of showing me around."

"Eh, it's not so bad," I smiled. "Besides, I really think you'll like this place."

She widely smiled. "I'm sure I will."

We eventually drove up Route 1, and I pointed out the nightclub I used to DJ at years earlier.

"We have plenty of little hick bars near my town," she said, "but you have to drive about an hour to find an actual dance club. That must have been so much fun to work there."

Lost in nostalgia, I nodded. I always loved working there, but now that it's been five years, I had a whole new appreciation of just how fun it was. If only I could turn back the clock eight or nine years, I thought.

Before my mind drifted and reminisced too much, Anna's voice snapped me out of it.

"What's that place?" she asked as we drove by the Ogunquit Playhouse.

I explained that it was an old playhouse (built in the 30's I think), and they did a lot of big musicals throughout the summer.

"It's a huge tourist attraction," I said.

"I bet it's beautiful inside. I love musicals," she said, "but I've never seen one in a classic old building like that."

Again, *if* I was romantically interested in Anna, I would have made a mental note to take her to a future show. But I wasn't, so there was no mental note taken, just a fleeting thought.

It had been awhile since I walked around downtown Ogunquit, but for the most part, it was the same as I remembered. We poked our heads in just about every store. Anna used the opportunity to buy more film and also add to her postcard collection.

Afterwards, we ended up grabbing drinks at Maxwell's pub in downtown Ogunquit. Anna's friendly and talkative nature continued as she befriended the older couple seated next to us. They were from Toronto, and by the end of the conversation, Anna (and I) had an open invitation to visit them whenever we wanted.

I wasn't the most social person with strangers, so I was more than impressed with Anna's ability to not only talk to whomever, but to leave them feeling like they've known each other forever. She had the same effect on my friends last night, including me.

After our browsing of stores and having our drinks, we headed down the street towards Perkin's Cove, where there were yet again, more tourists shops. Yay! Luckily, Anna made quick work of browsing, and we decided to grab dinner at Barnacle Billy's.

It was here that Anna Jensen had her first ever Maine lobstah.

Fun Fact (from Anna): 90% of the nation's lobsters are caught off Maine.

Let's just say, if Facebook was around then, she would have filled her timeline with photos of Larry the Lobster. Yes, she named her lobster, and yes, it was a boring and cliché name, but seeing how uncreatively she named her CD mixes, it didn't really shock me.

And if Facebook did exist then, my timeline would have been filled pictures of Iowa girl "attempting" to crack and eat her lobster. A hot mess? A beautiful disaster? Both of which came to mind. Before I had a chance to help her out, the woman sitting next to us came over (laughing), and she showed Anna the proper way.

Of course, this led to a friendly conversation, and long story short, Anna (and I) also have an open invitation to visit Albany, New York. I'm not sure why anyone would ever want to, but it was a nice offer.

There were many moments that would have been appropriate to end our day. After dinner was one of them, but for whatever reason, I suggested we take a walk on the Marginal Way. The Marginal Way is basically Ogunquit's version of the Cliff Walk in York. It winds its way for about a mile along the Atlantic Ocean from Perkin's Cove out to the Ogunquit beaches. It was a good thing Anna loaded up on film earlier because her fingers didn't stop clicking.

Our conversation during dinner centered around her relationship with her older brother and sister. They were both closer to my age and had moved out of Iowa a long time ago. Her brother was married living in Wichita, Kansas. Anna had a niece and nephew, but sadly said she rarely got to see them. Her sister was still single and living in Chicago.

Although Anna did most of the talking, she did make it a point to ask about my family as well. I politely responded, though I wasn't as detailed or as talkative as her. It wasn't until our walk on the Marginal Way that she pulled out the big guns.

"So, do you have a girlfriend?" she asked out of the blue.

Before I had a chance to respond, she quickly clarified.

"Not that I'm trying to hit on you! You know what, it's really none of my business. You totally don't have to answer."

"Relax, Anna. It's not a big deal. I didn't think you were hitting on me. And no, I don't have a girlfriend."

I suppose that would have been the perfect moment to return the question to her, but I assumed if she had a boyfriend, he would have been there on vacation with her.

She didn't delve into my lack of a girlfriend, instead, she continued taking pictures of the ocean. I think it was her polite way of giving me "an out" of the conversation.

I think we all know, you're never supposed to talk about your exes on a first date, but seeing as this was a friendly tour guide and NOT a first date, I offered a little backstory of my girlfriendless status. I didn't go as far back as Jane, but I did gloss over the Felicia situation.

"So how long did you two date for?" she asked.

"Two and a half weeks," I quietly answered.

Every time I heard myself answer that question out loud, I somehow felt embarrassed. Inside my head, it always felt longer… much, much longer.

"So she broke up with you just like that?"

"Yea. She said she wasn't ready for a serious commitment and she just needed to find herself, which I quickly found out was just a euphemism for wanting to date around."

"I'm sorry," Anna said.

"Thanks. I probably would have had an easier time moving on, except she always told me, if she ever settled down one day that I was the type of guy she would want to be with."

Again, hearing myself say that out loud made me realize just how much total bullshit that was. If Felicia knew I was the exact type of guy she wanted to be with, then why in the fuck would she need to date around?!?

"So, yea, she always had a way of making me think that someday we might get back together. Trust me, though, I've given up on that. It's been six months, and she's still doing a bang up job in trying to *find* herself."

You would think my little sob story would have brought the vibe down, but Anna simply gave me an encouraging smile and said, "Do you know what you need?"

I swear, if she would have fallen into Doug's camp and suggested that I just needed to "get laid," I would have jumped off the cliff into the ocean.

Fortunately, her suggestion was way more PG-rated than Doug's. It was actually quite G-rated.

"You need some salt water taffy from the Goldenrod."

"Oh, is that so?" I said.

"And by you, I kind of mean me," she giggled.

"Is that your way of saying the Goldenrod should be our next stop?"

"No. I'm only kidding. You've already gone above and beyond today."

She was right. I did go above and beyond. I was practically a tour guide extraordinaire! But as you probably already assumed, I continued our day, and we made our way back into York and to the famed Goldenrod.

It was dusk when we pulled into the Short Sands parking lot, and because it was a warm summer's night, the downtown area was packed. This, of course, meant the Goldenrod was also packed. I swear there must have been fifteen or twenty people standing at the big front window gawking at the sight of the taffy being made. I noticed Anna's eyes and smile widen as she too looked towards the window.

Before she got too mesmerized by the taffy machine, she looked over at me and smirked and said, "Don't worry, I won't embarrass you."

"Good," I joked. "For the most part, you've avoided typical tourist status today. Let's keep it that way."

We entered, and I watched as she eagerly picked out her taffy. I already explained on the ride over that I wasn't really a taffy kind of guy. It wasn't that I didn't like the flavor, I just didn't like the taffyness to it; just too much effort to chew it. I felt the same way about tootsie rolls, sugar daddy's, and gum. My jaw is not a big fan of working that hard. People usually think that is the most ridiculous thing they've ever heard, and Iowa girl was no exception.

After we left the Goldenrod, we walked up and down the sidewalks by all of the beach shops. We didn't enter any of them, we just walked and talked. Just watching her eat all of that taffy made my fucking jaw tired.

All of a sudden, Anna abruptly stopped walking and looked over at me. I was suspicious as I watched her smile get bigger.

"What?" I asked. "You want more taffy?"

She shook her head no and continued smiling as she pointed up ahead. I curiously looked over and saw she was pointing at Madame Rita's.

Madame Rita was our resident palm reader/fortune teller. Her storefront was a little 10X10 space with a curtain in the back corner. Behind the curtain was where the "magic" happened.

When I looked back at Anna, she was smiling as big as she had all day.

"Oh no, no, no," I said.

"Yup," she said. "We're totally getting our palms read! I know this will officially make me a typical idiot tourist, but…"

I immediately nodded in agreement.

"Oh come on Josh, it'll be fun. I'll even pay."

Whether it was her excited smile, or her overall cuteness, I don't know, but I went against my better judgement and agreed to her silly request. If she wanted to waste her vacation money on something as stupid as a palm reader, so be it.

"Do you mind if I go first?" she asked, bursting at the seams.

"Be my guest. I'll be right out here anxiously awaiting my turn."

She rolled her eyes and handed me her bag of taffy.

"Can you hold this for me?"

I nodded and took the bag.

"Don't eat any," she joked as she entered Madame Rita's curtained-off area.

I stood on the sidewalk and awaited Anna's return. I still couldn't believe she would waste her money on something as silly and transparent as a fortune teller. What did I expect though, she also wasted her money on coming to York for her big vacation.

As expected, Anna came out from behind the curtain with a giant-ass grin, and she motioned for me that it was my turn. I sighed, but didn't say a word as I handed her the taffy bag. I then entered behind the dreaded curtain.

This wasn't my first rodeo with Madame Rita, but it had been many, many, many years since my last appearance there. Growing up and working at the beach all those years, Madame Rita knew exactly who I was. I'm sure this played right into her fortune-telling spiel.

When we were finished, I exited through the curtain and was quickly bombarded by Anna asking, "That was so cool, wasn't it?"

As we headed back up the sidewalk, I said, "Please tell me you really don't believe in that shit, do you?"

"Oh come on, do you have to suck the fun out of everything? So what did she say to you?" she asked.

"Just the typical vague nonsense."

Anna seemed to ignore my cynicism and proceeded to tell me about her experience.

"After she read my palm, I paid for her to read my tarot cards too."

"For ten more dollars, you could have gotten the full-crackpot-charlatan special—crystal ball and all!" I laughed.

"You really do have to suck the fun out of everything, don't you?"

The way she said it, and the way she looked at me, told me that she was slightly annoyed at my sarcasm. We had only known each other for less than twenty-four hours, but this was the first time I'd seen that look from her. I didn't like it, not at all. I instantly felt like shit.

I remembered the first time I went to Madame Rita. I was sixteen or seventeen, and it was with Scott and two other girls we met at the Fun-O-Rama. Even back then, I wasn't really sold on the palm reading thing, but I do remember how excited we all were comparing our fortunes after. We all had so much fun and so many laughs that night. So just because I'm old and jaded now, I had no right to suck the fun from Anna.

"So what did she say to you?" I asked with sincerity.

Anna looked at me to see if I was being serious. I must have passed her eye test because she went on to tell me all of the "stuff" that Madame Rita told her.

"Oh, and the coolest thing, she told me was I was an old soul. My grandmother used to tell me that all the time."

I was definitely not a believer in the art of fortune telling, but I saw how happy Anna was afterwards. I guess there's something to be said about that.

"She kind of said the same thing to me," I said.

"She called you an old soul too?"

"No. She just called me old," I joked.

Anna gave a fake laugh, rolled her eyes then polished off the rest of her taffy. On our way back to the parking lot, I looked over at Here Hey Hoohahs. I almost suggested that we go grab a nightcap, but I thought better of it. If Doug knew I was still on my "tour guide" with Anna, he would surely give me shit. And by shit, I mean he would have gloated how he was the ultimate matchmaker.

He would then blast me with questions like: *Did you bang her yet? What kind of kisser is she? Soft and supple or a sloppy?*

Doug would then retell (20th time) the story of the chick who kissed so badly that he thought she was going to swallow his whole head.

At that point, Doug would probably start in on his stupid sexual innuendos. Yup, there wasn't a doubt in my mind that Doug would say something like: *So, did Iowa girl show you her field of dreams… as in, if you build it, she will cum?* Followed by him proclaiming just how fucking funny he was.

It was settled. There was no way I was going to bring Anna in there for drinks. Nope, not gonna happen!

I was, however, enjoying Anna's company, and although I didn't want to subject myself to Doug's comments, I did want to stretch the night out longer.

So, as we stood by my car, I made a suggestion.

"How about we leave my car here and I walk you back to your cottage?"

"Sure," she said. "But wait, that would mean you'd have to walk back to get your car."

I proceeded to tell her about our walkabouts; many of which took us down her road. I tried my best not to paint our walkabouts as just an occasion for stupid and silly guy talk. There were plenty of serious conversations that revolved around broken hearts or future dreams or whatever.

Anna listened intently about our guy-bonding walkabouts, and she even seemed a little jealous.

"I used to do late night walks too," she said. "But it was never usually a group thing. It was just me and my best friend, Rebecca. Of course, we certainly didn't have the beautiful backdrop of the beach and the ocean. We'd just walk down my road, which was a long, straight country road with farms and cornfields as far as the eye could see. Unless it was a full moon, it would be so dark that we had to carry flashlights because there were no street lights."

Speaking of no street lights, as we entered Railroad Ave. Ext, I'd forgotten how dark it was at night.

"Did you guys ever do your walks through the cornfields?" I asked.

"Yea, right! And take a chance on running into the children of the corn?"

"Ah yes, the children of the corn," I laughed.

"Thanks to your Mr. Stephen King, I'm forever scared to walk through the corn rows… even in the day!"

"I'll be sure and send your regards the next time I see him."

Her voice raised a notched as she said, "You know Stephen King?"

"Well yeah. Everyone from Maine knows everyone else," I said with a sarcastic smirk.

She covered her embarrassed face with her hand and said, "As you can tell, I was voted most gullible in high school."

"It's ok. You'd actually be surprised how many people think just because you're from Maine that you know Stephen King."

"I suppose I have now officially reached typical tourist status?"

"I hate to break it to you, Iowa girl, but you reached that a long time ago."

We both laughed as we stood at the head of her driveway, and for the first time all day, there was a brief moment of uncomfortable silence. And NO, it wasn't because there was the thought of a goodnight kiss looming in the air. At least not from my perspective, and I was pretty sure not from hers either.

I think our silence was more from the fact that this was probably the last time we would ever see each other, or at the very least, the last time we would hang out like this. I was the first to speak.

"Well, if I don't see you again, have a great vacation and a safe flight back home."

"Thanks," she said. "And thanks so much for today. I know your friends pressured you into it, but I appreciate it, and I really, really had a lot of fun."

"You're right," I smiled. "They did pressure me, didn't they?"

She nodded.

"I'm just kidding. Trust me, if I didn't want to show you around, I wouldn't have. I actually had a lot of fun too."

"Actually?" she said. "You didn't think you would?"

"Don't take it personally," I said. "I just think the novelty of this whole beach life has worn off on me. It's probably because I'm getting older... grouchier."

"You're really hung up on your age, aren't you? Older? Grouchier? You sound like you're an eighty-year-old man getting ready to yell at the kids to stay off your lawn."

"Soon enough," I laughed.

"Do you know what you need?" she asked.

"Taffy?"

"Ha ha. No. You need to go spend a summer in Iowa. Then maybe you wouldn't take this beautiful place for granted."

I didn't retort. I didn't feel I was taking this place for granted at all. Just because you're sick and tired of something, it doesn't mean you're taking it for granted. In my head, there was absolutely a difference.

Although there were a few moments of cynicism throughout the day, overall our conversations were good, really good. I decided not to end the night on a sour note, and besides, I knew she wouldn't ever fully understand where my negativity was coming from, and why would she, to her, York Beach was a new, shiny toy. So with that in mind, I decided to end the night on a positive note.

"If you ever get the craving for a blueberry ale… or, you know, just a Budweiser…"

She smiled and said, "I might take you up on that offer. Night, Josh, and thanks again. You're a great tour guide."

"Thanks," I laughed and waved goodbye. With that, we both turned and went our separate ways.

As I walked back down the darkened dirt road, I found myself replaying the day's events. I truly did have a fun day. Unfortunately, it wouldn't be enough to bring me out of my funk.

10

"MR. BRIGHTSIDE" – The Killers

The next morning, I met up with Pete and Doug at the batting cages at York's Wild Kingdom. I hadn't even seen my first pitch when they started in with their sarcastic comments.

"Sooo, how was your date yesterday with Iowa girl?" began Pete.

"Did she spend the night?" asked Doug.

I swung and missed then responded, "It was NOT a date. And no, she did NOT spend the night."

"Did she show you her field of dreams?" laughed Doug.

Do I know this guy or what? It was a damn good thing Anna and I didn't go in for drinks last night. I was, however, a little disappointed that Doug wasn't clever (perverted) enough to follow up his comment with the *If you build it, she will cum* line.

"So how was your non-date then?" Pete sarcastically said.

"It was fun. We had a good time."

Doug made solid contact with the ball then said, "Oh, I bet."

Again, I swung and missed.

"Guys, there was no kissing, no touching, no nothing! I just gave her a tour."

Doug turned to Pete and smiled. "And by tour he means…"

"Oh, for Christ sake!" I interrupted, "By tour I mean tour! Guys, we're not twenty-one anymore. I'm not looking for some random hookup or summer fling sorta thing. I've been done with that shit for a while."

The more irritated I became, the harder I swung the bat, and the harder I swung, the more missed by a mile. I probably would have missed even worse if my irritation turned to anger. That theory was about to be tested.

"She's not coming back to you, ya know?" said Doug.

"What are you talking about?" I asked.

"Jane?" questioned Pete.

"Nope," said Doug. "Felicia."

I shook my head in disgust at Doug, but that didn't stop him from running his mouth some more.

"She's not gonna get back together with you, so I don't know why you're wasting your time waiting around."

"Fuck off, Doug! Who says I'm waiting around?"

"Oh come on," laughed Doug. "When we went back to your place the other night, the first thing your eyes did was look over at the answering machine."

I gripped the bat tighter. I wanted to crush the stupid baseball.

"You didn't think I noticed that, did ya? You probably couldn't wait until I passed out to check it."

"I'm out of the loop here," said Pete. "Who's this Felicia chick?"

Let's go to the batting cages they said. It'll be fun they said. This is not fuckin' fun! Not only did I have to listen to their comments about my day with Anna, but now I had to listen to Doug fill Pete in on Felicia.

He painted a highly exaggerated picture of how bad our relationship was and how much of a bitch Felicia was. I didn't really have the energy to defend myself or her for that matter.

If I'm to be completely honest, maybe Doug's view wasn't that exaggerated. I mean, I wouldn't necessarily call Felicia a bitch, but in my heart, I knew she wasn't really the one for me. But still, I couldn't let Doug know he was right. I would never hear the end of it.

"Have you even gotten laid since she dumped you?" asked Doug. "Because that was like five or six months ago."

Again, my grip tightened on the aluminum bat. Not because I wanted to crush the ball, but because I wanted to crush Doug's face.

"What the fuck does that have to do with anything?" I said.

"I'm just saying, it's not like she's going without. I mean, I bet she's been with a half dozen guys since she was with you."

"Fuck you!" I yelled, yet knowing it was probably closer to a dozen. "Just because I haven't gotten laid doesn't mean I'm still hung up on her. And neither does me not wanting anything to do with summer girls anymore. Just because you're still living the playboy summer lifestyle, doesn't mean I have to!"

Doug said nothing. He casually waited for his next pitch and proceeded to line it deep into the netting. Unfortunately, his silence was short-lived.

"You're jealous of my penis, aren't you?" he asked, straight-faced.

I had no response. Absolutely no response. Pete on the other hand...

"I'm kinda jealous of it," laughed Pete.

They both smiled and gave each other a high five. This is one thing I DIDN'T miss about the good ol' days; getting teamed up on by my dumbass friends.

With the exception of some small talk, not much was spoken after that. Even though I calmed down enough to start crushing the ball deep, the damage was done. Doug's comments put a chink in my armor. He was an over-exaggerating fool, but he wasn't wrong... not completely.

Like I told you earlier, Felicia and I started dating less than two weeks after we met, and then we broke up less than three weeks after that. And by broke up, I mean she dumped me.

"I'm not ready to be tied down," she told me. *"I just need to find myself,"* she said. *"I kind of just want to see what's out there and have some fun,"* she said.

From that point on, I started treating it like a competition or some kind of challenge. I was bound and determined to prove to her that I was better for her than anyone else she could ever find. I know, I know, it sounds ridiculous— egotistical even.

I won't go into all of my feeble and lame attempts to win Felicia back, but let's just say, there might have been some letters, and poems, and sweet gestures involved. And yes, several bouquets of roses might have been sent.

We even attended a couple of concerts together after our breakup. We actually had a great time, in particular, the second concert—Radiohead. At several points throughout the night, we were holding hands and had our arms around one another. It felt like the sparks were flying again and that the fire was about to be rekindled. But after the show, when I attempted a goodnight kiss, she was quick to extinguish all fuckin' sparks and flames.

Needless to say, I fuckin' hate that band now. Sadly though, even that didn't deter me from continuing my pursuit of proving myself worthy to her.

Wow, saying those things out loud makes me realize that Doug was right, I really was fuckin' pathetic! And just maybe he was also right… maybe, just maybe I did need to get laid. But that being said, I still had no intentions on reverting back to summer flings or one night stands. I truly was fed up with that bullshit.

Anyway, my point is, the batting cages proved to be a wakeup call. I really needed to get Felicia out of my mind and move on.

I left the batting cages and went home and showered, and I'll have you know, I never once looked at the answering machine. True story.

11

"A GIRL LIKE YOU" – Pete Yorn

It was just Taylor and I for the first few hours of work that day. Doug was out running errands or doing whatever things Doug does. Even when he finally showed up, there was still a little bit of tension from our earlier banter at the batting cages. I knew it was only a matter of time before it would blow over, but for the moment, we kept to small talk.

As I was pouring a couple of drafts, Taylor gave me a nudge and pointed to the door.

"You're woman is here," she said.

My heart jumped, and I looked over expecting to see Felicia… or maybe even Jane. I guess that speaks volumes to just how screwed up my head was. When I saw it was Anna, I gave Taylor a glare.

"Don't you start in on me too," I said.

"Oh, relax, Josh," she said, then I swear she mumbled, "You really do need to get laid."

Before I had a chance to respond, Anna approached the bar. She was wearing a white sundress, her hair was pulled back, and it was blatantly obvious she had gotten way too much sun. Her skin was red and probably looked even worse in contrast to her white dress. Taylor and I did our best not to laugh.

"Go ahead, laugh," she said. "I fell asleep on the beach."

"Don't they use sunblock in Iowa?" I asked.

"Well, yea, but it was a little hazy at the beach, so I just assumed..."

We shook our heads at her then Taylor smiled and said, "Rookie mistake."

"I look stupid, don't I?" she said, sitting up on the bar stool.

"Nah, you look fine," Taylor said, then mumbled, "For a rookie tourist."

"You and you're mumbling," I said with a smirk.

Just then, we heard Doug's voice from across the bar.

"Holy shit! It's a frickin' lobstah wearing a sundress!"

Anna slid down on her stool and blushed. Well, I'm assuming she blushed, but it was hard to tell with her sunburn.

Doug approached her and joked, "Haven't they heard of sunblock in Iowa? Well, congratulations, Iowa girl, you're officially a dumbass tourist."

Doug raised his hand at her for a high five and said, "High five... or should I say, high claw."

Anna giggled and appeased him with a high five.

"You don't have to laugh at any of his stupid jokes," Taylor said. "None of us do."

Doug ignored her comment, for his attention was already focused on a table of girls in the back. A table of young girls.

His non-stop energy to flirt and schmooze with the new crop of summer girls never ceased to amaze me. And no, it's NOT like Doug said, I WASN'T jealous of his penis. At that point, I think I was more worried about his penis.

As Doug walked off, I slid Anna a beer. She started to take out some money, but I waved her down and said, "You're all set. It's free drinks for cute crustaceans' day."

My comment was met by strange stares from Anna and Taylor.

"What? Doug called her a lobster. I was doing a funny play on that. It was funny," I pointed out.

Taylor shook her head and looked over to Anna and said, "This is what I have to deal with on a daily basis."

Taylor then headed over to wait on a customer. Anna gave me a smile and said, "It was kinda funny."

In that split second, my mind began an internal debate. Should I have used the word cute? Did she think I was flirting with her? Maybe I should explain to her I was just being silly and that I was absolutely not flirting with her. Though I should probably omit the word absolutely. I certainly didn't want to offend the poor girl. I went back and forth but ultimately decided to say nothing about it.

"Thanks for the drink," she said. "I appreciate it. And thanks again for yesterday. I had fun."

"Yea, not a problem. So what's on your agenda the rest of today?"

"Besides purchasing a gallon jar of Aloe Vera, not too much," she smiled.

"You should come back by tonight," Taylor said, walking by. "It's ladies night, so they'll be a lot of cute guys here. Some of my girlfriends will be here too. I can introduce you to them. They will definitely show you a good time."

"Cool, thanks," Anna smiled. "Sounds like fun."

As I turned to walk away, Anna called to me.

"Hey, Josh? I was kind of thinking maybe tomorrow I could take you out for lunch or dinner or something."

Oh shit, I thought. She *did* think I was flirting with her earlier. I totally should have clarified my use of the word cute. Trust me, if this was any other point in my life, I would have been completely flattered and would have jumped at the chance, but—"

"I just wanted to pay you back and show my appreciation for yesterday," she said.

"Aw, that's nice of you, but it really wasn't a big deal. It was fun."

"Yea, it was." She then paused a few seconds and shyly said, "So, is that a no on tomorrow?"

I have to admit, I wasn't used to being on this side of the conversation. I was usually the one asking the girl out. She was a super-sweet girl, and I really didn't want to hurt her feelings.

I hesitated and said, "I really appreciate your offer, but I kinda have to be here all day tomorrow."

Yes, I knew Doug would give me any time off I wanted, especially if it involved a woman, but like I said earlier, if this was any other time in the past, I would have jumped at the chance, but my desire just wasn't there anymore.

"It's ok," she said, "I assumed you were probably busy."

I felt bad about turning her down, and I couldn't help but wonder if this is how the *many* girls felt that rejected my date offers. My quick calculations told me probably only 68% felt bad.

Feeling a bit awkward, I excused myself to the back office. I told her I had some phone calls to make which was more or less true. Doug entered the office a little while later. I was just getting off the phone.

"Hey," he said.

"Hey. So I just got off the phone with Atlantic Distributors. I noticed that they had double billed you for a delivery. It's all taken care of now."

"Wow, thanks. Are you sure you don't want to be partners? With all the paperwork and bookkeeping you do, you might as well be a co-owner."

"Ha, thanks. But I have a feeling if we were actual business partners we would be arguing more than normal."

"Speaking of which, I'm sorry about shooting my mouth off earlier. You know me, I never liked Felicia that much. I never thought she made you that happy when you were together, and she's only made you miserable since she dumped you. I know I can come across as sarcastic or a jerk, but it's only because I know you can do better… I know you deserve better."

Fuck! How am I supposed to stay mad at this idiot when he says things like that?

"If I'm being honest," Doug began, "I still don't see what you saw in her, but I promise I'll try and keep my mouth shut. What do I know anyway? I'll probably be single for the rest of my life."

"You weren't completely wrong," I said. "I don't even know why I'm still hung up on her. You were right, it was a lousy two and a half week romance. I really do need to move on."

Doug smiled a suspicious smile then said, "Speaking of moving on…"

"Oh God, here we go," I said. "I'm not gonna be your wingman with those summer chicks out there."

"Pffft," he scoffed, "I haven't needed a wingman in quite a while, thank you very much. Maverick is very capable of flying solo! Besides, the bar is my wingman. Chicks dig bar owners."

"Chicks dig free drinks," I laughed.

"That too," he smiled. "Anyway, what I was going to say was I heard that Iowa girl asked you out on a date but you rejected her."

"First of all, it wasn't a date. She just wanted to thank me for showing her around yesterday. Definitely not a date. And second of all, I didn't reject her. I politely told her that I had to be here most of the day tomorrow, which is the truth."

"Dude, you know I'd give you any time off you needed... especially for a chick... a cute chick at that."

"I know you would," I smiled, "but I was serious when I told you I was done with meeting girls here in the summer. No more fly-by-romances for me. What's the point? Even if we hit it off, she's gone in less than two weeks. I've had a hard enough time in the past dealing with long distance relationships from here to Massachusetts, never mind Iowa."

Before Doug could offer up a comeback, I continued on.

"Look, I know you still love the single life-summer girl-beach thing, and that works for you and that's great, but I would much rather have what Pete has. Maybe I just need to move away from this fucking beach town. With my luck, though, that dark cloud will probably follow me wherever I go."

When I was done babbling, I looked up to see Doug staring at me like I had three heads.

"You need some mental help, my friend."

"Why, because of the whole dark cloud and turning thirty thing?" I asked.

"No, because you wanna be like Pete. The dude has one and a third kids and his sex life is by appointment only. Seriously, he told me they plan in advance when to have sex. That's not right."

Just like I thought, Doug completely missed my point. He wasn't totally wrong, however... sex by appointment isn't right.

***

Later that night, it was Taylor, myself, and Dawn working the bar. Doug called Dawn in so he could be free to hang out with Pete. He offered to call in another worker so I could join them, but I declined. Pete and Doug sat up at the bar, so I was able to still interact with them.

Doug took great pride in filling Pete in on the new crop of summer girls, and although Doug highly exaggerated his sexual escapades, I could tell Pete enjoyed hearing them. It was like the poor guy was living vicariously through Doug's penis. Ok, maybe we both were. Let's just say, after hearing some of Doug's stories, I'm never sitting on the couch in the back office again. New rule: Not only does the bar top get sanitized at the end of the night, but before we open as well!

Midway through one of Doug's stories, a familiar face entered the bar. It was Todd from Murphy's restaurant. If you remember from *The Empty Beach*, Todd was my head cook back in '95. Even though we spent most of that summer butting heads, by the time it ended, we were, dare I say, friends?

Hey, what's up man?" I asked. "It's been a while."

Todd and Doug exchanged hellos and Todd made his way to a seat at the end of the bar.

"Sam draft?" I asked.

He nodded. I poured his beer, and as I set it in front of him, he stood there looking at the stool.

"You didn't put super glue on here, did you?" he asked with a smirk.

"Ha. You're never gonna forget that one, huh?"

"Nope. I wanted to kill you that day."

"Yea, I know. It made it that much sweeter."

He laughed and finally took a seat. He then began looking around at the bar.

"I was wondering when you'd pop in for a drink," I said. "Summer's half over already."

"I've been meaning to swing by, but every time I get out of work, I'm just too exhausted."

"Ah yes, the price you pay for running your own business," I said.

"It's also the price you pay for not being able to keep a decent manager for more than a week. My fucking employees keep running them off."

"Ahhh, karma's a bitch, huh?" I laughed. "Do you want to borrow my super glue?"

"Ha. No, but I could sure use some of Phil's duct tape to tape some of their mouths shut."

"Ah yes, good ol' duct-tape Phil. Have you heard anything from him?" I asked.

"I ran into his mom the other day. He's still one of the few and proud in the Marines. His four year stint is up in a few months."

I wasn't sure what was more shocking, the fact that Phil lasted four years in the Marines, or the fact that four years had gone by just like that. Sometimes it feels like it was just last summer I was running Murphy's, but then there are times that it seems like it was a lifetime ago.

"How's Mrs. Murphy doing?" I asked.

"She's doing okay, I guess. Definitely a lot better than back at the funeral."

"I really wish I could have gone. I didn't even hear about his death until after I got back in town. He was a good man."

Todd nodded then said, "Yea, that's kind of why I stopped in tonight. Before he passed away, he was actually in the process of selling Murphy's outright to me. Of course, all of that got put on hold when he died. I felt it would have been insensitive to pursue the deal with Mrs. Murphy. She had enough on her plate, ya know?"

I nodded as Todd continued.

"Anyway, a few weeks ago, she approached me and said she was moving forward with the sale as planned. So, as of tomorrow, I will be the new owner of Murphy's."

"Holy shit, Todd, that's great. Congratulations."

I was happy for Todd, but yes, I couldn't help but wonder: If I would have accepted Mr. Murphy's offer to lease the place four years ago, maybe I would be the proud, new owner. I know, I know, I was the one who turned down his offer in the first place. I wasn't jealous of Todd owning Murphy's. I think I was just jealous of yet another one of my friends finding their passion and running with it.

Todd had more to tell me, so my self-pity party would have to wait until later that night. That's when I could lay in bed looking up at my ceiling tiles as if they had the fucking answers to my life.

"Sometime next week, I'm closing early and having a little party at the restaurant. It's going to be a combination of a celebration party for me and an ode to Mr. Murphy. I certainly wouldn't be where I am if it wasn't for him… or you."

"Me?"

"Mr. Murphy wanted to lease the place to you, but not only did you turn him down, you stuck your neck out and highly recommended me. Don't think for a second that I've forgotten that."

I was speechless, literally speechless. Todd's comment and gratitude wouldn't fully resonate with me until later on, but it still left me searching for the right response.

All I could manage was, "Thanks, man, but I'm sure he would have chosen you whether I put in a good word or not."

As if not buying into my statement, Todd shook his head and continued.

"I've been trying to contact and invite as many old employees of Mr. Murphy's as possible. I even got a hold of a few from way back in your day."

"Ha! Way back in my day, huh?"

We both had a laugh at that one.

"So, can I count you in?" asked Todd.

"Of course. I'll definitely be there. More so to pay homage to Mr. M, rather than celebrate your little ownership thing."

"I would expect nothing less," he laughed as he finished his beer.

He stood up, shook my hand and then headed out.

***

Todd wasn't the only familiar face to show up that night. Iowa girl returned to the bar and Taylor introduced her to her friends. Doug thought he had a chance with one of Taylor's friends, so needless to say, most of their drinks were on the house.

I was glad Taylor introduced Anna to her friends. I kept thinking how much it would suck to be on vacation by yourself, especially hanging out at a bar alone watching everyone else drink and laugh and have a great time. There was no way I could do that.

Even though Doug had one eye on Taylor's friend, he had his other eye on Taylor. The same dude (Charles in Charge) from a few nights ago was there and was once again making his moves on Taylor. The dude's carefree demeanor and the way he had Taylor laughing at his jokes seemed to get under Doug's skin. I think partly because he reminded Doug of himself, but mostly because Doug obviously had a thing for Taylor. Either way, every so often, I'd catch Doug staring and mumbling something to Pete.

Pete only hung out until 11 ish. I'm not sure if he was just tired or if Michelle had given him a curfew. Maybe it was because he had appointment-sex to get home to.

At one point, I headed into the back storage room to get some more cases of beer.

"Hey, ya need a hand?"

I turned to see Doug standing there.

"Nah, I got it, thanks."

"Dude, have you seen the guys that Taylor has been flirting with lately? Fucking losers! Especially that Charles in Charge dude."

"Have you seen some of the girls that you flirt with?" I asked.

"Don't even compare!"

"Ashley? Sue? That Kendra chick? Need I go on?"

"Alright, alright, point taken," he sighed. "Anyway, I see that Iowa girl came back tonight. Two times here in one day."

"What's your point, Doug?"

"I'm just saying she's a pretty nice girl. Easy on the eyes too."

"We're really not gonna do this again, are we," I asked.

"Just hear my theory out, okay?"

"Oh God. You have a theory about this?"

"Maybe Felicia will change her mind and want you back. Or maybe Jane will settle back here for good and you two can finally get together and live happily ever after. But until any of that happens, I just don't think you should put your life on hold. More importantly, your happiness. And I'm not talking about summer flings, or one night stands. I get that it's not your cup of tea any more. Personally, I fucking love that cup of tea, but this isn't about me. And I'm also not even talking about getting laid. I'm just talking about having fun again. Although, getting laid is pretty damn fun too. Anyway, I think life is too short not to have fun. You and Iowa girl obviously like each other's company, so I see no reason to walk away from fun. Even it's only for two weeks."

"You and your theories," I said with a slightly impressed smile.

"Well, I've said all I will say. I will leave you alone with your dark cloud above your head."

With that, Doug turned and headed out. Before I could process his long-winded theory, he reentered.

"Oh, by the way, Drunk Dave is here… and he's drunk."

"Of course he is," I replied. "That's why we call him Drunk Dave. What's your point?"

"Nothing. Except he's sitting up at the bar."

"The girls know never to serve him. Either ask him to leave or call the cops. You've done this routine a hundred times, Doug. Seriously, what's your point?"

"No point. No point at all. Except he's kind of sitting next to Iowa girl, and it seems like he's hitting on her pretty hard, but I'm sure the innocent country girl can handle an obnoxious drunk. Man, he's really shitfaced tonight."

I shook my head at Doug and amusingly said, "Is this your attempt at reverse psychology? First your theories and now this?"

He smiled, and with a shrug he said, "Dude, don't let my exterior fool you, I can be quite deep. Remember, Josh, even a blind man can cry."

As his nonsensical words hung in the air, Doug turned and once again left. I didn't even try to decipher his ramblings. I simply grabbed two cases of beer and headed back behind the bar.

Taylor was busy clearing some tables, and it looked like her friends had left already. It also looked like Doug was telling the truth, Drunk Dave was indeed sitting next to Anna.

I really wasn't that worried about him. For a drunk, he was fairly harmless. He was in his 40's and still lived at home with his mom. He knew we would never serve him, but he'd always come in and try. Mostly, I think, he just liked to interact with people. We usually let him babble a bit before telling him he had to leave. Ninety percent of the time, he stumbled out without an incident. The other ten percent we were forced to call in one of the summer cops to escort him out.

Sometimes, it was his sixty-something year old mother who came in looking for him. Nothing worse than being a grown ass adult and having your mother grab you by the ear and drag you out.

I nonchalantly moved closer to them so I could assess the situation better. As I stocked the beers in the cooler, I overheard Drunk Dave making his move.

"So, you're from Ohio, huh?" Drunk Dave slurred.

"Umm, Iowa," she hesitantly said, backing away from his alcohol-laden breath.

Did I mention, the more drunk he was the more he turned into a close-talker. He loved to lean right into your face.

"Ahhh, Iowa," he smiled. "The Sunshine State. Ya know what, you should let me be your tour guide. I'm like a professional tour guide and shit."

Again, he leaned in closer to Anna to speak. And again, she did her best to back away. He was swaying so much, I seriously thought he was going to fall off his stool. It wouldn't have been the first time.

"Maybe we can go park up at the lighthouse and wait for the light to turn green… if you catch my drift? Or maybe we could watch the submarine races… if ya know what I mean?"

"Umm, I actually have no idea what you mean," Anna said, now completely freaked out.

Those two phrases he just used were classic code words for *hooking up* at the Nubble Lighthouse. By now, Taylor was by my side listening to his lame drunken banter.

"You'll have to drive," he slurred. "My car is, umm, in the shop. So, what time do ya wanna pick me up tomorrow, sweetie?"

When I saw him put his hand on her shoulder, I knew it was time to step in.

"Hey, are we still on for tomorrow?" I asked Anna.

She was caught off guard at first, but quickly realized I was throwing her a life preserver.

"Oh… yea. We are still on for tomorrow." She turned to Drunk Dave, casually removed his hand then politely said, "Sorry, I forgot I had plans with Josh."

Even drunk as a skunk, he realized he was getting shafted.

"Pfft, whatever. Like I'd wanna waste my time with a chick from Idaho."

After he wiped the spit that flew from his mouth, he turned his attention to Taylor.

"Can I get some service here or what?"

Both Taylor and I shot him a look. Before Taylor could say a word, I stepped in.

"Oh, by the way, Dave, while I was in the back just now, you're mom called looking for you. I told her I hadn't seen you, but she said she was gonna come on down here anyway."

Drunk Dave's eyes widened, and he quickly slid his ass off the stool and stumbled his way out. Anna gave me a smile and an appreciative nod. I returned the gesture and continued restocking the beer.

Anna hung around until closing time, and as Doug locked the doors, she stood up and said, "Well, I should head out and let you guys close up."

"We're heading over to Portsmouth for a late night bite to eat. You coming?" asked Taylor.

As soon as she saw Anna hesitate, she emphatically said, "You're coming! I'm not dealing with these two idiots alone!"

Anna gazed over at *us two idiots* then nodded in agreement to Taylor.

12

"DESIGNS ON YOU" – The Old 97's

After we closed up, we all headed over to Portsmouth. We drove to Bickford's restaurant on the Portsmouth traffic circle. It was one of the only places around which was open all night. It was great for all of us in the service industry who got out late. It was also great for all the starving drunks after last call. Who it wasn't great for was the wait staff of Bickford's. It was bad enough dealing with drunks until 1 AM, but I could never deal with them after that. Obnoxious times ten!

I have found, however, that 79% of drunks are excellent tippers. Not necessarily because they're overgenerous, but because they can't count for shit. Of course, then there's the 21%.

Take for instance, the table next to us. They left zero tip, but the guy did leave his phone number and a message that read *Ur hot!* (all written in ketchup on the table).

The four of us sat, ate, talked, and laughed. We filled Anna in on Drunk Dave. The best story was when he stumbled onto the basketball court and joined in on one of our games. He kept telling us he tried out for the Globetrotters back in the day, but they didn't accept him because he was too white. This story led Doug to invite Drunk Dave to join us on our famous Globetrotter passing drills.

Doug started it off by manipulating the ball between his legs, around his back, and finally hitting it off his forehead as a pass towards Drunk Dave. Dave first attempted a simple dribble, which didn't go so well. He then attempted to follow Doug's "ball handling skills." This also didn't go so well. In his attempt to go around his back, the ball kept getting caught on his hip and falling. The situation got even worse when he tried to go between his legs and ended up jamming the *ball* into his *balls*. Yea, too white... that was the reason the Globetrotters rejected him.

Throughout the rest of our meal, Doug kept Anna (and us) entertained with many stories of our past summer shenanigans.

"Wow," Anna began, "I am so jealous. This place sounds like such an amazing place to grow up in."

Leave it to me to sprinkle a little reality on the conversation.

"Well, it's not all sunshine and roses. This place has its downside as well."

I felt the all too familiar look from Doug and Taylor. Doug shook his head then turned to Anna.

"Yea, you gotta watch out for that big black cloud that constantly looms over York Beach. Ironically, it only follows a certain pessimist around though."

"I'm not a pessimist... I'm a realist," I mumbled.

"That's the great thing about you three guys," said Taylor. Pete is the happy-go-lucky guy who sees the glass as half full.

Josh is the slightly pessimistic one, who sees the glass as half empty."

"And what am I?" interrupted Doug.

"You're the dumbass one who looks at the glass and just wants a refill."

Doug pondered a second then said, "Nice. I'll take it."

I would have joined them in laughing, but I was still in shock that everyone thought I was a pessimist. I mean, yea, I've been known to go a little over the top with my depression sessions over girls, but all in all, I have always been an upbeat, happy dude.

See, this is exactly what I'm talking about! This fucking beach is sucking the positivity out of me. Luckily, my internal rant would have to wait, for Doug was about to bust out another one of his theories…or observations… or whatever you want to call them.

"When I come back in my next life," Doug boasted, "I'm coming back a chick. A hot chick. Life would be so much easier."

"Don't even go there," snapped Taylor.

"If you take away the monthly period thingy and the whole pushing a kid out of your vagina thingy, you girls have it made."

Both Taylor and Anna shot Doug a glare.

"Oh come on! You get your drinks, your meals, and your cover charges all paid for you." Doug then looked over at me and said, "You agree with me, don't ya, Josh?"

Before I could answer, Doug continued on.

"Actually, didn't you once pay for a girl's car payment?"

"No!" I said, then murmured, "It was her rent payment."

"See, see!" Doug excitedly said. "Hell, I once paid for a girl's shopping spree at Victoria Secret."

Anna smiled and said, "Well, at least you were able to reap the rewards later."

I more than eagerly responded with, "Too bad the spree was for her boyfriend."

Both girls looked over at Doug for confirmation, and he acknowledged by lowering his head in shame.

"See, that is exactly why I'm coming back as a chick in my next life," said Doug.

"So some guy will buy you lingerie?" joked Anna.

Taylor and I both cracked up laughing.

"Go ahead and laugh, Josh, but you know I speak the truth."

I continued to laugh, but yes, Doug was definitely not wrong.

"Trust me," said Taylor, "It's not easy being a woman. Not by a long shot."

"And we don't get everything for free," Anna added.

"Oh really?" questioned Doug. "How many drinks did you pay for tonight, Iowa girl?"

I smiled and looked over at Anna, wondering how she was going to get out of this one.

"Um, I didn't pay for any… but I would have…"

"But you didn't!" Doug said with a smirk. He then turned to Taylor and said, "And you! You love using that big cleavage of yours to get whatever you want!"

Taylor smiled, shrugged knowingly, then said, "It's not our fault guys are stupid."

"Exactly my point!" yelled Doug. "We see skirts, tight shirts, and big cleavage and we turn into stupid little creatures. Yup, a hot chick, that's what I'm gonna come back as! Not to mention, you can get laid any time you want."

"Well that's a crock of shit," spouted Taylor. She paused a second, smirked and said, "Well, at least not with a quality looking guy."

Anna smiled and nodded in agreement with her.

"What's a quality looking guy?" I asked. "A six or higher?"

Taylor thought for a moment, looked at Anna then answered, "I'd say a seven or higher."

I saw Doug's wheels a turning and knew he was up to something. I'm sure it was no good, but I was also sure it would be quite amusing. I was right on both accounts.

He scanned the room then stood up and announced, "Excuse me guys, but I'm taking a little poll here. Could you raise your hand if you would have sex with this lovely girl right here?"

He pointed to Taylor and watched as both she and Anna turned a bright shade of red. There were about thirty customers throughout the restaurant with a pretty even split of guys and girls. The room went quiet as everyone stared over at Doug and then to Taylor. Even the wait staff stared blankly at our table.

But then it happened; one by one, hands were raised. By my count, the final tally was nine guys (and two girls) who raised their hands.

Doug carefully observed each of them then turned to Taylor and said, "I'm not gay, but in my opinion, I see at least five who are a seven or higher on the quality scale."

For whatever reason, Doug looked over at me for confirmation. I hesitantly sized up the nine volunteers then nodded in corroboration.

"You all can go back to eating," yelled Doug. "This was just a survey and not an actual proposition."

As the customers went back to stuffing their faces, Doug proudly looked over at Taylor.

"See, I told you, Taylor. You can get laid whenever you want. Shall I do a survey for you, Iowa girl?"

Her mouth fell open, but before she could protest, Taylor jumped in and motioned to our waitress.

"Check please," Taylor said, then glared over to Doug. "You made your point, okay?"

Doug smiled a victorious smile then polished off the rest of his fries. The waitress dropped the check off on our table. Taylor picked it up and scanned it. When Anna began to reach for her purse, Taylor waved her off and smirked. While Doug continued stuffing fries down his throat, Taylor made a quick adjustment to her shirt so that her boobs and cleavage were even more exposed.

Out of her purse she pulled out a pair of glasses... sexy glasses. She put them on, lowered the bill into the valley known as her cleavage then squinted down at the bill.

"I'm having a hard time figuring out what Anna and I owe. Can you help me with it, Doug?" she asked in a voice made for soft porn.

Doug looked up from his plate at the check... and then at her cleavage... and then to her perfect boobage. After five or nine seconds, he reached for his wallet and said, "Fine! Give me the check, I'll pay."

"Aww, thanks Doug," said Taylor.

"Yea, thanks, Doug," echoed Anna.

"Hmmm, maybe you're right," said Taylor. "Maybe it is pretty great to be a chick." Both girls giggled then stood up.

"Do you need some money from me?" I asked. "Or should I flash you some skin?"

"Ha fucking ha," he said. "Fuckin' cleavage! I swear it'll be the death of me."

I threw down some money and smiled, "You and me both, my friend."

"I'm not even sure why I fall for that either," he said. "I'm not even into big boobs."

"Everyone's into big boobs," said Taylor. "Hell, I'm into big boobs," she laughed.

"Well not me," said Doug. "I'm more of an ass guy. I actually prefer small boobs. Little fried eggs are all I need."

"Fried eggs?" laughed Anna.

"Yup," he answered proudly. "Kind of like Taylor's friend, Jen has. Nice little fried eggs. Although, in the outfit she had on earlier, they looked more like two sunny side up eggs."

Taylor curiously looked from Doug to me. I simply shrugged. It was just another case of Doug being Doug. That being said, I know we just ate, but I was kind of craving eggs.

***

We dropped Anna off at her cottage, and as she got out of the car, I asked, "So, what time do you wanna meet up tomorrow?"

She seemed a little taken aback.

"I know you were just saving me from that drunk guy. You don't really have to hang out with me tomorrow," she said.

"It's okay," interrupted Doug, "I gave him the day off."

"Oh, that's great," she said. "I'm hitting the beach in the morning if you want to join me?"

"The beach, huh?" I said.

"What?" she said. "Is laying out on the beach not cool for locals?"

Again, Doug interrupted. "Are you kidding me? Laying out on the beach is great. I might even join you guys."

"You're more than welcome to," Anna smiled.

"Nah, you kids have fun. I'm sleeping in."

After Anna headed in, I dropped Doug off at his place and drove home and went to bed. Apparently, I was hitting the beach in the morning.

13

"I HOPE THAT I DON'T FALL IN LOVE WITH YOU" - Tom Waits

The next morning I met Anna at the beach store I had worked at for the last three years. We grabbed iced coffees and some supplies and then made our way across the street to Long Sands. For the last four years, I lived exactly 72 feet away from the beach, but I bet I had only been down there a handful of times at best.

We walked down the ramp and claimed a piece of real estate behind the bathhouse. It was an all-too-familiar spot. Back in the day, my friends and I must have sat down here hundreds of times. The bathhouse area was kind of the "local" spot. As a matter of fact, as we settled our chairs in the sand, I noticed many familiar faces around us. To our left was the "brew crew."

They were a large group of friends who had been lounging on the beach together for as long as I could remember. They were about five years older than us, and although their crew had shrunk over the years, they still carried on their tradition of hitting the beach every day. No, seriously, they were at the beach every nice day of the summer. I'm sure they all had real jobs at night(maybe?), but during the day, sitting their asses on the beach was their full time gig.

The brew crew was led by beach bum Willy. You might remember him from *The Empty Beach*. He was the dude who ran the small movie theater down in Short Sands. You know, the guy who hooked me up with the private movie for my date with Elise.

I've only been back to that theater a few times since then, but each time I go, my thoughts return to that fateful night. Even though things ended the way they did with Elise, I still consider that night one of my favorite dates ever.

Anyway, back to the brew crew. With their giant blue cooler filled with "beverages" and with each of them holding red solo cups, it was obvious why we called them the brew crew.

I gave a wave over to Willy and the crew then sat in my chair next to Anna.

"Josh?" a voice from behind me said.

I turned around to see Jasmine Ewing. Like me, she was also a York resident. We had known each other since we were kids and our paths had crossed many times throughout the summers (never in a romantic way). We had never so much as even kissed. And no, I never made a mixtape for her!

"Hey, Jasmine, how are you? I thought you moved to Providence?"

"Yea, I was there the last couple years, but now I'm back. I'm meeting my cousin down here."

She pointed to a girl laying out about ten feet in front of us next to one of the lifeguard stands.

"We're checking out the new crop of lifeguards," she smiled.

I gave a quick look over at the lifeguard and said, "He's like twenty-one at the most."

"So. I'm only twenty-eight. Besides, you know age means nothing in York Beach." With that, she turned and winked at Anna.

"Oh, Jasmine this is Anna. Anna, this is Jasmine: the cradle robber."

"Ha," she laughed. "I think you have me mistaken for your buddy, Doug."

"Good point," I said.

"Well, I'm gonna head over to my cousin. Nice meeting you, Anna. Watch out for this guy's lines. He's a smooth talker."

"Get out of here," I joked.

"Oh, by the way, if you see me drowning today, don't rescue me," she said, eyeing the young lifeguard.

"Don't worry, I won't," I said.

After Jasmine headed over to her cousin, I finally settled into my chair and took a long swig of my iced coffee. I put on my sunglasses and pretended not to notice Anna removing her shirt and shorts. Underneath she wore a jet black bikini, and I have to admit, my look lingered way longer than it should have.

I still had no romantic intentions with her, but I would have been a liar if I told you I wasn't attracted to her. Out of her bag she pulled a bottle of sunblock and proudly showed me.

"That a girl," I said.

Her skin was still red from the previous day, and I watched as she began rubbing the sunblock on. And when I say *watched,* I mean, discreetly out of the corner of my eye behind the glasses. And if I'm going to be completely honest, there was a part of me that was hoping she'd ask me to rub her backside. I know, I know, totally a pervy guy-thought, but what can I say... I might have been almost thirty, and I might have had a dark cloud looming over me, but I was still a pervy guy at heart, I guess.

The only thing that interrupted my mesmerized staring was the all-to-familiar sound of, "Da ha ha ha."

I looked to my right, and there sitting on a beach chair was Geoff. If you read *The Empty Beach* then there's no way you'd forget "A little left Geoff." Besides being four years older, he was exactly the same. From his laugh, to his sweater-like body hair, to his classic talk of burning things down, he was the same.

I'd seen him quite a bit the last few years while I was running the store across the street, but now that I was working at the bar, I rarely saw him. This would actually be my first run-in with him this year.

"Hey, what are you laughing at over there?" I said.

Geoff stopped his laughter and immediately scanned the beach for who had yelled that. Finally, his eyes found mine, and he got up and walked over. He wore Hawaiian shorts, a blue visor, and his nose was completely covered with sunblock. I knew Anna was in for a treat.

"What are you doing here?" Geoff asked. "Why don't you work over there anymore?" he said, pointing across the street.

"Remember my friend Doug? I work for him now down at Short Sands."

"Where?" Geoff asked, overly curious.

"It's a bar where the Golden Fortune Cookie used to be."

Geoff began to smile widely, and I knew what was next.

"Why are you laughing, Geoff? Are you thinking about burning it down?"

His smile disappeared and he snapped, "No! I don't talk like that anymore."

I knew better, but said, "Oh, I see. Well, that's good."

Less than a second later, his smile returned and he said, "But would you laugh if it burned down?"

"I would laugh," I said, "and then I would roast marshmallows by the fire."

"Da ha ha ha!" he laughed then said, "Are you joking or serious?"

"I'm joking, Geoff. Why would I laugh if my friend's business burned down?"

"Is that your girlfriend?" he said, looking at Anna.

"No, it's just my friend Anna. She's visiting here from Iowa."

Geoff immediately bombarded her with question after question like: Why did you come to York? What do you do for work? What are your parents' names? Do you have a dog?

"Jesus, Geoff, enough with the questions. The poor girl's head is gonna explode."

"Da ha ha ha! Her head is gonna blow up."

Before I could say a word, I could tell by his big smile that his mind was already thinking about something else.

"Remember that time I was in the bathroom touching my twang. My twaaaang."

"Okay, Geoff, I think you need to go back over to your chair now."

Geoff knew I was serious and *not* joking, so he da ha ha ha'd all the way back to his beach chair. Anna's face and reaction was priceless.

"What... in the heck... was that?" she said.

I proceeded to fill her in on everything a little left Geoff, and yes, I even told her about the two infamous incidents involving ex-lax and his twang. She went back and forth between being disgusted and laughing her ass off.

When I was finished she asked, "Does he really fart on people?"

"He absolutely does. I'm surprised he didn't rip one while he was over here."

After the Geoff talk faded out, we moved onto other similar topics. I told her about some of the other classic beach characters over the years, and she informed me of some strange characters from her hometown as well. The next thing I knew, two hours had passed.

"Wow, it's been years since I've laid out down here," I said.

"Really?" she said shocked. "If I lived here I would be at the beach every day!"

"Every day, huh? Even in the rain?"

"Heck yea! There's gotta be nothing better than dancing on the beach in a warm summers' rain."

"Heck yea," I mimicked. "Nothing better."

"Go ahead, make fun of the country-girl tourist."

"I'm just giving you shit, Anna. I actually spent almost every day of my teens and early twenties sitting right here. It feels like a lifetime ago."

"So what made you stop hanging out down here?" she asked. "And don't tell me you're too old for the beach."

Anna motioned over to the brew crew, who were laughing and having a great time.

"They still seem to be enjoying themselves," she pointed out.

I explained to her that my summer crew of beach friends used to be just like that. On any given day, there could be a dozen of us sitting down here together, but unlike the brew crew over there, our crew either drifted apart or simply moved away. Even though she had no idea who I was talking about, I went down a partial list of all the old summer friends who had faded away.

As we sat there, her eyes darted all around the beach, and she excitedly made one observation after another:

"Aww, look at those sand castles over there."

"What game are those people playing?"

"I want to fly a kite! So cool."

"We should go get a Frisbee."

"Don't you just love the smell of suntan lotion?"

It was like I was sitting next to a wide-eyed five-year-old, who was visiting the beach for the first time. Finally, her attention focused on a group of kids jumping into the waves.

"Let's go swimming!" she said.

"Ummm, that would be a big fat no," I answered. "Do you know how cold it'll be?"

"It's like 85 degrees out. I'm sure it's warm by now. Besides, those kids seem to be enjoying it."

"That's because they're kids. They don't know any better."

I'm not sure what age exactly, but there was usually a certain age that most kids lose their fascination with all the things that she was mentioning. Not Anna.

"Just because it's hot outside, it doesn't mean the water is anywhere near warm," I said. "This isn't some swimming hole in Iowa," I laughed. "This is the Atlantic Ocean. Didn't you go in the other day when you were here?"

"No. It was too hazy and I figured it might be cold."

I laughed as her attention returned to the kids.

"Come on, Josh, let's go in," she pleaded.

I looked from her to the ocean and then back to her. I finally conceded, and we made our way down by the shoreline. She started to test the water with her toes, but I stopped her.

"The best way to do this is to just run and jump in. No toe-testing, no hesitation, just run in full steam."

She nodded in agreement, and I motioned for her to lead the way. She smiled, took a deep breath then bolted into the water. Reluctantly, I followed close behind.

We dove into the oncoming waves, and when we popped back up, she exclaimed, "Holy shit! That's cold!"

She immediately covered her mouth and looked around to see if anyone heard her.

"Nice language, Iowa girl."

We made our way to our chairs, shivering the whole way back. We wrapped ourselves with our towels and sat down.

"I did warn you," I said.

"It really wasn't that bad," she said with chattering teeth.

I gave her a playful nudge then turned my attention over to Jasmine and her cousin. Jasmine was talking (flirting) with the lifeguard. She kept doing this smiling, giggling thing while kicking the sand with her toes.

"Pathetic," I said.

"Oh, come on, Josh. You've never flirted with someone on the beach before?"

And just like that, a Rolodex of moments flooded my mind. I thought about my teenage days, flirting the summer away with the cute, Fun Float girls.

I thought about the countless times playing Frisbee on the beach with Pete, Doug, and Scott. We would show off doing Frisbee-dive-catches, and we would purposely throw the Frisbee so it landed on or next to a group of cute chicks. Conversation would ensue, and if we were lucky, we would hit it off and be partying with them later that night. Success rate was around 22%.

I also thought about the time I sat near a girl (Melissa), who was laying out listening to her Walkman. I noticed the cassette tape sticking out of her bag was The Lemonheads. Fortunately for me, I had that same tape packed in my backpack. Also fortunately for me, I had my boom box with me.

I popped in the Lemonheads tape, cranked it up, and before I knew it, her headphones were off and she yelled over to me, "Hey, I'm listening to the same tape!"

I used that as my *in,* and proceeded to head over and chat with her. Unfortunately, it was the last day of her family vacation, and they were heading back to Massachusetts later that day. This didn't deter me. By the time track 4 ("Rudderless") was playing, I had gotten her digits.

I called her that night, and we had one of those long "in common" conversations. You know, music, movies, TV shows type stuff. I ended the conversation with, "I should come down to see you sometime."

She responded with, "Yea, that would be cool."

Long story short, the following week I decided to give her a visit. Yup, I drove down to Lunenburg, Massachusetts, looked up her address (phone booth & phonebook), and showed up at her doorstep for a visit... a surprise visit.

Her parents were surprised.

She was surprised.

Her boyfriend was surprised.

And not only was I surprised, but I was fuckin' outta there!

Definitely a top ten embarrassing moment in my life. Maybe I shouldn't have tried to be cute and surprise her, but come on, she should have mentioned the boyfriend on the phone calls. Or here's a little idea: How about you DON'T give a guy your digits when you have a fucking boyfriend!!

Anyway, I still think of that Lunenburg chick when I hear the Lemonheads.

"Hello? Josh?" Anna said, bringing me back to the present.

"Oh, sorry. What were you saying?"

"I said you must have had your share of flirting with girls on the beach."

I shrugged. "Maybe a few, I guess."

"Uh huh," she smiled. "I bet you and the guys were quite the players."

I was just about to explain the difference between flirters and players, but I noticed another friend up ahead. It was old man Ugo. He was in his seventies stood about 6'1... 6'4 if he could straighten out his back. He was a big man with gigantic mitts for hands. He wore an unbuttoned short sleeve shirt with a white tee shirt underneath, a dirty pair of blue Dickies, and a wide-brimmed Huck Finn style hat (with a seagull feather sticking out).

There were two young children following close behind pulling a little red wagon full of cans and bottles. Anna and I watched Ugo approach the garbage cans and dig in them for cans, bottles, or anything returnable.

Anna watched curiously then whispered, "What's he doing?"

"He hits all the garbage cans on the beach for returnables then cashes them in at the redemption center."

"Is he... homeless?" she asked.

I laughed and shook my head no, but like most people on the beach, it was a typical assumption. I explained to Anna how he was actually quite well-off and how he even owned a brand new Cadillac. The collecting of the cans thing was just something he had always done.

"He's actually a retired police chief from down in a small town in Massachusetts," I pointed out. "Those kids are probably his great grandkids."

I explained to Anna how I met Ugo. Although I had seen him down here for years, it wasn't until I started running the store across the street that I actually met him. The store opened at six in the morning, but Ugo would show up around 5 AM and unbundle and organize all of the newspapers on the shelves outside.

As soon as I opened the doors, Ugo would come in and proceed to pour coffees for the customers. He thoroughly enjoyed the banter.

"High test or decaf," his booming voice would ask. This was quickly followed with, "Are you here for the week or summer?" And that was predictably followed with, "Where are you from?"

The customers loved the early morning repartee with the larger than life old man. The most amusing thing about Ugo was he said exactly what he was thinking. If he saw someone shuffle in hungover, he would say, "Boy, must have been some party. You look in rough shape."

He also had no edit button when it came to women wearing skimpy bikinis. Like the time he asked if she bought the bikini that way or did her dryer shrink it three sizes too small?

Every time a pair of big boobs approached the coffee station, his eyes would widen and he'd fake like a heart attack was coming on. It totally reminded me of Sanford and Son. *"This is the big one, Elizabeth."*

No matter how risqué the comments, most every girl just laughed at him. It was almost like they thought it was endearing. It's no secret that I am dreading turning thirty, but

I tell you what, I can't wait to be in my seventies. To be as pervy as you want and it be seen as endearing? Sign me up!

I gave Ugo a wave, and he made his way over to us. He asked how my new job was, and before I could introduce him to Anna, he said, "Is that the Lunenburg chick?"

"Ugo, that was three summers ago," I said.

He knew it wasn't her, but ever since I told him the story, he's never stopped joking about it with me. When he found out Anna was from Iowa, he made some corny jokes. Literally, they were about corn.

Before he headed to the next garbage can, one of his great grandkids approached Anna and offered her something. Anna held out her hand, and the little girl gave her a small collection of shells. Anna's face beamed.

"Aww, thank you, sweetie," said Anna.

The little girl giggled and rushed off to catch up with Ugo. For the next ten minutes, the smile didn't leave Anna's face as she studied each of the shells over and over.

Eventually, our attention turned back to Jasmine, sitting up ahead of us. She had this dumb smile on her face as she stared longingly up at the lifeguard. She could at least put on her sunglasses and stare out the corner of her eye like I did. She was definitely being obvious. Luckily for the swimmers, the lifeguard's attention was on the water and not the horny Jasmine behind him.

He must have felt her eyes burning the back of his head because he slowly turned and gave her his own creepy smile. He wasn't even hiding the fact that his eyes were going up and down her bikini-clad body, and Jasmine wasn't hiding the fact that she was enjoying it. She even did the cliché move of twirling her finger in her hair.

"Are you watching this?" whispered Anna.

"Pathetic, isn't it?" I said.

They were both literally eye-fucking each other. Jasmine was so focused on the young, flirtatious lifeguard that she didn't even notice Geoff approaching her from behind.

Just when she was about to do another hair twirl, it happened: Geoff put his ass right in her face and ripped a loud fart in it. Her face turned bright red and she quickly covered her nose as the stench hit her.

"Da ha ha ha! I farted on you," laughed Geoff as he walked off.

When Jasmine gained her composure, she hesitantly looked up at the lifeguard stand. To her disappointment, it was empty. Her young, studly lifeguard was on his way down to the water. Nothing ruins flirting and eye-fucking like getting farted on.

***

Long after the lifeguards and the Fun Float girls had packed up and left the beach, Anna and I remained in our chairs, talking. Without a doubt, this was my longest beach day in many, many years.

At one point, I suggested that we pack up and go out to eat somewhere, but I could tell by her expression that she was very content where she was. I then suggested we walk over to the Oceanside Store and grab some takeout. This idea was met with a more than happy nod.

Burgers, fries, and chocolate milkshakes ended up being the perfect beach dinner food. By now, the beach had thinned out considerably. Jasmine and her cousin were long gone, and a little left Geoff had da ha ha ha'd his way off the beach hours earlier. Even the brew crew had disbanded for the day. There was no one sitting within twenty feet of us... except the family from hell.

It was a family of five... six counting the screaming newborn. They didn't arrive at the beach until 6-ish. Apparently they wanted to avoid the prime sun hours. This was pretty ironic considering they spent the first twenty minutes lathering up their kids in sun block. The parents then spent the next twenty minutes arguing over how to open and secure their giant beach umbrellas. Yes, umbrellas plural. They finally gave up and tossed them aside.

Did I mention, all of their kids were under the age of six? And did I mention they were loud? Obnoxiously loud. Come to think of it, the screaming newborn was the quietest one there. I swear, they never had a normal or quiet conversation. Even if they were five inches away from the other, they would talk loud enough for the whole beach to hear.

Fortunately, Anna and I had done most of our talking throughout the day, because there would have been no way we could have concentrated with this shit-show going on in front of us. We certainly didn't need to introduce ourselves to know their names... all of their names.

With milkshakes in hand, we simply sat back and enjoyed the entertainment.

"This is better than TV," Anna whispered.

At one point, one of their kids (Sammy) not only had a staring contest with me, but he did it while picking his nose the entire time. Our amusement only lasted a short time before it turned personal. Apparently, three full beach baskets of toys weren't enough to hold their attention, because one by one the kids made their way over to our chairs.

One of the kids (Kimmy) held out her hand for Anna to give her one of her fries. The other kid (Johnny) didn't bother asking, he rudely reached over and grabbed himself some fries. The third kid (Sammy) began playing with my radio. I shit you not, he started twisting all of the knobs trying to find a station that he approved of. I snatched the radio from him, giving the little shit a *Don't fuck with my music* glare.

What did their parents have to say about their kids' obnoxious behavior?

"Kimmy and Johnny love their fries. They'd eat them for breakfast if they could."

Are you kidding me? That's what their mom had to say about her little thieves stealing our fries? The Dad's response wasn't any better.

"Sammy loves his music. He's gonna be a rock star one day."

Are you fucking kidding me? This is called parenting? They spent the first hour yelling and screaming at their kids for every little thing they did, yet they think it's cute that Sammy has his fingers all over my damn radio! The same fingers, I might add, that were deeply implanted up his nose earlier.

If they wanted a battle, I was about to give them a war! If it was fries they wanted, fries they would get. I waited until the kids finally scampered back to their loving family, then I turned to Anna and told her the game plan. It was an age-old game plan and was only used in situations just like this.

When the family's attention was focused elsewhere, Anna and I began tossing bits of fries near them—lots of French fry bits! Just as planned, within seconds, the family from hell was invaded with dozens of seagulls. The family found it amusing at first watching all of the seagulls scattered around them in the sand.

What they didn't find amusing was the dozens of other seagulls flying and circling directly above them. Anna followed my instructions, but I don't think she fully understood the entirety of my plan—not until it happened.

Let's just say, the parents should have worked harder to put their umbrellas up earlier. With huge amounts of seagulls, comes huge amounts of seagull shit. In between us laughing our asses off, I counted at least six direct hits. Two of them were on Sammy. That'll teach you to touch my radio, you little nose-picking shit!

We used their yelling and screaming as the perfect distraction to pack up our stuff and get the hell out of there. We laughed the whole way back to her car.

"Now that was a very fun and interesting day," she said.

"It always is down at the beach," I said.

"Thanks for hanging out with me all day."

"Not a problem. It was fun."

"You do realize you paid for everything today? So I still owe you a dinner or something."

"Nah. You don't owe me anything, Anna."

"I totally owe you. How about breakfast at the Goldenrod tomorrow?"

After having that much fun two days in a row, I found it hard to turn her down.

"Breakfast it is," I said. "I'll swing by and get you around nine?"

"Cool, then it's a date," she said, getting into her car. "Thanks again for today. I'll see you in the morning."

After Anna drove off, I headed back into my apartment. I felt both exhausted and rejuvenated.

Exhausted, because I forgot just how tiring it was sitting on a hot beach all day.

Rejuvenated, because I forgot how fun it was hanging out on a hot beach all day, especially with someone as fun as Anna.

I thought about going to the bar to watch the Sox game but decided to crack a beer and watch it on my couch.

It wasn't until the fourth inning that I noticed the blinking light on my answering machine. I was sure it was my mom wondering why I hadn't called her back, so I didn't actually check the message until the seventh inning. The voice was not that of my mother. It was Felicia.

"Hey Josh. I'm sorry I haven't called in a while. Things have been crazy with my new job. I'm actually in upstate New York right now at a training seminar. I'll be home in a couple days and would love to get together if you're free. It's been too long. I miss hanging out with you. Anyway, I'll call you when I'm home. Bye."

I am fully aware that I recently told Doug I needed to move on with my life and put Felicia in the rear view mirror. But... well... that was before I actually heard her voice on my machine. Her voice telling me how she "missed me" and how she would "love" to get together.

I knew I shouldn't read too much into her 64 word message, and I knew in my heart that Doug was right; she wasn't the right girl for me, but after all these months of trying to win her back and creating multiple scenarios of how great it'd be if we were dating again, I couldn't help but be a little bit excited.

After I listened to her message for the sixth time (I had to be sure I wasn't reading too much into it), I reached in my top drawer and pulled out an envelope of photos that were taken during the very brief time we dated. It's funny how the mind can convince you of things you know are just not true.

As I flipped through the photos, two things popped into my head:

1. Doug was going to give me sooo much shit for this.
2. Anna's voice saying, "Cool, then it's a date."

I knew she didn't really mean *date, date*, and I knew it was just an innocent expression, but still, it got me thinking—overthinking maybe, but thinking nonetheless. Was I hanging out with Anna too much? After all, she was leaving in just over a week. Even though I didn't have high hopes that Felicia wanted to get back together, there was still a possibility.

I decided I needed to stick to my original guns and not get involved in any sort of summer romance. Yes, I knew Anna and I were just hanging out as friends and that romance hadn't even crossed our minds, but I did kind of stare at her in her bikini for longer than a "friend" probably should have.

If I met her out for breakfast that would have been three and a half consecutive days hanging out together. I definitely needed to pump the brakes with this sweet, country summer girl.

14

"HONEY DON'T THINK" – Grant Lee Buffalo

My intention was definitely not to hurt Anna's feelings or make her feel bad. My intention was also to make my speech short and sweet. I think you all know from *The Empty Beach* that I might do sweet—but I don't do short.

When I pulled into Anna's driveway the next morning, she had no idea what she was in for. She was expecting Josh, but instead she got—the King of Babble.

Before I had a chance to knock, she opened the door. She wore her hair up with a black sundress on. My mind immediately replayed seeing her in her black bikini. Fuck! What is wrong with me?

"Morning," she said. "Are you ready for breakfast? I'm starving."

"Ummm, yea, about breakfast… I'm not sure it's such a good idea."

"No? Are you not feeling well?" she asked.

I knew I couldn't dance around it, I just needed to rip the band aid off all at once.

"I don't think we should be hanging out as much. It has nothing to do with you. You're sweet and fun and funny… and yes, you're quite easy on the eyes, but… but the truth is: If this was a few years ago, I would jump at the chance to hang out with you, and I'm not talking about sex or hooking up. I'm talking about hanging out and getting to know you. But now isn't a good time. In fact, it's a real bad time. I'm still sorting through my feelings for Felicia and when you used the word 'date' last night, it kind of freaked me out. Not that going on a date with you is freaky… not at all…And I know it was just an expression, and you didn't mean 'date' in a romantic way, but… well, like I said, this is just a bad time for me. The fact that I'm almost thirty only makes matters worse. Seriously, what's there to look forward to after that? Retirement homes in Florida? AARP? Senior citizen cruises? Shuffleboard?"

I paused for a moment just to catch my breath, and when I finally made eye contact with Anna, she was looking at me like I was bat-shit crazy. She looked speechless and overwhelmed—definitely overwhelmed. Sadly, I wasn't close to being done babbling.

"It just feels like most of my friends are way ahead of me; career-wise, relationship-wise… Doug has his own bar, and Pete and Michelle are on their second kid, and now they're in the process of buying a house, which I'm sure will have a white picket fence. And I bet they're even gonna buy a pet dog soon too. And here I am still living in a one bedroom apartment, no idea what I wanna do with my life… no wife, no kids, and not even a girlfriend. I don't even have a dog for fuck's sake! It's bad enough I have this dark cloud over me, but you don't need to be caught under it too. Don't get me wrong, you should still come by the bar sometime. My friends love you, but I just don't think we should do the one on one thing any more, that's all."

I stopped long enough for Anna to finally say something. All she was capable of was, "Ummm...I see."

Actually, she probably would have said more, but I kind of interrupted with my final babble.

"Just so we're clear: You—sweet girl, fun, funny. Me—twenty-nine and a half years old, black cloud, no dog. Okay? Okay. I think I'm gonna leave now. Hopefully you'll come by the bar again. I'm gonna leave now though. See you later, Anna."

While babbling all of this, I slowly backed my way down her driveway. She was no longer overwhelmed as she waved goodbye to me. In fact, it looked as though she was fighting back laughter. I didn't overwhelm her, I fucking amused her.

Not only was I still the King of Babble, but I was the king of the idiots as well. This would be thoroughly pointed out to me later that night when I made the mistake of telling Doug and Pete during our walkabout what I had said to Anna.

15

"THIRTY-THREE" – Smashing Pumpkins

That night's walkabout started from Doug's bar. We walked up Long Sands into the harbor and then back again. It was one of our longest walkabouts in many years, and on that night, it needed to be.

Anna didn't come by the bar at all that night (I couldn't really blame her), so I didn't feel the need to inform anyone what had happened earlier. Around seven o'clock, Doug informed me that Steph and Hillary were coming in to work the rest of the night for us. He said Pete was coming down and suggested we drink a little then do a walkabout like old times. Who was I to argue with my boss? A drinking night it was.

After a few drinks at the bar, we filled a backpack with some beer bottles and then headed out on our way. By the time we walked by the Cutty Sark Hotel on Long Sands, I was loosened up enough to reveal what I had said to Anna that morning.

"You said what to her???" exclaimed Doug.

Pete laughed and shook his head. "Whoa, that is some serious Josh-babble."

"Yea, and he needs some serious Josh-professional help too," added Doug.

"Shut the fuck up, Doug. You have more issues than all of us. Besides, it really wasn't that bad."

"Wasn't that bad?" laughed Doug. "You show up at Iowa girl's cottage, and you proceed to babble about dark clouds, white picket fences, and… dogs? I absolutely stand by my assessment—you need professional help."

"Oh relax you two," said Pete. "We all probably need professional help."

A few steps later, Pete followed up with, "Are you really that hung up on turning thirty? And regarding all that other stuff, you do know it's not a competition, right?"

"I know, I know, but… it's just that I'm nowhere near where I'd thought I would be, ya know?"

"Maybe that's part of your problem," said Pete. "Maybe you shouldn't have a timetable. I never set out to get married or have a kid by a certain age. It just happened when it happened."

I shrugged and nodded in agreement.

"I guess it still bothers me not knowing what I wanna do with my life," I said. Before Doug could open his mouth, I added, "I know what you're gonna say, Doug. And I appreciate the offer, but owning the bar with you isn't in the cards for me right now. Don't get me wrong, I love working there, but I'm just not sure it's what I want to do, but thanks though."

By the time we reached the Sun & Surf restaurant, not only was the backpack lighter, but so was Doug's original sarcasm with me. Dare I say, for the rest of the night, he was more human than he usually was.

"Do you wanna hear my theory?" asked Doug.

"Not really, but that's never stopped you before," I said.

"Did you ever think because you're so hungry for a serious relationship, that is why you've held onto the notion all these months of Felicia being the right one?"

Before I could question Doug on using the word *notion,* he continued.

"I'm sure you guys had some fun times and maybe even some meaningful conversations. And I'm sure the sex was great. After all, psycho chicks are always the best ones in the sack."

Pete nodded in agreement. I said nothing and continued to drink and walk, but internally, I was kind of nodding too.

"You guys only knew each other a couple of weeks before you started 'dating' and then you only 'dated' for another couple of weeks."

"Two and a half," I mumbled.

"Whatever," he said. "All I know is you've spent the last six months or so pining and whining, and scheming and dreaming of how you can get her back."

"What's your point?" I asked, getting annoyed.

"What exactly would you be getting back? Was your relationship in those two and a half weeks so earth shattering?"

I was annoyed, but I didn't have a comeback.

"I think over the past months, you've wanted a relationship so badly that you might have lost track of what was real and what was fantasy. I'm just saying, I think you took those two weeks and made it into something it wasn't. In your head, you've made it into what you *wanted*... not what it *really* was."

Fuck, fuck, fuckity, fuck! Did I mention, I hate it when Doug makes sense?

"Hey, we've all done it, bro," said Pete.

"Totally," agreed Doug. "Remember that waitress chick from the Gaslight that I dated back in '90?"

"Ahh, Kelly," answered Pete. "How long did you guys date? Wasn't it like only a couple of weeks?"

"Exactly my point!" exclaimed Doug. "I have no fuckin' clue how long we actually dated, but I was so into her that I made it seem like we were together for months, if not years."

"Oh, I remember," smiled Pete. "You were a mess all winter."

I joined Pete in smiling and said, "Yea, you even borrowed my Depression Session mixes."

Doug slowly nodded and said, "I haven't seen her in eight years, but sometimes I still think she was the one."

"I'm sure Josh still has his Depression Session mixes if ya wanna borrow them," laughed Pete.

"That I do, that I do," I said.

"Anyway, my point is, Josh, I think you've taken what your ideal relationship is and superimposed it into what you and Felicia actually had."

Pete nodded and said, "Strangely, I think Doug is right."

"Thanks," said Doug. "Wait! Why do you say strangely? Just so you know, I can be very deep."

Pete and I looked at each other and couldn't help but laugh.

"Go ahead and laugh at me, but just remember— sometimes even a deaf man needs earmuffs."

Again, Pete and I looked at each other. We had no idea what he was talking about.

"It's like he's a walking, talking fucked-up fortune cookie," said Pete.

Doug proudly smiled and we all clinked our beers. By now, our walkabout had taken us into the harbor, where we turned around and started to head back.

"We should stop by Scott's house and drag his ass out," suggested Pete.

"Good luck with that," I said. "We tried a few times last year, but he always had a lame excuse why he couldn't join us."

"What the hell happened to that guy?" asked Pete.

"Your guess is as good as mine," I said.

Doug finished off his beer then said, "I miss when Scott used to ask us stupid questions on our walkabouts."

"And I miss your equally stupid answers," said Pete.

"Like, would you have sex with an alien to save the world?" I smiled.

"I would still totally do it," Doug said proudly.

Just then, a motorcycle drove by and Pete started to laugh.

"Remember when Scott asked us how much money it would take for us to have sex with a ninety-year-old woman?"

"Oh, shit, I remember," I said. "That was a long time ago. I think my answer was a cool million."

Pete thought for a second then said, "I think I only said a hundred thousand. I was knee deep in college loans, so I just wanted them paid off."

"Do you remember your answer, Doug?" I asked.

"Yup! I would have banged her for a motorcycle."

Pete and I cracked up.

"I still have no idea where you came up with that," said Pete.

Doug shrugged and said, "Fuck, I'd still do it for a motorcycle. Sex is sex! I'd give her some calcium pills, make sure there's a defibrillator handy, and then go for it!"

"And you think I need professional help?" I asked.

"What? What's the big deal? We're just talking intercourse. No kissing or foreplay, right? Brush away the vaginal cobwebs, squirt some WD40 to get rid of the creaks, and you're good to go."

"Vaginal cobwebs? Creaks? You're making it sound like her vagina is a haunted house," said Pete.

Doug stopped in his tracks and thought about it.

"Fuck that!" exclaimed Doug. "If I see any ghosts or bats fly out, I'm upping the bet to two motorcycles!"

Anyway, that was our walkabout that night. It started off pretty deep and emotional and ended with a vagina being compared to a haunted house. Did I mention how much I loved our walkabouts?

It was nearly 11 PM when we got back to Short Sands. We were going to shoot some hoops, but Pete wanted to get back home to his pregnant wife, and Doug had his eye on a cute blond sitting up at the bar. It had been a long day, so I decided to head home and hit the sack.

Before he left, Pete said, "Hey, my parents are taking Kayla up to Storyland in the White Mountains sometime next week. They're staying overnight."

"Party at Pete's house then?" asked Doug, hopefully.

"Absolutely," said Pete.

"Count me out," I said. "I'm closing most every night next week."

"Fuck that shit!" said Doug. "We're both taking the night off. I told you, Hillary and Steph are going away for like ten days in August. It's like this giant hippie retreat thing up in Vermont."

"Yea, what's that all about?" I asked.

"I don't know," shrugged Doug. "I didn't really listen to their details. It's some hippie thing in the woods. They probably just run around naked smoking pot, listening to the

Dead and playing hacky sack. Anyway, when they're gone, you and I are gonna be working a shit-ton. So until then, I'm gonna work their asses off. I already told you to take some time off this week, remember?"

"Yeah, but I thought you were just trying to get me to hang out with Anna."

Doug pondered a second then said, "Well there you go, it's a win, win."

"So, party at my house is a go?" asked Pete.

"It's a go," Doug and I both said.

After that, Pete headed home to his wife and daughter, Doug headed over to make the moves on the cute blond, and I headed home for bed.

16

"ALMOST GOLD" – The Jesus and Mary Chain

I thought about dusting off one of my Depression Session mixes but decided against it. I didn't want any music on or the TV for that matter. I just wanted to lay in bed with my thoughts. My thoughts being: Just how much sense Doug made tonight. It was apparent more than ever that I had turned my little two and a half week relationship with Felicia into something it wasn't.

Was I trying to win her back just for the sake of *winning*? Did I really want a relationship so badly that I was willing to hold onto things that just weren't there? I was starting to think yes to all of the above.

That being said, I still felt depressed about where I was in my life. I meant it when I said I was nowhere near where I thought I'd be. I also meant it when I said how fucking tired and jaded I was by the whole summer-in-York Beach-lifestyle thing.

As I continued to toss and turn in bed, I tried to pinpoint when my bitterness began. Was it the summer of '95 and Elise? I put my heart and soul into getting to know her, only to have it blow up in my face and end horribly. So horribly, I vowed to stay away from summer romances from then on.

I did revert back to flirting and pursuing summer girls in '97 and then briefly in '98. Most of those, however, were purely sexual for both parties concerned (this basically meant there were no mixtapes iven out). Still though, even that left me feeling empty. I really, really don't know how Doug does it.

As the clock hit midnight, my thoughts turned to Anna. I felt bad about my babbling session at her door earlier that day. Maybe Pete and Doug were right, maybe I shouldn't try to label things so much. And yes, maybe Doug was right, if you have fun with someone you should keep doing it until it's not fun anymore, and the truth was, every time I hung out with Anna I had fun.

By the time the clock read 12:27, I had my mind made up. First thing tomorrow morning, I would go to her cottage and apologize for my babble and then invite her out for breakfast. Even if she was only here for another week or so, I was all in on having fun!

And no, I wasn't talking about sex. Besides, she didn't seem like the girl who would meet a guy and have sex with him in a two week span. She was too sweet and innocent for that. Not to mention, I was not looking for that anyway. I just wanted to be around someone who I could relax and have fun with. Yup, the next morning I was going to pay Iowa girl a visit! I closed my eyes and prepared for a nice deep sleep.

Have I ever mentioned that I have zero patience? Zero. By 12:49, I was in my car with a bag full of wet laundry, and I was driving down the dark and bumpy Railroad Ave Ext.

I made a deal with myself. If there were no lights on in her cottage, I would drive straight home to bed and come back tomorrow morning as planned. But, if there was a light on (lamp, TV, candle) then I would knock right then and there and get my apology out of the way.

Long story short, a light was indeed on, so I knocked. A few moments later, she opened the door.

"Josh? What are you doing here?"

"First of all, what are you doing opening up the door this late at night without even asking who it was? I could have been a psychopathic killer."

"They have those in Maine?" she smiled.

"Well, yea! Where do you think Stephen King comes up with his stories?"

She giggled as she held up his latest book, which she was just reading.

"Seeing as I looked out the window and saw your car, I figured I was safe. I am safe, aren't I?" she smiled. "So what brings you here at this hour?"

As I fumbled for the words, I gazed at her outfit. She wore pink sweats and a black, well-worn Cranberries concert tee. To be deadly honest, it could have been a fuckin' In Sync shirt and she would have looked adorable as fuck.

I took a moment to soak in her cuteness, and I also took a moment to mentally recite my top three favorite Cranberries songs.

1. "I Will Always"
2. "When You're Gone"
3. "No Need to Argue"

Once that was out of the way, I began to speak. I tried my best not to babble or use run-on sentences.

"I couldn't sleep, so I decided to do some laundry. It wasn't until they were washed that I remembered my dryer was broken. I hate leaving wet clothes overnight, so I decided to head down to the all-night laundromat at the beach. I took a short cut down your road and happened to notice your light on, so I figured I'd stop in and see if you maybe wanted to tag along."

"Wow," she said.

"Wow what?"

"I've heard of late night booty calls, but never late night laundromat calls. That's a new one to me."

"Sooo… is that a yes?" I asked.

"Sure. Why not. I suppose I better change though."

"Nah, you look fine. Besides, I'm sure we'll be the only ones there."

We arrived at the beach laundromat, and just like I predicted (hoped), we were the only ones there. I threw my bag of wet clothes into the dryer. I then sat next to Anna and debated the best way to explain my long-winded babble from yesterday morning.

The debate quickly faded though as we began talking about… actually, I don't even remember what we started talking about first. All I know is our conversation flowed easily from one topic to the next.

When our first moment of silence hit, Anna looked around at the empty laundromat and then at the clock. I noticed a smile creep over her face.

"What?" I asked.

"Is this a thing you York boys do? Take random tourists to the laundromat late at night? Is this how Maine does the booty call?"

"No." I answered defensively. "This is totally not a booty call!"

"I'm just kidding, Josh. Relax."

I *relaxed* for exactly 7.7 seconds then said, "And for your information, I've never brought a girl here before... for laundry or a booty call. Although, I do believe Doug has."

"Somehow that doesn't surprise me."

"If memory serves, I think her name was Sarah," I pondered.

"Ah yes," she smiled, "good ol' spin cycle Sarah."

I laughed out loud. There's something to be said about a girl with a great sense of humor—a girl who doesn't take themselves too seriously—a girl who looks cute as fuck in pink sweats and a tee—at 1:30 AM in a laundromat.

At that very moment, I was so tempted to lean over and kiss her, but I didn't. I was enjoying her company too much, and a kiss would only complicate matters. My self-control won out, and I didn't lean in for the kiss. Instead, I walked over to the dryer and fed it some more quarters. I'm sure they were already dry enough, but I didn't want to leave yet.

Amazing conversations, physical attraction, and that overall excited newness feeling—these are what you hope for when you meet someone. I think my main problem over the last twenty-nine and a half years was I always read into those feelings too much.

Just because you share those *feelings* and *moments* not does mean a relationship is in the cards. Plain and simple: the excited newness feeling doesn't mean she's your soulmate. For the first time in as long as I could remember, I didn't read into it. I made a conscious decision to just live in the now with Anna. No plans. no expectations.

"So, apparently two of the girls who work for Doug are going on vacation for a couple weeks in August, so the rest of us will be working a ton. Because of that, Doug is cutting my hours for the next week or so."

Anna looked on, wondering where I was going with this.

"So anyway… I'll have some free time if you want to hang out or whatever. I'm sure I can find plenty of other cool sights and places to show you."

Anna said nothing. She just sort of smiled and laughed at me.

"What? What's so funny?"

"Hang out with me, huh?" she said. "What about all of those things?"

"What things?" I asked.

"Um, let's see… nearly thirty years old… black cloud… no dog…"

I knew it was only a matter of time before she would bring that up. This probably won't come as a shock to you, but I was about to respond to my babbling by babbling even more.

"Oh… yea… those things," I said. "Well, what I said earlier is more or less true. I know thirty is just a number, and I know I probably shouldn't put timetables on my life, but I just can't help feeling I should be further along in my life… in my career… in my relationships. And I know it sounds dramatic, but yea, I kind of do feel like a black cloud is following me sometimes. You see, I promised myself not to get involved with any more summer girls…"

"I didn't realize we were involved?" she interjected.

"No, we're not. Not at all. That's my point. You and I just have fun together. Well, at least I think so. Sometimes I tend to overthink things, that's all. The bottom line is it doesn't matter how long you're here for, what matters is that we enjoy each other's company and we have fun. I was reminded by one of my friends that when you have fun with someone, you should keep having fun until it's not fun anymore."

"Your friend sounds like a smart guy," she said.

"He's actually a dumbass, but in this case, I think he might be right."

At that point, Anna just sat there, digesting my latest babbling session. Finally, she smiled and said, "I *am* a pretty fun girl."

"Yes, yes you are," I said.

"I suppose we could hang out some more while I'm here."

"Good. I would like that," I said.

"Do I need to buy an umbrella? Ya know, in case your black cloud decides to follow over me?"

"Nah," I said. "Besides, they don't feel so black when I'm with you."

I know that sounds like a super-cheesy line, but I swear I was just being sincere. But yea, as soon as it left my mouth, I was like, *Oh man! That was some cheesy-ass shit, Josh!*

I cringed at my comment then slowly looked over at Anna. I fully expected her to burst out laughing at any second, but to my surprise, she didn't laugh. She didn't even smirk.

The look on her face said that she took my line as sincere and sweet—which it totally was! Her look also said it was the sweetest and most amazing thing anyone had ever said to her! Okay, maybe I'm stretching her look a little bit... a lot a bit. But she did seem sincerely touched by my statement.

I'm not the best person when it comes to eye contact, but at that moment, our eyes locked in. I noticed her green eyes when we first met, but right here and now was the first time I looked into them. Like, really looked into them. All I could think of was how beautifully green they were.

Well, I also thought about one of my favorite marbles as a kid. It had that same green hue to it. I wondered what ever happened to all my marbles... my mom must have given them away. Too bad.

Anyway, I continued to stare into her eyes. They were like a sea of green, which also started me thinking about The Cure song "From the Edge of the Deep Green Sea." Great fuckin' song!

Other than that, my thoughts were solely focused on her eyes... and then to her lips... her full, lip-glossed lips... the kind of lips that just look kissable.

And yes, "Lips Like Sugar" by Echo & the Bunnymen might have popped into my head. I know, I know, my passion for music can be a gift... and a curse.

Maybe it was her green eyes, or maybe it was her full lips, or maybe it was those kick-ass songs I mentioned... or maybe it was the fresh scent of fabric softener in the air...

Whatever it was, it caused me to lean in and go for it. I kissed her. She kissed me back. Our first kiss lasted for at least a seven Mississippi count.

After a brief pause and pull-away, she was the one who initiated kiss number two, which not only lasted a solid nineteen Mississippi count, but it involved my hand running up through her hair.

Not to brag, but I've kissed a lot of girls over the years, but I tell you what, that was one of the best nineteen Mississippi kisses I had ever experienced. When we finally pulled away, we were faced with that infamous moment of awkwardness of what to say.

Speaking of which, here are a few things you *shouldn't* do or say after a great kiss like that:

1. "That was awesome!" (Offer her a high five)

2. "Wow, that was way better than the girl I kissed last night."

3. "So, do you like, wanna do it now? I have condoms."

4. "Wow! That kiss was... was too legit, too legit to quit!"

5. "That was the best kiss I've ever had. Please don't go... you're the only stable element in my universe."

6. "Oh baby, you taste like butterscotch."

And by the way, NO, I have not done or said any of those things before! Well, maybe one of them was a true story, but there is no way I'm going to reveal which one to you guys! I'll take that one to the grave.

Anyway, as I sat face to face with Anna, I searched for the right thing to say, but my mind was blank. Don't get me wrong, the kiss was amazing, but I just didn't know what to say.

Just then, the dryer buzzer went off. I was saved by the bell, or so I thought. When my eyes made their way over to hers, she looked at me and said the dreaded words NO guy wants to hear after kissing... or after sex.

"What are you thinking about?" she softly asked.

I was now on the spot, so I said exactly what I was feeling at that moment.

"I'm actually not thinking about anything. Or I should say, I'm not overthinking or overanalyzing anything that just happened. For the first time in a long time, I'm just trying to live in the moment, and the moment we just shared was nice, like, really, really nice."

Anna looked at me sweetly, and I returned the look. I have to admit, I was pretty God damn proud of myself. Usually, when I get put on the spot with the famous *What are you thinking* question, I usually panic and end up babbling my ass off, but just now—I fucking nailed it!

"How about you? What are you thinking about?" I asked.

I watched her sweet smile grow... and grow. It grew so much that it became less sweet and more amused.

"What? What are you thinking about?" I insisted.

She stood up and began taking my clothes out of the dryer. She then turned to me and said, "Late night laundromat? This was totally a booty call."

"No! No it wasn't. Not at all," I defensively argued. "This was most definitely not a booty call! Besides, all we did was kiss. There was no booty action involved."

"Relax, killer. I was just giving you crap," she giggled.

"Oh, okay," I said as I helped her unload my clothes.

"But I do agree with you," she said. "The kiss was nice. Really nice."

17

"CAN'T HARDLY WAIT" – The Replacements"

The next morning I met Pete and his little girl down at the beach playground. When I arrived, I stood on the outside of the chain-link fence and just observed. I watched how Pete interacted with Kayla. He was a good Dad.

As he pushed her on the swings, I thought about all the times we had invaded the playground after drinking all night. I thought about the night Doug pushed us so fast on the merry-go-round that Scott hurled all over the place. I also remembered the detailed description Doug gave of what Scott's puke looked like. Don't worry, I'll save you from that one.

I thought about all the times we brought girls here late at night. Our younger teenage selves would simply act obnoxious and show off for them. Over the years, this playground was also the scene of many a late night hookup... for all of us.

And besides just hooking up, I also know for a fact, there were times each of us brought girls down here to just hang out and talk late into the night (yes, even Doug).

As Pete continued pushing his daughter, I smiled at the memory of all the times we had "swing contests" of who could swing the highest and jump the furthest. Doug usually won the highest contest, but Scott always won the furthest contest. You would think because Doug swung the highest that he should be able to jump the furthest, but this was never the case.

The swings had the typical rubber seats which conformed to your ass. For whatever reason, Doug could never make a clean jump. His ass always got caught, which caused him to awkwardly and amusingly fall flat on his face in the soft sand. At first we thought he was doing it on purpose, you know, just to be funny. But after the 33rd time in a row face-planting in the sand, we thought differently.

I guess my whole point is, in one form or another, we all had great memories down here at the playground. So, as I watched Pete push his adorable daughter in *our* playground, I couldn't help but think, sometimes, it's pretty God damn beautiful to see things come full circle.

Pete spotted me and waved me in. As I walked closer, he pointed me out to Kayla and said, "Look, it's Uncle Josh. He's come here to swing with us."

She crinkled her nose and smiled. I might have been a little jealous of where Pete was in his life, but it's pretty cool being referred to as Uncle Josh to your best friend's kid.

She rushed over and gave me a hug. We had only experienced a handful of encounters over the years, so I was pleasantly surprised how easily she took to me. If only grown women shared this attraction, I would be all set!

"Hey kiddo," I said as she led me to the swings. "Where's Michelle?" I asked Pete.

"She's running a few errands. She'll be here in a bit. I think Doug is on his way too. I figured once Michelle gets here we can shoot some hoops."

I wanted to tell Pete about *the kiss*, but I held off. I figured it would come out soon enough. Besides, it was just a kiss—one with no expectations tied to it.

When Kayla spotted Doug, she climbed off the swing and rushed over to him. Doug scooped her up and helped her climb the ladder to the big, winding slide. They both slid down, laughing the whole way. I suppose it shouldn't have surprised me that they got along so well. After all, they were basically on the same maturity level.

Doug and I scampered around the whole playground, taking Kayla on every piece of equipment there. Michelle and Pete stood by with their arms around one another and watched us get run ragged by a three-year-old.

Once we hit the courts and began shooting around, I started to casually hint about the kiss.

"Hey Doug," I said. "If you're still offering, I think going easy on my schedule this week would be good."

"Yea, sure," he said as he missed a ten footer.

I grabbed the rebound and waited for him to ask what I had planned. When neither of them did, I took it one step further.

"I was thinking about playing tour guide some more with Anna."

Pete and Doug exchanged smiles. I took a jump shot then awaited what was sure to be a barrage of sarcastic comments.

"That's cool," said Pete.

Doug followed with, "Good for you. Just let me know what you want to work this week."

That was it? That was their barrage of comments? I know what you're thinking, if I always hate hearing their wise-ass comments about my personal life then why am I so disappointed when they say nothing? What can I say, I'm a complicated dude.

"I actually saw Anna last night after our walkabout. She went to the laundromat with me."

There was no way they could resist this tidbit. It was on! Bring on the sarcasm, boys!

Pete was up first. "Laundromat? Doesn't your mom still do your laundry?"

Wait... what?? This unforeseen comment caused me to brick a simple ten foot shot.

"My mom doesn't do my laundry. Not anymore," I mumbled.

Surely I could count on Doug for a doozy of a comment.

"Why did you go there?" asked Doug. "Didn't your landlord just install a new washer and dryer for you?"

What the fuck was wrong with these two????

He wasn't wrong, however. I did have a new washer and dryer, so I may have just got my clothes wet and then bagged them up last night. Don't judge!

But seriously, what the fuck was wrong with these two? I couldn't take it anymore, so I blurted out, "Anna and I kissed last night!"

Pete picked up his dribble and looked from Doug to me.

"You fuckin' dog!" he smiled as he threw the ball at me. "You and Iowa girl kissed?"

I picked up the ball, smiled then nodded.

"Did you bang her?" asked Doug.

"No," I answered.

"Blow job?" asked Pete.

"No," I snapped. "We just kissed."

"Did you finger-bang her?" asked Doug.

Before I could respond, Pete blurted out, "Hand job?"

"Jesus Christ, guys! There was no banging or jobs of any kind! All we did was kiss!"

Those were the exact barrage of perverted, sarcastic, and annoying comments I expected when I baited them, yet, I baited them anyway. I told you, I'm a very complicated dude.

"All you did was kiss?" asked Pete.

I nodded.

"Good kisser?" asked Doug.

I smiled and nodded again.

"Well that's good," said Doug. "Nothing worse than a bad kisser. Did I ever tell you guys about that chick who I made out with on the dance floor at Goodnight Ogunquit?"

I knew it was only a matter of time before he retold this story.

"Worst kisser ever! Wet, sloppy, and at one point, I swear I thought she was gonna swallow my whole fuckin' head! It was like I was this wild boar, and she was an anaconda. I felt helpless as I watched her jaws unhinge extra wide and attempt to swallow me whole! Scary shit, I tell ya."

"Wow, we've never heard that story before," Pete laughed. "Anyway, back to Josh and Anna... so, what happened after the kiss?"

"Nothing really," I shrugged. "After that brief moment of *what the fuck do we say*, we just talked for a few then I brought her back home."

"She didn't pull the typical, *what are you thinking about*, did she?" asked Pete.

Again, I nodded.

"I hate when they do that," yelled Doug. "Especially after sex. Like I'm really gonna say, *I'm thinking how long do I have to lay here before I can go home to my own bed'.*"

Pete laughed and said, "Or, I'm thinking, *'where did I put the remote control? Sportscenter is on in a few'.*"

It'd be easy to say my friends are shallow idiots, except I too have had those same thoughts cross my mind. And before all of you girls out there get high and mighty, think about your REAL thoughts after kissing/sex versus what you actually say!

"So how was the kiss?" asked Pete.

"It was good. Really good."

"So what did you say when she asked what you were thinking about?" asked Pete.

"Please tell us you weren't stupid enough to use the *'It was too legit, too legit to quit'* line... again?"

I shot Doug a hot glare and said, "No, no I didn't."

So much for taking that one to the grave.

"Stupidest line ever!" laughed Doug.

"At least I got another kiss out of it," I said, defensively. "Better than your stupid butterscotch line."

"What butterscotch line is this?" asked Pete.

It was Doug's turn to give me a glare.

"Go ahead, Doug, tell Pete about your *brilliant* line."

Doug continued his glare then slowly said, "Fine. It was years ago at the Aqua Lounge, and I was on the dance floor kissing and grinding with this summer chick. I think Neneh Cherry's 'Buffalo Stance' was playing." Doug pondered a second then said, "Ramona. Her name was Ramona, and she had these sexy tattoos all over her arms, and she had a smokin' hot tramp stamp. It was some sort of bird... a phoenix, I think."

Do you guys find it funny that Doug can remember all of those details of a girl he was grinding with ten years ago, but he can't remember the name of the girl he banged last week?

Anyway, back to Doug's story:

"So, after the club closed, we made our way across the street to the beach. We started making out on the sand, and I assumed beach-sex wasn't far off. But just to seal the deal, I decided to offer her a sweet kissing-compliment."

Pete was already chuckling in anticipation.

"When we were done making out, I said, '*Oh baby, you taste like butterscotch*'."

"Oh God! What did she say?" asked Pete.

Doug hesitated then continued, "She said, '*Yea, and that line tasted like bullshit.*' With that, she got up and left. Needless to say, the butterscotch line did NOT seal the beach-sex deal."

We all cracked up laughing and continued shooting around.

Oh, and just so we're clear regarding the *two legit line*… I was very intoxicated that night, not to mention, I was in the middle of my brief hip hop phase. And just to be crystal clear, she apparently also thought the kiss was *too legit to quit* because we continued making out 'til the break of dawn! Word!

I went on to explain to Pete and Doug that I had zero expectations regarding Anna. I was simply taking their advice and having fun. I was also quick to point out, that even though I had fun with Anna, and even though I enjoyed our kiss, I still had NO intentions of having sex with her. She was only here ten more days, so the fewer complications the better. This was not going to turn into another classic summer-girl fling. It wasn't.

18

"TIME FLIES TOMORROW" – Paul Westerberg

So, even though this wasn't a summer-girl fling, and even though I had no expectations, Anna and I ended up hanging out a lot over the next few days. None of it felt forced or overly thought out. We were just enjoying each other's company.

One of the days was spent doing some hiking around York. We started off crossing over the Wiggly Bridge and hitting the trails over in Steedman Woods.

Fun Fact (from Anna): The Wiggly Bridge is considered the World's smallest suspension bridge!

I also took Anna on a tour of Old York. Some of the highlights were the 18th century schoolhouse, the Old Burying Ground, and the Old York Gaol (Jail).

Fun Fact: The Old York Gaol is the oldest jail in the country.

We ate dinner up at the famous Maine Diner in Wells, where Anna completely devoured and raved about their homemade blueberry pie.

Fun Fact (from Anna): 99% of the country's blueberries are from Maine.

We finished the day by hiking a bunch of the trails up at Mount Agamenticus. We hung out at the top of the mountain and watched the perfect sunset.

Later that night, we met the whole gang (Pete, Michelle, Doug) down at the York Beach Cinema. Thankfully, Doug spared me the embarrassment by not bringing up the "Elise movie night."

With all of us hanging out at the beach cinema, it definitely felt like old times. Needless to say, it would have been even better if Scott was there too, but it is what it is!

The movie we saw that night was *American Pie*. That might have been the most laughing I had done at a movie since Doug and I saw *There's Something About Mary* the summer before.

What also made it feel like old times was the loud "Da ha ha ha's coming from behind us. A little left Geoff was a fixture at the cinema. He went to almost every movie in the summer and always sat in the same seat.

Of course, in addition to his signature laugh was his signature farting... loudly. Why we sat directly in front of him, I'll never know, but I suppose it was better than directly behind him. I think we sat so close so Doug could spend the night razzing him and getting him going.

For example: The apple pie scene. After we all laughed our asses off, Doug turned to Geoff and said, "I bet you've stuck your pecker in a pie, huh?"

Geoff responded with a firm, "No!"

He then proceeded to give Doug an angry, evil stare down. Within eight seconds, however, Geoff emitted the all-too familiar "Da ha ha ha... my pecker in a pie. Pecker in a pie!"

Yup, just like old times.

***

The next day we took an Isles of Shoals cruise out of Portsmouth. We had a picnic out on the scenic Star Island. Between those two days, Anna went through roll after roll of film. She was just getting started, however. The next day would be the ultimate picture-taking trip.

We left York bright and early and headed north along the coast. We spent the entire day touring a bunch of lighthouses in the southern and mid-coast area of Maine.

Fun Fact (from Anna): Maine has 65 lighthouses still standing.

We didn't even come close to seeing a quarter of them, but we started up at the scenic Portland Head Light and made it as far as the Rockland Breakwater Lighthouse, located at the foot of the beautiful Samoset Resort in Rockland.

Time was limited, so in order to see as many sights as possible, it was more of a quick whirlwind-tour of each. We also made time to do a few side trips. It wouldn't be a Maine-cation without visiting L.L. Bean and the giant-ass boot.

We also stopped in Phippsburg at Popham State Park. It was directly on the coast and was also home to another old and very cool fort (Fort Popham). Anna was in tourist heaven. Just a hunch, but I think that was Anna's favorite day yet.

What tipped me off to that was Anna saying, "This is absolutely my favorite day yet!" She also repeated about six times the phrase: "This is exactly why I wanted to come to Maine! Exactly why!"

We had a long, full day of sightseeing, and by the time I dropped her back at the cottage, it was just after 9 PM. Just like the previous two days, I was sound asleep before my head hit the pillow. I think I was more exhausted than if I worked at the bar the last three days.

You guys are probably wondering why I ended up taking Anna on the coastal lighthouse tour. Especially considering I said earlier, that a lighthouse tour would be the perfect date—*if* I was trying to romance or pursue something serious with her. Trust me, guys, I only ended up doing it because I knew she would really enjoy it. Besides, she had already purchased dozens of lighthouse postcards and a *Lighthouses of Maine* calendar to boot. That being said, I simply figured it would be considerate of me to show her some of them in person.

Yes, I know that a lot of the things we did the last few days were usually reserved for actual "dates," but I convinced myself it was just a case of me showing a sweet and kind out-of-towner a fun time. Period!

Trust me, if I was really trying to romance this chick, I would have pulled out all the stops. I would have taken her up to the White Mountains for a day or two—as in, a drive along the scenic Kancamangus Highway. Or an even more scenic train ride through the mountains—with a chance to take countless pictures of the famous Old Man of the Mountain.

And if I was really, REALLY trying to woo her, there would have been an excursion planned to Bar Harbor—as in, Acadia National Park—with romantic sunset cruises—and whale watches. Now THAT would be romancing her!

I did mention to her that we should spend a day in Boston before she left. She not only loved the idea, but she suggested we do it on the day before she flew out. And SHE (not me) suggested we take two cars and drop off her rental that Friday morning.

Seeing as her flight wasn't until 5 PM on Saturday, SHE (not me) suggested we get a hotel and make it a day and a half of sightseeing before she flew out. Of course, she was also quick to point out we could get separate hotel rooms. I thought the whole plan was a great idea, and I immediately started coming up with the perfect Boston itinerary.

See, the fact that she suggested separate hotel rooms proved that she didn't think our many trips throughout the week together were romantic.

19

"TENDERNESS" – General Public

When Doug didn't show up for our golf threesome with Pete, I should have known something was up. Doug was the one who set up the tee time, and he must have reminded us ten times throughout the week. We were slightly concerned, but eventually we assumed Doug must have just gotten lucky the night before. We figured he was either too hungover, or he stuck around for morning sex. Either way, we knew we were in for a big story later on.

Pete and I went on and played without him. For the record, we only lost nine balls, and we only hucked our clubs three or five times. Overall, not a bad day on the course.

After about a week of spending nearly every day with each other, I figured it would be good if Anna and I took a little breather. That being said, we did meet out at Hoohahs later that night for drinks.

***

When Anna and I arrived at Hoohahs, it was packed. It wasn't a big place, so it didn't take much to fill it up, but it was one of the busiest nights I've seen yet. Taylor, Hillary, and Steph were straight out but seemed to be handling it fine, which was good because Doug appeared to be of no help. He was slouching on a stool at the end of the bar with a shot glass and a bottle of Jägermeister.

Anna made her way into the ladies room, and I made my way over to Doug. Within seconds, I knew something was up. It's not uncommon for Doug to have a few drinks throughout the night, but I had never seen him like this at work. He was drunk off his ass. Usually when he was this drunk, he would be loud and obnoxious but in a funny Doug sort of way. That particular night, however, he seemed angry.

I walked over to him with the intent of giving him shit about not showing up for golf. Before I could say a word, he offered me a shot of Jäger, and when I declined, he called me a fucking pussy and poured himself another. I figured now wasn't a good time to bust his balls about golf.

Over his shoulder, I spotted Michelle hanging out with an old summer friend of ours, Caitlin. Pete and Michelle used to lifeguard with her back in the day. I made my way over and gave Caitlin a hug.

"Hey you. I haven't seen you in forever," I said, and then gave Michelle a hug too. "Where's Pete?"

"At home watching Kayla. You can't hang out with him every night. Mama needs some girl time."

"Yea, well, that better be water you're drinking there, Mama," I joked, then turned to Caitlin. "You're married now, right, Caitlin?"

"I am," she said. "We actually have a three-year-old daughter as well."

"Our girls are so cute together," added Michelle.

"So where are you living?" I asked Caitlin.

"We were living down in Mass, but we just built a house over in Wells."

Internally, I grimaced. Yet another old friend; married, kids, and a new fucking house. My jealousy only lasted a brief second, I was more concerned with Doug's condition.

"What's his deal?" I asked, motioning to Doug.

"I was going to ask you the same thing," said Michelle.

"I haven't seen ol' Doug like this since nickel draft night at Captain Nick's," laughed Caitlin.

Just then, Anna returned and I introduced her to Caitlin.

"He hasn't taken his eyes off that cute bartender," said Caitlin.

"More like, the guy she's been talking to all night," added Michelle.

I looked over, and sure enough, Doug was focused on Taylor and that dude that had been flirting with her the past week or so.

"Is something going on between Doug and Taylor?" asked Michelle.

"I don't think so," I said. "They're constantly trying to one-up each other with wise-ass remarks, and I suppose there's some flirting mixed in, but I never thought much of it."

"Well, I definitely think he's jealous of that guy," said Michelle.

"Nah," I said. "That guy is an idiot. Taylor is probably only flirting to get a bigger tip."

"They've been sleeping together the last few nights," said Anna, out of the blue.

"What? Really?" I said.

Anna nodded and said, "Yup, she told me earlier today."

I had no horse in the race, and I certainly had no designs on Taylor, but if Doug did, I could see why he'd be angry and jealous. When I thought this guy was simply "trying" to get with Taylor, I thought he was just a tool bag... but in an innocent way. But now that I knew his cocky, smug, lame lines had led to him having sex with Taylor, he went from tool bag to douchebag status.

Come to think of it, I never had an actual conversation with this guy, but every time I saw him, he always acted like we were best friends or something. Worst of all, he was the type of dude who would address you with words like: Pal, Buddy, Boss, Captain, or Bro. I hate that!

What the fuck was Taylor thinking? I was on Doug's side on this one. So much so, that I went over and did a shot with him, which caused his earlier irritation with me to subside a bit. I didn't bother bringing up Taylor... or the douchebag. I figured I'd wait until sober Doug showed back up.

"Hey, can you go crank some real tunes on?" asked Doug. "This shit is what happens when I let the hippie chicks be in charge of the music. If I hear another Dave Matthews, or Grateful Dead, or a fucking Phish song, my head is gonna explode!"

Once again, Doug and I were on the same page.

"What are you in the mood for?"

Doug thought for a second then said, "Something with a beat to it. Maybe some of that classic dance shit you used to play at Goodnight Ogunquit."

I smiled and nodded. "I'm on it."

"But no fuckin' depression session shit... not yet anyway," he drunkenly smirked.

I happily removed the girls' crappy CDs and put in a couple of my mixes. The first song that came on was Naughty by Nature's "OPP".

The tie dye twins looked over at me in disdain. I glanced over to Doug, and he had a smile on his face and was doing some sort of hip hop gestures with his arms... or maybe he was having a seizure. Either way, it was obvious he approved of my musical selection.

I made my way back over to the girls. Michelle and Caitlin hung out for another half an hour or so. Every time we heard a classic club song, we would reminisce about the good old days. Anna seemed quite amused with our many stories of Sunday nights at Goodnight Ogunquit.

When Marky Mark's "Good Vibration" blared out, we informed Anna about the infamous underwear ritual. I think I covered this in *The Empty Beach*, but long story short: Marky Mark Wahlberg used to do Calvin Klein underwear ads. So naturally, whenever I played his song at Goodnight Ogunquit, a handful of my friends would drop their pants and dance in their underwear. By the end of the summer, the club was full of underwear dancing freaks, including some chicks and even some of the bouncers.

The more I reminisced, I slowly looked over to Doug to make sure he wasn't getting any ideas to relive his underwear-dancing glory days. He did get off his stool, and he simulated pulling his pants down, but thankfully it remained just a simulation.

Once Michelle and Caitlin left, Anna and I found entertainment in people-watching. We played that game where you choose two people and make up your own dialogue about what they're saying. Doug and I did this all the time behind the bar. We're actually pretty fucking funny at it. Yes, we amuse ourselves. Surprisingly, Anna was pretty good at it in her own right.

Hillary and Steph might have been pissed at me for overriding their music, but the majority of the crowd was loving my mixes. As a matter of fact, at one point, people started dancing in the back, darkened part of the bar. By the time "Rump Shaker" cranked on, two people turned into four, turned into a dozen or so, and all of them were laughing, drinking, and dancing. I might be almost thirty and over the hill, but I can still get people dancing.

During K7's "Come Baby Come," Doug stumbled his way over to us and began to sway; not from the pulsating beat, but from his plethora of Jäger shots. While we snickered at his condition, Doug focused his attention out to the darkened, makeshift dance floor.

He gave me a nudge and slurred, "I know I'm fucking drunk, but I think that hot chick is giving me the look. Have you ever seen her in here before?"

It was too dark for me to know for sure, but she didn't look familiar. I shook my head no.

"Is that a sweet ass or what?" he said.

"Go dance with her," urged Anna.

I shot her a look. We already avoided a Marky Mark pants drop, there was no telling what Doug would do on the dance floor in his condition. Before I could advise against it, he was already on his way to the dance floor.

As the song faded out, they began conversing. Just then, a loud foghorn sound effect echoed throughout the bar. This was Doug's idea on how to signal last call. Kind of cheesy, but just like the name of the bar, it had kind of grown on me.

"Last call for alcohol," yelled Taylor to a bunch of groans.

The next song was Sophie B. Hawkins'-"Damn, I Wish I was your Lover." It's a great tune, but it's not really dancing material. Apparently, however, it was grinding and groping material.

We watched as Doug went for a firm ass grab, and to our shock, the woman began groping Doug's crotch area. I shit you not. We watched in dismay, yet were laughing the whole time.

"She does have a sweet ass," I said.

Anna jokingly gave me a nudge and we continued our amusement at the dance floor. When the song was over, Doug excused himself to the bathroom. When I noticed he was in there longer than normal, I went to check on him. He was in the stall hurling into a toilet. By the time he got most of it out of his system, most people were filing out.

I led Doug back to his stool at the bar and got him some water. One of the people who hadn't left yet was Taylor's new man. While Taylor was closing up, he made his way over to us and offered up a snarky comment.

"Whoaa, looks like somebody's gonna have quite the hangover tomorrow. You really shoulda paced yourself, Chief."

I didn't need to look at Doug to know he was about to punch this guy in the throat. I quickly stepped in to quell the situation.

"Yo, pal, it's closing time. I think you need to head out," I said, looking at Taylor for some backup.

Taylor knew how drunk Doug was, and she also knew how much he hated this guy.

By the way, the reason I keep referring to him as "this guy" is because I never did actually find out what his name was. We always just referred to him as either the Charles in Charge dude or the giant bag of douche dude. Mostly the latter.

Taylor told the giant bag of douche that she'd meet him back at his place after. He left, but it was obvious that the thought of her going to his house to have sex, left Doug even more jealous. I was surprised, but I guess he really did have a thing for her.

I did my best to try and change the subject.

"Hey, where did your dance partner go?" I asked, giving him a smile and a nudge.

It took him a second to process my question, but then he returned my smile.

"Yea, where did she go?" he said, and curiously gazed around.

There were a handful of stragglers in the back.

"Dude, did you see her grab me? She totally knew how to touch a guy."

"She should," said Anna with a slight giggle.

"Why do you say that?" asked Doug.

"I might just be a country girl from Iowa, but I do believe that she is a he."

Anna pointed to the front door. Doug spit his water out when he saw his "dance partner" in the now well-lit doorway. It was vividly and disturbingly apparent that we had a crossdresser in our midst. She/he gave Doug a wink and blew him a kiss before exiting the bar.

Doug let out a loud, tortured groan then grabbed a random leftover drink off the bar and began chugging it.

"Dude, she fondled my package," he said.

"Actually, *he* fondled your package," Anna said, fighting back her laughter.

Another groan emitted from Doug's mouth as he pounded down another random drink.

I smirked and shook my head at him and said, "You couldn't tell?"

Anna shot me a shocked look.

"What?" I said.

"*She does have a sweet ass,*" mimicked Anna.

I recalled my earlier observation then hastily followed Doug's lead by grabbing a random drink and swigging it down.

After everyone had exited, Doug looked up at us and solemnly asked, "Does this mean I'm gay?"

"Yes," yelled Taylor.

"I wasn't fucking talking to you," snapped Doug. "Don't you have a boy-toy to go play with? And you can tell him if he ever calls me chief again, I'm gonna kick him in the balls."

Taylor rolled her eyes and shook her head at him.

"You're not gay," I reassured him. "You've just had way too much to drink, that's all. Not to mention, it's really dark back there."

Doug looked towards the still-darkened back wall and nodded.

"Yea, it was really dark back there. Too dark. We gotta get some more lights over there. Like a fucking floodlight or something."

I gave him a pacifying nod then said, "See, I told you you're not gay. Besides, it's not like you had a hard on, right?"

Doug thought for a quick moment then lowered his head into his hands and uttered, "Not full-on, but… but I definitely had a semi."

"Maybe you're semi-gay," laughed Taylor as she headed towards the backroom.

Doug shot her a glare, but when she was out of the room, he turned to us and quietly said, "Maybe she's right. Maybe there's a part of me I don't know about?"

"Oh shut up," I said. "You're not semi-gay. Semi-stupid maybe. Come on, let's go. We'll give you a ride home."

Doug shook me off then started to stagger towards his office.

"Thanks, Josh, but I think I'm just gonna crash here tonight. I've got some things to figure out about myself… and my sexuality."

Again, Anna and I fought back our laughter.

"Okay, buddy. Good luck," I said. "Call me if you want me to come get you."

"Thanks, Josh. You're a good friend. Night guys," he said, entering his little office.

Anna and I shut off the lights then headed out, locking the door behind us.

20

"EVERYTHING FALLS APART" – Dog's Eye View

Late the next morning, Anna and I met Doug out for coffee. His hair was disheveled, and he still had on the same clothes from the night before. Dark sunglasses covered up his bloodshot eyes and he sat with his head down.

"Jesus, you look like shit, dude," I said, sitting down.

I thought about calling him chief but figured it was too soon.

"I'm never drinking again," he said, sipping his coffee.

"Hmmm, I've never heard that one before," I said.

Before Doug could tell me to fuck off or whatever, Anna cut right to the chase.

"Was last night about Taylor and that guy?"

When Doug didn't answer right away, I prodded some more.

"Yea, what's the deal with you two? You got a thing for her or what?"

"Nah," he said. "That ship sailed a long time ago."

"What ship? Did you guys have sex?" I asked.

As soon as Doug paused, I knew they had.

"When was this?" I asked.

"A couple of years ago," he shrugged. "It was when we both worked over in Portsmouth together."

Again he paused, but this time it was more like a stoppage, as in, end of story.

I wasn't letting him off that easy. I needed to hear more.

"Come on, Doug, spill it," said Anna.

Shit, she just read my mind. This chick is getting cooler by the day.

"Yea, come on, Doug, spill it," I echoed.

He shook his head and sighed, but ultimately he caved in and told us.

"Fine, but no judging me, and this stays just between us!"

Anna and I nodded, and Doug reluctantly began.

"We started working together in the summer of '97. We pretty much hit it off immediately. We had other things in common too, but we definitely had the same sarcastic sense of humor, and I guess we kind of used it to flirt with one another. For most of the summer and fall she had a boyfriend, but by the time we had our Christmas party at work, she had been single for a couple months."

As soon as we heard "Christmas party," Anna and I knew where this was headed.

"There were a lot of people at the party, but Taylor and I ended up hanging out together most of the night. We just talked and laughed… and drank… a lot. The next thing I knew, we were checking into the Sheraton in downtown Portsmouth."

I wanted to turn the tables and make a "Doug comment." I wanted to ask him if they banged, or finger banged, or if he got any kind of the "jobs," but I didn't. I figured Doug was too hungover to be amused, and Anna wouldn't have gotten my references anyway. Besides, Doug was opening up to us, so the least I could do was not be sarcastic or graphic. A lesson that would be nice if he and Pete followed it as well.

I left my hint open-ended.

"So, I assume you guys…"

"Had sex?" said Doug. "Well yeah! We banged the whole fucking night. Like, crazy sex too. Loud crazy sex. She was like a banshee for Christ sake."

Well, it's a good thing I chose not to be graphic, I thought.

Anna and I smiled at each other. Like I said earlier, as soon as we heard him say Christmas party, we knew the outcome, and the word hotel definitely sealed the deal, but what we weren't expecting, was the next part of his story.

"We slept in until checkout time, and then we went our separate ways without really talking about it. The whole thing felt a little different to me. I had the next couple days off, so it gave me time to think about things."

"Felt different how?" asked Anna.

"Well, usually when I have a one night stand, the only things that run through my mind are: *Please don't offer your number and ask me to call you.* Or *How am I gonna sneak out without her noticing?*"

"Doug! That's horrible!" scolded Anna.

Doug just shrugged and said, "Sorry, but I'm just being honest. And it's even worse if the one night stand takes place at your own house."

"Why is that?" asked Anna.

"It's easier to find an excuse to leave her house rather than an excuse to kick her out of yours. One night stands are one occasion where home court advantage is bad."

Compared to Doug, I wasn't as well-versed with one nighters, but he wasn't wrong; home court advantage was bad.

"Is that how you felt with Taylor?" said Anna.

Doug paused then said, "No, not at all. I liked waking up next to her, and I would have had no problem hanging out or calling her later."

"Did you tell her that?" I asked.

"No. But over the next day or so, I couldn't shake what I was feeling."

"Which was what?" asked Anna.

"I liked her. A lot. As in, I could see having a relationship with her."

"Jesus Christ! Why didn't you tell me this before?" I asked, slightly offended.

"I didn't tell anyone. It was bad enough that I was about to pull a Josh."

"Pull a Josh?" Anna curiously asked.

Oh shit. This was not going to be good, I thought. I quickly ran through my personal checklist of things that might constitute "pulling a Josh."

"You made her a mixtape, didn't you?" I blurted.

"Fuck no! I don't have patience for that shit."

I'm glad Doug used the word patience. It did take a lot of patience... and skill. Making a good mixtape was a God damn art form! A highly underappreciated art form, by the way. Doug's next comment snapped me out of my mini internal mixtape rant.

"What I did was worse than a mixtape," he softly said.

This time, my mind went to Doug's famous "kiss of death" list of things NOT to do when you like a girl.

1. Give a girl flowers.
2. Tell her that you *like* her before she tells you.
3. Make her a mixtape.

"You told her that you liked her, didn't you?" I said, too excitedly.

I could tell by his expression that I had hit the nail on the head, but I could also tell there was more.

"And you bought her flowers too!" I said, as if I just won a contest.

Doug lowered his head in his hands.

"That's *pulling a Josh*?" asked Anna. "I think it's super sweet."

"Pfft! Super dumb, you mean," he scoffed.

Sympathy oozed from Anna's face as she softly asked, "What happened?"

Doug took another sip of his coffee, sighed, then continued his tale.

"On the way over to her apartment, I stopped and bought her a dozen white roses."

I crossed my fingers and prayed Anna wouldn't ask why white and not red. No such luck.

"Red roses would be the triple kiss of death, for fuck's sake!" he snapped. "The only time you give a chick red roses are if you're married to her or if you fucked up. And if you're married to her AND you fuck up, you better make it two dozen! Besides, a few months ago, I overheard her tell someone that white roses were her favorite."

I gave Anna a look that said, please, no more questions like that. She smiled and let Doug continue.

"Just like Josh probably would have, I had the whole thing planned out. I put the flowers in the back seat, and I was going to ask her if she wanted to take a ride and talk. I was gonna drive up to the Nubble and give her the flowers and tell her how I really felt about her."

Wow, he really was going to pull a Josh. Of course, a mixtape would have been a cherry on top, but whatever.

Doug continued. "I knocked on her door, and she invited me in. Before I could say anything, she said she wanted to talk to me about something. I'm not gonna lie, my gut told me she was feeling the exact same way as me."

I looked over at Anna. She was practically on the edge of her seat. She was such a sucker for romance. It was sweet.

"Taylor said, and I quote, 'I just hope our big mistake the other night doesn't affect our working relationship or our friendship.' Pfft, so much for my gut feeling. Obviously, my gut's a dumb fuck!"

The romantic air was just released out of Anna's face.

Still deflated by Taylor's comment, Anna asked, "What did you do? What did you say to her?"

"What the fuck was I supposed to say? It was clear that she didn't feel the same, so I told her that I agreed it was a mistake and assured her it wouldn't affect our friendship. She offered me a drink, but I told her I had to get going."

Anna and I sat there in silence as Doug zoned out for a second. When he returned, he finished up his story.

"I drove home along the beach. It was dark out and had just started snowing. I remember parking on the side of the beach, and the longer I sat there, the angrier I got. Not at her but at myself. I got so pissed at myself, that at one point, I started yelling at myself and beating the shit out of my steering wheel."

Been there done that, I thought. There had been many a night I had TKO'd my steering wheel.

"Before I drove off, I happened to glance in the back seat and saw the fucking roses. The next thing I knew, I threw them into the ocean and watched the waves crush the shit out of them."

Anna sweetly reached over and touched Doug's hand and said, "I'm sorry."

"Yea, I'm sorry, man," I said. "You really should have told me this though."

"Eh, it's no big deal. I got over it pretty quickly, and it really didn't affect our friendship. Within a week or so, we were back to exchanging quips with each other. And before you overanalyze this, Josh, the answer is no; I'm not still into her like that."

"First of all, I don't overanalyze things… that much. And second, you seemed pretty damn jealous last night."

Anna nodded in agreement.

"Last night was more about that douchebag than her. The guy is bad news. I just don't want her to get hurt, but trust me, that's where my feelings end. Taylor and I have a good thing going."

"I don't know," I skeptically smiled. "You were pretty worked up."

Doug shrugged and said, "It was just a bad day—all the way around."

"What do you mean?" I asked.

Doug hesitated, then said, "I went to see my mom yesterday, and when I got there it was obvious that she had been crying. On the table next to her was a bunch of old photos. He's been gone for 25 years, but the asshole can still make her cry. I fucking hate that."

It was then I realized Doug might be telling the truth; last night was probably less about Taylor and more about his mom. The feelings he had for his mother... and for his father, ran deep. It was one of those topics he rarely talked about with us, and if he did, it was kept brief. This was another one of those times.

Doug finished his coffee and stood up.

"I think I'm gonna head home and get some sleep in my own bed," he said. "Not that there's a point to it. I have to be back at the bar in a few hours anyway."

"I'll cover for you today," I said.

"Really? You guys don't have plans?"

"Nah," I said, looking over at Anna.

It would have been nice to hang out with her today, but I knew Doug wasn't in any condition (mentally or physically) to go into work.

Anna nodded in agreement and said, "Yea, we didn't really have any plans today anyway."

"You sure?"

"Seriously, go home and get some sleep. I'll take care of the bar."

"Thanks," he said, then headed out.

After Doug was gone, we sat quietly drinking our coffees.

"Umm, Josh? What is he doing?" Anna said, pointing up ahead.

I looked up, and about thirty feet away was good ol' Geoff. He stood there staring and smiling at us while he pretended to be striking a match.

"That's Geoff's way of saying he's going to burn down my house, that's all."

"Oh. Should we be worried?" she asked.

"Not at all," I said as I returned Geoff's match-striking

gesture back at him.

His smiled was replaced with a look of worry.

"You better not!" he yelled. "My dog Ivan is in there!"

I continued striking my pretend match at him.

"Are you joking or serious?" he said.

"Oh, I am very serious, Geoff! Da ha ha ha."

I probably shouldn't have said that because it caused Geoff to approach us, warning me if I burned his house down that I would go to jail. To which I almost replied that I had been to jail many times and I liked it there. I smartly held off, knowing full-well it would only cause him to remain talking to us.

After Geoff walked off, and after our laughter subsided, Anna turned to me and hesitantly asked, "So, what's the deal with Doug's mom?"

I went on to explain to Anna the general history of Doug's parents. I say general because Doug had never gone into full details with any of us. Apparently, when he was four or five, his dad left him and his mother high and dry. As far as I know, there wasn't another woman involved.

From what I understood, his dad had a lot of personal issues; drinking, drugs, gambling. I'm not positive, but I don't think he's even seen his dad since then. His mom had a few serious relationships, but never remarried. Every so often she goes through these bouts of depression and blaming herself.

I can't imagine growing up with an absentee father, never mind trying to deal with a mother who goes through these depressive episodes. Once again, it put any of my own family problems over the years in perspective, and after hearing me tell her all of this, I think it put Anna's parents' divorce in perspective as well.

Considering I told Doug I'd cover for him, and considering I had Todd's celebration party to go to later that night, I assumed I wouldn't see Anna again until tomorrow. So, we finished our coffees, said our goodbyes, and headed off in different directions.

21

"LIGHTHOUSE" – Antje Duvekot

I knew Taylor was going to ask what the deal was with Doug's drunkenness from the night before. I was vague and short with my answers. I figured it was Doug's place to fill her in on the details if he wanted.

When she asked if it had anything to do with her and that dude, I told her no. I did tell her that both Doug and I thought that he was a major douchebag and that she could do better. She just gave me a wink and said she had it under control.

Hillary and Steph came in at six, and I ended up hanging out until around seven. After that, I left Hoohahs and headed over to Murphy's for Todd's party. Seeing as social media was not yet invented, I was surprised how many old employees he was able to get a hold of. Most of them were from Todd's tenure there, but there were a handful from the late 80s and early 90s. In other words, way back in my day. A couple of them I hadn't seen since then.

We recounted one crazy story after another. It's funny what you remember from ten years ago. It was also funny how embellished those stories had grown over the years.

A lot of our conversations started off like this: "Hey, what was the name of that dude who cut his finger off on the slicer?" Or "What was the name of that waitress who got caught having sex in the bathroom with her boyfriend?"

Two of the people I knew the most there were Kent McCall and Stevie Wendell. We worked together in the late 80s.

Kent's claim to fame: He was the guy who got a spindle stuck through his arm. For those of you who don't know what a spindle is, it's a thin pointed metal rod on a base. It's used by the wait staff to impale their order slips.

Doug and I had swung by Murphy's on our night off to pick up Kent for a big party. We waited for him in the dining room while one of the waitresses moped. Not realizing the floor was wet, Kent rushed out of the kitchen and immediately went airborne and landed on his ass.

That in itself would have hurt, but what hurt worse than that was on his way down, he slammed his arm on the spindle next to the register. Apparently, the pointed metal rod entered and exited his forearm and then entered his bicep.

None of us knew what happened until he slowly stood up and revealed that his arm had been shish-kabobbed. Needless to say, the party was put on hold for a trip to the emergency room.

Stevie Wendell only worked at Murphy's for one summer, but it happened to be the summer of the infamous toilet papering night. After work one night, Doug, Pete, Scott, Stevie and I decided we were going to be the first people to ever toilet paper the statue in the center of York Village. The three busy roads that converged at the statue made it a nearly impossible task to pull off.

So, for all you Millennials or I-Gens, let me break it down for you. Back in the 80s, back before Facebook and Snapchat, and back before cell phones and Netflix and whatever else consumes your time, people found it amusing to go around TP'ing houses.

It wasn't just a matter of throwing rolls of toilet paper into random trees. Pfft, that was for amateurs. The real fun and talent was turning it into an art form. After a while, we needed more of a challenge than just doing someone's house at 2 AM, especially if they lived on a quiet dead end street. Boring. That's why we decided on the statue in the center of town... in the middle of summer... at late o'clock at night.

Wendell was our getaway driver and was parked across the street with the engine running. Two of us stood as lookouts about a hundred feet down two of the busier roads. The other two quickly TP'd the statue. It had to be a hurried job, so unfortunately it lacked artistic integrity.

Apparently, about thirty seconds in, a good fucking Samaritan spotted us out his window. Not only did he call the cops, but he ran outside for an apparent citizen's arrest. Seeing this, we bolted towards our getaway driver, only to see that our getaway driver had already gotten away. The fucker!

The dude chased Doug, Scott, and myself behind all of the village businesses. We ended up ducking down in some tall brush behind York Town House Pizza. Long story short, one of us (me) stepped on a twig, causing Mr. Good Samaritan's flashlight to land on us.

He then escorted us back to the scene of the crime. By now, there were two cruisers with their blue lights flashing. There were also two cops standing there questioning Pete.

"Oh shit," I mumbled.

"Don't worry," said Scott, "Pete's not gonna tell them anything."

Less than five seconds later, one of the cops said, "Which one of you is Josh Wentworth, Doug Andrews, and Scott Ouellette?

Fucking Pete.

Luckily for us, the cops were cool about it and only gave us a stern warning. So, despite having our getaway driver leave without us, and despite having Pete narc us out, it was a successful night. Our only regret was not getting a picture of our accomplishment.

I continued to reminisce with Stevie and Kent, and eventually Todd made his way over to join in. Todd and I retold some of the classic Freddy and Phil stories, and we all shared in telling some equally classic Geoff stories as well.

"Da ha ha ha," said a voice from behind us.

We turned to see Megan standing there. Megan, as you might remember, was my feisty and sassy waitress from the *Empty Beach* book. She was loud and rough around the edges, but she always had a good heart. It wasn't long after the summer of '95 that Megan got pregnant and had a kid.

She gave Todd a hug then came over and hugged me. I wasn't positive, but it almost looked like she was pregnant again. I think everyone knows NEVER to congratulate a woman on her pregnancy until you know for sure she is actually pregnant.

I waited until she wandered off and then asked Todd.

"Hey Todd, is it me or is Megan—"

"Pregnant again? Yup. Baby number three."

"Number three?" I exclaimed. "Holy shit!"

Todd looked around to make sure she was far enough away

then whispered, "Three different kids, by three different fathers."

I shook my head in shock.

"I knew she was always on the promiscuous side," I said, "but... wow. It's too bad, she's actually a really nice girl, but she—"

"Can't keep her legs closed?" said Todd.

"Um, I was gonna say she has a hard time staying away from losers and deadbeats, but yea, mostly what you said."

We both laughed and continued talking about some of the others from 1995.

"Have you seen or heard from Freddy at all? I haven't seen him since that summer ended."

Todd smiled and said, "I saw him a couple of times last summer. He's living down in NYC and has been doing some off Broadway plays."

I laughed out loud. "That is so perfect for him."

Todd nodded and said, "He's living with three or four roommates and works at some popular diner where the wait staff sings to the customers."

"I've heard of that place. It's like the Starlight or Stardust diner or something. Yet another perfect job for him."

I almost asked Todd if he ever had an Elise sighting, but I decided not to bring it up.

Apparently though, I must have worn my thoughts on my face because Todd said, "Did you ever see that Elise chick again?"

I slowly shook my head no.

"That's too bad. She was a pretty cool chick, and I honestly thought that she dug you."

"You and me both," I sadly smiled. "Oh well, it's not the first time I misread a girl, and I'm sure it won't be the last."

Before the moment got too depressing, I spotted Todd's girlfriend, I mean, his wife, Kerri. As she walked towards us, my eyes glanced down at her very pregnant belly. There was definitely no mistaking if she was pregnant or not, but just to be sure, I gave Todd a curious look and said, "Is she…"

Todd smiled and proudly said, "She's due September 3rd. It's a boy."

"Jesus Christ! Why didn't you tell me earlier? Congrats, man."

I shared those same sentiments with Kerri. Just as they were going over their top three baby names, I noticed the front door open and Mrs. Murphy entered.

The mood in the room lowered a bit, and I watched from a distance as one by one everyone approached her. I'm sure some of them attended the funeral, but most, like me, were offering their condolences for the first time.

When she finally made it over to where I was standing, she gave me a warm smile and a long embrace. We sat and talked for about twenty minutes. It was probably the longest conversation I'd ever had with her, certainly the deepest.

She told me how I was always one of Mr. M's favorite employees over the years. She also told me that they were both more than a little surprised when I turned down his offer to lease the place four years earlier. She asked me what my career aspirations were, and I responded with a laugh and told her I wish I knew.

She gently put her hand on my hand and sweetly offered words of encouragement. The gist of which was that things will happen when they're supposed to happen. I couldn't help but think her statement went beyond just my career aspirations.

After our little chat, I said my goodbyes to everyone I knew, and I headed back over to Hoohahs to check on things. Taylor told me that although Doug never came in, he did call to see how things were going. I knew his absence at work had more to do with his mom than him still being hungover.

I planned on checking on him in the morning, but for now I'd give him some space. Taylor and the girls had everything under control, so I really didn't need to be there. I sat up at the bar and cracked a beer, but I don't even think I took a sip of it. I just sat there and stared at the bottle and thought about the last two hours.

It was great to reminisce with my old co-workers, and it was great knowing that not only was Todd the new owner, but that he and Kerri were having a baby. But there's a Ying and Yang to every situation, and tonight's Yang left me feeling old, unaccomplished, and certainly behind the times when it came to marriage and kids.

As my eyes stared fixatedly on the beer bottle, I also thought about Mr. Murphy. I tried to remember the last time I saw him, and the last thing we said to each other.

I was so deep in thought, I didn't even hear the bar crowd or the loud music being played. The only thing that snapped me out of my trance was a hand on my shoulder. After I jumped, I turned to see Anna standing there.

"Sorry, I didn't mean to startle you," she said. "I called your name, but I guess you were really into that beer bottle."

"Oh, sorry. I was just deep in thought, I guess."

"Well, I won't interrupt your thinking. I just wanted to come over and say hi."

She started to walk back to her seat.

"Hey, Anna… do you wanna go for a drive?" I blurted out.

"A drive? At this hour? Where are we gonna go?"

"I don't know," I shrugged. "I just feel like driving around and listening to some tunes."

Her green eyes glistened underneath the bar lights. She smiled and replied, "I would love that."

We swung by my apartment so I could pick up some mixes for the ride. One of my favorite things to do is drive around (especially at night) and listen to music. I do some of my best thinking while driving. Most of this book was conceived while I was behind the wheel. I usually do this by myself, but on that particular night, with Anna riding shotgun, it turned out to be one of my most favorite drives ever.

Some of the best drives are ones where there are no destinations in mind, and that night was no exception. We drove one backroad after another all around southern Maine. The songs were usually the centerpieces to my drives, but on that night, the conversations between Anna and I took center stage.

Throughout the week our topics ranged from silly to serious, but on our drive, they leaned more towards the serious side. I told her about my night at Murphy's, and I told her in pretty good detail about my history there. I told her all about the many years I worked there, and I filled her in on Mr. Murphy's offer to me. And yes, I even told her about the infamous summer of Elise. As we continued through the backroads of Maine, my thoughts turned back to Mr. Murphy's passing.

"You wanna hear something weird? I'm nearly thirty years old and I have never actually been to a funeral. A couple of distant relatives, but no one who I was that close with."

"I'm not sure if that's weird, but it's definitely pretty lucky though. I've been to three. My grandfather on my dad's side, my grandmother on my mom's side, and when I was fourteen, one of my classmates died from cancer."

"I'm sorry."

"We weren't close friends, but we grew up together, and it was hard seeing someone so young go through that. I think my grandmother's passing hit me the hardest though."

"You two were close?"

"Very."

It was now Anna's turn to carry the conversation. She told one story after another about her and her grandmother.

"It was because of my grandmother that I decided to become a nurse."

"She was a nurse too?" I asked.

"No. Not at all. But the last year of her life, I watched how kind and compassionate the nurses were with her, especially when she was put in Hospice care. They went above and beyond to make the last few months of her life as happy and content as possible. I was originally going to go to school for business, but after seeing how dedicated they were and just how well they cared for my grandmother, it changed my outlook on my future. I knew their job was super hard and tiring, and for the most part, thankless, but at the end of the day, they made a huge difference. That's what I wanted—to make a difference."

At that moment in my life, I would have settled for half of her passion. Before I could offer my thoughts, R.E.M's "You are the Everything" came on the radio.

"I love this song!" she said, cranking it up.

I fucking love that! There's nothing cooler than when someone not only loves the same song as me, but they crank it up. Well, it has to be the opposite sex though. It does nothing for me if Doug or Pete got excited and cranked one of my favorite songs up.

When the song ended, she turned it down then asked out of the blue, "What would say is your biggest fear?"

"What? Where'd that come from?"

"Dunno. I was just curious."

"Hmm, I'll have to think about that one. Why, what's yours?"

She thought for a quick moment then said, "Regrets."

"How do you mean?" I asked.

"I don't want to be seventy-years-old sitting on my rocker regretting all the things I didn't do or say. Heck, I don't wanna be twenty-three with those type of regrets. That's one of the reasons I forced myself to come here on vacation alone. I have to admit, when Vanessa cancelled last minute on me, I was so close to scrapping the whole trip, money and all. I've never been very good at being independent, but I've been trying harder the last couple of years. I knew if I didn't come here alone, I would regret it forever, and I'm tired of living my life like that."

Through the darkened interior, I gave her a smile and said, "Well, I admire the hell out of you for coming here alone. I think you'll be just fine sitting on your rocker one day."

I didn't need an interior light to know that she was slightly blushing.

By now, I had made my way off the backroads and entered the city of Lewiston. It was well after midnight, so I crossed my fingers I could find a gas station open this late. We got lucky, not only did we find a gas station that was open, but one that had coffee.

After I filled my tank, we grabbed two extra-large coffees, some junk food provisions, then hit the road again.

"If we take the highway from here we can be back home in just over an hour, or we can slowly head back off the beaten path again. Your choice."

"Oh that's totally up to you," she said. "You're the one

driving."

I took a sip of my large coffee and said, "Backroads it is."

"I was hoping you'd say that," she said, also taking a sip of her coffee.

Over the next few miles, nothing much was spoken. We just drank our coffee and listened to "The Same Deep Water as You" by the Cure. I was, however, still thinking about her question from earlier.

"I think my biggest fear is going through life without finding it," I said as the song faded out.

"It?" she curiously asked.

"Yea, you know, that one thing that drives you. That one thing you're passionate about."

"Like a career you mean?"

"A career… a job… hell, I'd settle for a hobby."

"You really have no desire to partner up with Doug?" she asked.

"Not really. Don't get me wrong, I really like working there, and as far as jobs are concerned, it's probably one of the best places I've worked, but no matter what, I'll always look at it as Doug's place. He's talked about owning a bar forever. It was always *his* dream, his—"

"His *it?*" she said.

"Exactly. Here Hey Hoohahs is Doug's *it*."

"Despite your old, old age," she joked, "I have confidence that one day you'll find *it*. I can definitely see you doing something creative."

"Ha ha," I laughed. "Were you eavesdropping on my palm reading session?"

"No. Why? Is that what Madame Rita told you too?" she said excitedly. "See! I told you she was good!"

"Pfft. She also told me that she could sense I was a huge

animal lover," I said.

"Are you?"

"Besides a goldfish I had when I was five, I have never ever had a pet in my life. I haven't even been to a zoo in over ten years!"

"Geesh, you're such a pessimist."

"No I'm not. I'm just a realist."

"Whatever. Either way, I think you'll end up doing something creative."

"Oh yea? Like what?" I asked.

Anna thought for a second then enthusiastically said, "I got it! With all the crazy stories you and your friends have, you should write a book!"

This caused me to laugh out loud.

"What's so funny?" she asked.

I went on to tell her about my screenplay fiasco back when I was nineteen. I told her how I had this big, stupid, ridiculous idea that not only was I going to write a movie about me and my friends growing up here in the summer, but that I was going to have it filmed right here in Maine. To my surprise, Anna found it neither stupid nor ridiculous. I even told her I originally wanted John Cusack to play the lead. Anna did think that was slightly humorous.

"You really burned it?" she asked.

"Yup! I lit the whole notebook on fire. I even burned the pen too."

"Aww."

"Trust me, the writing was horrible. What was in my head just didn't come through on the paper."

"And you haven't written anything since?"

"Not a word."

Just then, "April Skies" by the Jesus and Mary Chain came

on, and I reached over and turned it up. I turned it up because I liked the song, but also because I was hoping to change the subject. I hated thinking about my failures or about my silly pipedreams.

Despite the volume being turned up, it didn't drown out my thoughts. If truth be told, although I had never attempted to write another word since I was nineteen, I had thought about the "movie" over the years. For whatever reason, I decided to share this with Anna.

"Sometimes," I said, turning the volume back down, "sometimes I find myself thinking about the movie. The storyline has definitely changed in my mind over the past ten years, but I do find myself filing things away. Sometimes when something happens to me, whether good or bad, I find myself saying, *Hey, that would make a great scene.* Or when Doug says something completely off the wall, I think, *that would make a great dialogue in the movie.* And don't laugh, but I even have the soundtrack picked out."

"No laughing here," she said. "I think you need to sit down and try again."

"Nah. I've never even taken a writing class, so I'm sure the thoughts in my head would still come out like shit on the paper."

Again, Anna pointed out that I was being a pessimist, and again, I used the word realist. It was too dark in the car to see, but I could feel her rolling her green eyes at me. Luckily for me, Depeche Mode saved me from further getting lectured. Their song "It Doesn't Matter" came on, and I pointed out that I had seen them twice in concert. This led to a concert comparison conversation. I rattled off at least twenty shows ranging from U2, the Cure, Sting, Radiohead, New Order... you get the picture.

It really wasn't much of a comparison. Besides a few obscure one hit wonder bands from the 80's, the only two real concerts Anna had been to, were Alanis Morissette and the Cranberries.

"The closest city that most of the bigger bands play is Chicago," she said. "I would have to drive three plus hours in order to see them. Yet another reason you should feel lucky. Not only do you live next to the ocean, but you have easy access to see all of those great shows. I would love, love, love to see U2!"

I suppose she was right. There were at least four or five great concert venues within two hours. It wasn't until I started listing all the shows that I realized how fortunate I was.

Anna's distraction was short-lived. Five minutes after our concert conversation, she went right back to my screenplay idea.

"I really think you should try and write your screenplay again. I'm not sold on the idea that you're a bad writer, and I'm also not sold on the idea that you need to go to school to be a writer. Maybe you just needed to gain some real-life experience first. I might just be a silly, naïve country gal, but from what I've heard so far, I think you've gained plenty of life experience. For what it's worth, I'd definitely watch your movie!"

"Thanks," I laughed.

I should have left her sweet comment and pep talk alone, but, well, the glass half empty side of me took over. Again.

"Even if I did write it, and even if it came out the way I wanted, it would still be a nearly impossible task to actually get it made into a movie. I would first need to land an agent, and what kind of agent worth their salt would take on a dude from Maine with no prior resume?"

I went on to point out at least five more likely roadblocks.

"So, long story short," I said, "I don't want to be seventy-years-old in *my* rocker looking over at my screenplay, which by then would have three inches of dust on it. A screenplay, mind you, that I put my heart and soul into all those years earlier. And at that point in my life, I'd be so old and shaky, if I tried to light it on fire again, I would probably end up burning my whole house down. Who wants that?"

The scary thing was I was only half joking. I noticed Anna slowly nodding her head.

"Yup. Definitely a pessimist," she said.

"Just a realist," I mumbled.

Anna knew it was useless to continue her debate, so she resigned to just sit there, enjoying the tunes as we got closer to home.

It was nearly 3:30 AM when we arrived back in York. Whether it was all the late night coffee I drank, or all of the interesting conversations we were having, but I still wasn't very sleepy.

"I don't know about you, but I'm really not that tired."

"Same," she said.

I took a chance and asked, "Do you want to go up to the Nubble and wait for the sunrise?"

"Yes!" she said, nearly jumping out of her seat.

Even though we still had an hour and a half before sunrise, there were already a couple of other cars parked up there. While we sat there killing time, I told Anna about our big statue toilet papering caper from ten years ago. I was also reminded of a part of the story that I left out earlier.

Before we TP'd the statue that night, we did a "warm-up" job that was equally as legendary. We thought it would be funny if we came up to the lighthouse and TP'd a car while there were people inside it making out (or doing other stuff).

Stevie Wendell kept his car running and parked at the foot of the lighthouse road at Fox's Lobster House. The rest of us walked up the hill to the Nubble's parking lot, in hopes of finding the perfect car to TP; preferably, one with the most fogged up windows. To our pleasant surprise, we hit the jackpot. There was a long, black limo parked front and center.

We huddled up and made a quick game plan, which consisted of two of us on the driver's side and two on the passenger's side. Depending what was going on inside the limo, we figured we had twenty seconds, tops.

As discreetly as we could, we took our positions. The two on the passenger side threw their rolls of TP over the top of the limo. The other two caught them and rolled the TP back to them underneath the limo. We got a solid three and a half limo-wraps before the driver's door swung open and out popped a huge chauffeur. He must have been 6'8, maybe even 7'8.

We froze for a second then all four of us took off running down the hill towards the getaway car. One of his strides equaled two of ours. If this was a horror movie, one of us would have surely tripped and been killed. Fortunately, it wasn't. We were all young enough and in our athletic prime, so we were able to easily outrun the giant driver.

We all packed in Wendell's car, and as we sped off, I remembered looking back at the huge limo driver standing there (out of breath), shaking his huge fist at us. It was not unlike a scene from Jack and the Beanstalk. If only Wendell's getaway driving ability could have lasted one more mission!

"See!" laughed Anna. "Yet another great, potential movie scene."

I couldn't argue with that imagery, so I shook my head in agreement.

"I really can't believe we drove that many hours tonight," she said.

"Like I said earlier, it's one of my favorite things to do. When I went down to Florida to see my dad earlier this year, I drove by myself and loved it! One day, I would actually love to pack up my car, grab a bunch of CDs, and just drive around the country."

"By yourself?" asked Anna.

"Sure."

"And you make fun of me for going on vacation by myself?"

"No, I never made fun of you for coming by yourself. I made fun of you for choosing York, Maine for your big vacation destination."

"I really don't think you give your town or state enough credit," she said. "So where would you go on your solo vacation?"

"I'm not really a big city guy, but I'd like to hit Chicago, Seattle, San Francisco... oh, and definitely New Orleans."

"I would love to go there!" she said.

"Basically, I'd just like to drive around and see all the different landscapes of our country. I would definitely have to stop at some of the cliché places too. The Grand Canyon, the Rocky's... and most definitely Iowa!"

"Awww, to see me?" she sweetly said, then quickly caught on. "Oh, you were referring to that silly baseball field, weren't you?"

"I suppose I could visit you too," I joked. Anna gave me a playful glare.

Outside, the darkness was slowly giving way to the light. At any moment, the sun was ready to poke its head up over the horizon. By now, the parking lot was filled with cars. People were mulling about with their tripods and cameras just waiting to take the perfect sunrise picture.

"So why don't you do it?" she asked. "Why don't you take a major road trip and see everything you want to see? No offense, but it's not like you have anything tying you down here. No wife, no kids, it's just a matter of saving up for it, right?"

I was prepared to give Anna multiple reasons why I couldn't possibly go on a road trip like that, but... they weren't really reasons, they were more like excuses. I was the master of that; the master of excuses and not following through. There were times when justifying shit like this was second nature to me. There were also times that my excuses and justifications disgusted me.

Anna awaited my response but suddenly became distracted with something out the windshield. I followed her eyes and saw the top of the sun rising behind the lighthouse. Anna's smile grew as she grabbed her camera and quickly exited the car.

I watched as she navigated her way onto the rocks and began to take one picture after another of the sunrise. Even when the entirety of sun was visible in the sky, it was apparent that Anna was going nowhere. She sat on her rock marveling at the sky, yet shivering from the cold early morning ocean breeze. I grabbed her sweatshirt from the backseat and joined her down on the rocks.

"I can't believe I haven't come here sooner to watch this," she said. "Every time I planned on it, I always overslept. I guess the key is to just stay up all night," she smiled.

Do you ever have those moments when you feel like you're exactly where you're supposed to be? Usually, those were few and far between for me, but as we sat next to each other and watched the sun make its way above the lighthouse, and as I watched the sunlight reflect off her green eyes, I felt one of those moments.

I mean, we were just sitting there on a rock. That's pretty random and insignificant, right? But I guess it's not really about what you're doing or where you are... it's more about a feeling.

I didn't overthink or overanalyze it, I just took it in and enjoyed the moment. I knew the endgame was near. Anna would be heading back to Iowa in a handful of days, and I knew this would all soon be just a distant memory, but for whatever reason, that moment was good enough for me.

It was nearly 7 AM when I dropped her back off at her cottage.

"Thanks for keeping me company last night... and this morning," I said.

"No, thank you. I think it was one of my favorite nights since I've been here," she said.

"Really? Even more than doing late night laundry?" I joked.

"I said *one* of my favorite nights," she clarified with a smile.

"I don't know about you, but I'm gonna sleep all day," I said.

"Me too! Oh, wait, I'm meeting Taylor for lunch today."

"You guys have been hanging out a lot."

"Yea, I really like her. She reminds me a lot of one of my old best friends."

I was sure there was a story why Anna referred to her as her "old best friend" but I was too exhausted to ask her about it now.

"Do you want me to pick you up tonight?" I asked.

Anna gave me a puzzled look.

"You're going to Pete and Michelle's party, right? They did personally invite you. As a matter of fact, I think they invited you before they invited me."

"It's because I'm funnier," she said as she exited my car.

"You really are overtired, aren't you?" I said.

Anna laughed and said, "I'll see you tonight."

She continued walking towards her cottage but stopped. She turned back around and said, "Thanks again for the drive... and the sunrise."

"You're welcome," I said, then slowly backed out of her driveway and headed home to bed.

22

"WITH OR WITHOUT YOU" – U2

Growing up, there weren't a lot of parties at Pete's parents' house. This was mostly due to the fact that his parents rarely went out of town. The three things you could always count on when Pete did have a party were:

1. Some sort of sporting event would be on TV. He was obsessed with watching sports. He's been known to switch on *Sportscenter* while having sex. True story. And don't even get me started about Spring Break in Daytona Beach. Let's just say, Spring Break coincided with the NCAA tournament. 'Nuff said.

2. If there was music playing at his party, it would be either U2 or Fleetwood Mac. Period. I have nothing against either. U2's *Joshua Tree* is one of my top five albums of all time, but I swear, if he could, Pete would bang Bono. I'm sure he'd do Stevie Nicks too, but definitely Bono first. I think it was the

sunglasses.

3. Drink coasters. Pete's family were big coaster fans. No matter where he was in the house, he could always hear if a glass or bottle hit the surface of a table, and before you could blink, he was right next to you sliding a coaster underneath. A coaster ninja, if you will.

When Anna and I arrived, I was pleasantly surprised to see a dozen or so people already there. Apparently, Pete and Michelle had run into a couple of our summer friends from back in the day and they spread the word. It certainly wasn't like our old house parties, but it was nice to see a few of the old summer crew.

Caitlin was there and she invited a couple of former lifeguards that she still talked to. They were more Pete, Michelle, and Doug's friends than mine, but I did remember partying with them back in the day.

I introduced them to Anna then we headed to the kitchen to get a drink. Oh, by the way, the Sox game was playing on the living room TV. We entered the kitchen, and just as I handed Anna a beer, there was a loud voice from behind me.

"DJ Melancholy!"

Without turning around, I knew exactly who it was.

"Hang, the DJ, hang the DJ," another familiar voice yelled.

I turned around to see Mike Forbes and Adam Slater... and their wives.

Adam's middle name was Christopher, so we used to call him AC Slater. You know, like that guy on *Saved by the Bell?* Not that I've ever watched it. I might have seen one episode at best.

"What kind of party doesn't have music?" said Mike, giving me a hug. "You should get the fog machine going," he joked.

"No shit. I'm sure you have some mixes in your car," said

Adam, also giving me a hug.

I absolutely had mixes in my car, but before I could offer them up, Pete's voice yelled from the doorway.

"You guys want some tunes? I'm on it!"

When Pete left, we all shook our heads and laughed. Anna asked what was so funny, and I told her she'd see soon enough. I introduced them all to Anna, and they introduced me to their wives.

Just as we expected, we were interrupted by Bono's Irish voice informing us that "This song is not a rebel song. This song is Sunday Bloody Sunday."

As the drums kicked in, I turned to Anna and said, "I hope you like U2."

"And Fleetwood Mac," laughed Mike.

She didn't completely understand, but by the end of the night, it would be crystal clear. To be fair to Pete, at least he had much, much better taste than Hillary and Steph. I could most definitely handle U2 and Fleetwood Mac over their hippie shit any day.

After talking with them for a bit, I found out that Mike was just in town for the week visiting family. He now lived out in La La Land working for some big company doing graphic design. No kids yet, but I did find out their condo was only a three minute walk to the beach.

"You guys should totally come out to visit us," offered Mike.

"That sounds like a plan," I said. "We should set something up."

I explained to Anna later, that both of our comments were what you'd call "polite party BS." It's especially used when you haven't seen someone in a while. The whole *'Hey, we should get together'* or *'Absolutely, let's do that'* lines were thrown out more times than I could count that night.

Don't get me wrong, I knew that Mike would love to have us visit, and he knew that we would honestly love to visit, but we both also knew the chances of it happening were slim to none. It's just a given that these are the types of conversations you have when you haven't seen someone in a while—"polite party BS."

That being said, I had a great time that night catching up with everyone. If you recall from *The Empty Beach*, Mike was the guy who was famous for his after-party streaking habits. I asked Mike whatever happened to his streaking sidekick, Andy. I hadn't seen Andy in nearly four years. Apparently, neither had Mike. Andy had pulled a Scott. He just slowly stopped hanging out or responding to calls. The one difference being, Scott lived only two miles away from here, and Mike had no clue where Andy was living.

When Pete and Mike began talking about their jobs, I did my best to gather information on what the hell Pete actually did for work. It was obvious that Mike was some sort of graphic designer, but Pete's job was still tough to pinpoint. I did hear the words *IT* and *startup company*. I quickly lost interest when they began talking about some Y2K/end of the world thing that was coming up at New Year's.

This was the first time I'd seen Mike since he moved to Cali a few years ago. Adam and I, on the other hand, crossed paths a handful of times a year. He owned a surf shop over in Ogunquit, and yes, I was jealous. Not of his success, but jealous of the fact that ever since he was a teenager, he knew exactly what he wanted to do with his life. Here I was knocking on the door of thirty, and I still didn't have a fucking clue what I wanted to do.

I had zero interest in surfing, but I loved listening to Adam talk about his store or hearing him talk about the killer wave he rode during last week's storm. Actually, I loved listening to anyone talk passionately about their career. I didn't talk that way about anything.

I snapped out of my wallowing long enough to pose a question to Adam.

"Anna mentioned to me the other day that she would love to try to surf at least once before she headed back to corn country."

The word surf was all it took. Adam's face lit up. Not only did he tell Anna that he'd take her in the morning, but he would hook her up with a wet suit and board for the day. Anna's face beamed with excitement.

Mike was in town another couple days, and said he'd love to join them. Doug overheard and wanted in as well. Adam laughed and pointed his finger at Doug.

"Don't pull what you did last time."

We all knew what he was talking about, but Anna stood there with a curious look on her face.

Adam turned to Anna and said, "The last time we went surfing, this kook over here must have yelled shark at least twenty times."

Doug proudly smiled and said, "Oh come on. It was funny seeing everyone's reaction."

"It was funny for the first two times, tops," smiled Adam.

Doug looked at Anna and said, "More like the first eight times… then it was kinda overkill."

As everyone laughed at Doug, Anna immediately took the opportunity to thank me for hooking her up. I don't know about you, but the girls that show the sincerest appreciation for the littlest things are the ones you want to do the biggest things for. Does that make sense?

The party rolled on for another couple hours. I use the word *party,* lightly. There might have been a handful of our old summer crew there, but this was far from one of our old parties. There were no drinking games, or keg stands, or watching people try to flirt and hookup with someone. There was no Frank Clines playing his guitar and having Doug and I make up songs.

Those were real parties—kegers, bashes, ragers. What we were doing tonight was more like a get-together. Actually, it was worse than that; it was more like a *couples'* get-together.

Even though Anna and I showed up together, I had to point out to almost everyone there that we were not dating and that we were just friends. Other than us and Doug, everyone else there was married or dating, and most had kids too.

At one point, while Anna was over talking to the other girls, Pete and Doug approached me. Pete was the first to speak.

"So, you and Anna have been hanging out a lot, huh?"

"Yea, what's up with that?" said Doug. "You haven't been kissing and telling us shit lately. Have you tapped that ass yet?"

"Eh, you wouldn't believe me anyway," I said.

"Try us," said Pete.

"We've kissed a few times, but as far as sex is concerned, absolutely not! I'm not gonna complicate things more than they are, and sex will definitely complicate things. Besides, she'll be gone in less than a week."

They looked at each other and simultaneously said, "You're right, we don't believe you."

"Whatever. But I'm telling you the truth. It's not about the sex. We just have a fun time together. She's different than a lot of girls I've met."

"What the fuck are you talking about? She's got tits, she's got an ass, what's different about that? What, does she have a dick or something?" laughed Doug.

"Do you really want to talk about chicks with dicks?" I asked.

Doug's laughter quickly subsided. Pete hadn't yet heard the crossdresser story, so he looked on a bit confused. Doug was spared for the moment as we were joined by Mike, Adam, and their wives.

The more I was around all of these couples, the more I felt weird and like a loser for being one of the only single ones there. Ironically, Doug probably thought everyone that *wasn't* single was weird. What started off as mostly reminiscing about the good ol' days, quickly turned into talking about their kids, or the Caribbean vacation they just took, or how outrageous property taxes were in their towns.

I love my friends. I love kids. I love my friends' kids. But I swear, if I heard another adorable potty training story, I was going to jump through the window. It got so bad, I secretly prayed that Doug would tell some stupid, crazy, perverted story… even if it involved making fun of me.

The summer gods must have heard my prayer because less than five minutes later, Doug got his groove on. His opportunity came when somebody asked Anna where she was staying. When Doug heard she was on Railroad Ave Ext, he turned to me.

"Is she at the party house?" he asked.

"No. Anna is staying in the tiny cottages across the street from the party house," I said.

"A lot of parties there, huh?" said Doug, then began to reminisce. "The Worcester girls, the Assumption College girls, the Ashland girls, the Toronto girls…" Doug sighed. "A lot of memories."

Most of us in the room nodded in nostalgic agreement.

"Hey, Pete," chuckled Doug, "remember when I walked in on you and that girl, and she was giving you a—"

Doug stopped short and looked over at Michelle then altered his thought.

"… she was giving you a beer. Um, a Rolling Rock, I think."

Doug knew he had stepped in it, so he offered Pete and Michelle an apologetic smile, especially Michelle. I have to admit, I was impressed. Doug never edited his thoughts. Maybe good ol' unfiltered Doug was finally growing up.

Michelle looked at him with a straight face then burst out laughing.

"It's okay, Doug. We both had quite the crazy life before we dated. It WAS before we were dating, right?" she said, smirking at Pete.

"Yes, dear. Wayyyyy before."

Doug seemed dumbfounded. "Wait. Are you telling me it doesn't bother you to hear about Pete's hookups?"

"Why would it?" smiled Michelle. "We both had our share of summer fun before we dated."

"I told you, Doug, she's not the jealous type at all," Pete said, putting his arm around Michelle.

It was like a weight had been lifted from Doug. With that, he once again became good ol' unfiltered Doug.

"It wasn't really a beer she was giving him… it was a blow job," Doug specified.

Everyone laughed and Michelle played along.

"Really? You mean it wasn't a Rolling Rock?"

"More like a swollen cock!" laughed Doug as he turned and offered Pete a high five.

Pete's face turned red and he half-heartedly hit Doug's hand.

Michelle smirked and shook her head at Doug, who was still

shocked at her easy-going nature.

"There's no way you can be cool hearing about this stuff."

"Doug, we've been married for four years and are going on our second kid, not to mention we've been dating forever. I think I'm secure enough to hear about a little BJ from a lifetime ago," said Michelle.

"It wasn't really a *little* BJ," said Doug. "The chick was going to town on Pete… as in downtown! And she had some serious DSLs too."

Anna leaned into me and started to whisper in my ear. Doug saw this and clarified for her benefit.

"Dick Sucking Lips, Iowa girl."

Anna immediately turned a bright red. Doug was just getting warmed up. This was great! This was the perfect remedy for all the baby, family, and career talk. Best of all, none of Doug's stories involved making fun of me.

Doug looked at Michelle and said, "Well, seeing as you're so cool and hip about all of this, I've got another good story. He turned and addressed the rest of us.

"At one party we were at, I was passed out on one bed and Pete and some bimbo were in the other bed next to me."

Pete's eyes widened and he began giving Doug the *don't say another word* look.

"Relax, dude. Your wife said she's fine with it." Doug refocused and continued. "So anyway, I woke up in the middle of the night, and when I looked over, all I could see in the dark was Pete's white-as-snow ass jackhammering this bimbo from behind."

Everyone started cracking up. Everyone except Pete. He pounded the rest of his beer, set it on the table (on a coaster), then hung his head in shame.

"Seriously guys, it was like he was trying to jackhammer his way to China for Christ sake! Oh, and the best part was the noises that the bimbo was making. It was this loud, quick-panting sound, which makes sense… they were doing it doggie."

Pete finally had enough and stood up and said, "Okay, okay Doug, we get the picture. Story time is over."

Doug looked over at Michelle for help. "Does this bother you?" he asked.

"Who, me?" she said, pointing to herself. "Why would it bother the *loud, quick-panting bimbo*?"

Doug's jaw dropped and his face went blank.

"Oh fuck! That was you?" he said.

Michelle's deadpan glare slowly broke into a smile and she gave Doug a smack on his arm.

"You knew that was me, you little shit."

"No, I swear I forgot," he said, looking over at a still embarrassed Pete. "If it's any consolation, Michelle, you've always been my favorite bimbo of his."

"Aw, thanks, Doug. And you've always been my favorite dumbass friend of his."

Michelle smiled and put her arm around Caitlin and said, "It's not like we didn't have our share of fun back in the day."

Both girls clinked their drinks and began reminiscing.

Caitlin nudged Michelle and said, "Remember those guys from Montreal that we had an all-nighter with?"

"Oh my God, yes! Around 2 AM you and I split up. You guys *hung* out in the playground, while we *relaxed* on the basketball court."

"Hey! We play hoops there!" I exclaimed.

Pete followed with, "And we take our daughter to that playground!"

Doug just stared them both down and said, "You soiled our

hallowed ground with French fuckin' Canadians? You girls disgust me!"

Both girls laughed and clinked their drinks. Pete shook his head at the two of them then headed into the kitchen for a well-deserved beer. Michelle finished off her drink and set it down on the table… with no coaster.

Doug made a loud siren sound and I announced, "Code red, code red! We need a coaster, stat!"

We all laughed and looked towards the kitchen, and there in the doorway was Pete… not laughing.

"What is this, pick on Pete night? You guys know my parents are sticklers for coasters. I'm just respecting their house, that's all."

Say what you will about Pete, but he was always adamant about respecting his parents' house. I couldn't help but laugh as I looked over at his parents' dining room table. It must have been about ten years ago, but I remembered all of us sitting around the table playing drinking games with the crazy *Marshwood girls*. Drunk Heather and drunker Trish taught us this stupid drinking game called Thumper. It involved a lot of hand drumming on the table, all the while the girls would drunkenly yell out, "WHAT'S THE NAME OF THE GAME? "THUMPER!"

"AND WHY DO WE PLAY THE GAME?"

"TO GET FUCKED UP!"

Beyond that, I can't remember how the stupid game was played. I just remembered those loud, obnoxious phrases and the even louder drumming of hands on the table.

Did I mention, all of the girls' fingers were adorned with rings… especially that Kim Shirk girl. Many, many rings. The kind of rings that would do some serious damage to a nicely polished dining room table… far more damage than a coasterless beer.

As those drunken hands and rings slapped on the table, I swear to God, I thought Pete was going to have a heart attack. He was morally and sexually torn. Morally, because he wanted to respect his parents' rules and their scratch-free dining room table.

Sexually, because he was trying to "get with" one of the chicks. He certainly didn't want to be the guy to bring down a game of Thumper. Smartly, he compromised by putting down a heavy duty tablecloth. Sadly though, he still didn't get lucky.

Anyway, back to Pete and Michelle's party. It was only 11PM but most of the couples had to get back home; babysitters and whatnot. Back in the day, 11PM was when our parties usually got going. Oh well, I suppose it could have been worse. They could have broken out the Pictionary.

After Anna helped Michelle pick up a bit, we decided to head out.

Doug looked at the clock and said, "Why is everyone leaving so early?"

"I don't know," I said, then looked at the speakers and smiled. "Maybe a landslide brought them down."

Doug laughed and gave me a solid high five.

"Ha fucking ha, guys. Go ahead, make fun of my music," said Pete.

"Oh, relax," I said. "U2 and Fleetwood Mac are solid choices."

"I agree," said Doug. "By the way, Pete, which one do you think about more when you masturbate? Bono or Stevie?"

"You guys are such assholes," Pete said, shaking his head.

"We're outta here," I said. "Do you need a ride, Doug?"

"Nah, Pete and I are gonna play a little Tiger Woods golf

on Playstation."

I left them to their golf and headed out to drive Anna home.

23

"ANNA BEGINS" – Counting Crows

After the party, Anna and I were both wide awake, and I suggested that we hit the courts for a late night shoot-around. I told her in addition to our late night walkabouts, we also loved coming down to the courts for a late night shoot-around. I also told her that even without my friends, I used to love to come down here at night and just shoot and think.

"So you guys would play here all day then sometimes come back late at night?" she asked. "Sounds kinda boring."

"No, not at all," I said, launching a shot. "The cool thing about the four of us was we could do nothing, yet it would still be something fun. Does that make sense?"

"Yea, I think know what you mean," she said, shooting a two handed shot. "I really like your friends. Everyone is so nice."

"They all like you too," I said, chasing down her third air

ball.

I picked up the ball and gazed around at the court.

"There were many times we would hang out here all night long just shooting and talking, especially Scott and I."

"I hear his name a lot. What exactly happened to him?"

Before I had a chance to say a word, there was a loud yelling coming from the park behind us. We both turned to see who or what it was. Off in the distance, underneath the sporadic lamp lights, we saw a person running towards us. I couldn't make out who it was or what he was yelling. It wasn't until he was about thirty feet away that I caught what he was saying.

"Alley-oop! Alley-oop me!"

The next thing I knew, I was throwing up an alley-oop pass to a buck neked Mike Forbes. He missed the shot badly then continued streaking towards the beach. Of course, I don't think Anna noticed him missing the shot, her eyes were drawn somewhere else.

"Ummm, was that—"

"Mike from the party? Yup," I said. "He used to do this all the time back in the day."

"Hmmm, interesting. You and your friends are very, very interesting," she smiled. As Mike's white ass faded into the night, Anna said, "Yet another classic movie scene."

Eventually, we got back to the topic of Scott. I explained to her how he just sort of faded out of our lives with no apparent reason why.

"When is the last time you guys saw him?" she asked.

"I saw him a couple years ago at a grocery store. It was just your run of the mill BS conversation."

"What does that mean?" she asked.

"Hey, how are you doing?"

"We should all hang out sometime."

"Yea, sounds good. Give me a call."

"Blah, blah, blah."

"Ahhh," she said. "Polite party BS" type conversation."

"Exactly," I said. "Anyway, Doug saw Scott last year at his wedding."

"You didn't go?" she asked, shocked.

"No! He blows us off for years and I'm supposed to go to his wedding?"

"Yes. Yes you are. That's what good friends do."

I'm not sure why, maybe it was how she said it, but right then and there I started to get pissed off at her. She had no fucking clue how many times we tried to get Scott to hang out with us.

"Hey! Don't make me out to be the bad guy here!" I snapped. "I tried to stay in touch!"

"Whoa, relax. You don't need to get so upset," she calmly said. "You kind of take things too seriously sometimes, ya know?"

Anna launched another air ball that bounced into the vacant parking lot. I walked, not ran, to go retrieve the ball. With every step I took, flashbacks of emotion flooded my mind.

I thought about the disintegration of Scott's friendship, and the disintegration of most of my summer friendships and relationships.

I thought about the stupid party tonight; how successful and far along with their lives they all were.

I thought about the many summer girls I had shown interest in, only to have them leave and lose touch. There was that Elise girl, who I spent a whole summer chasing. And then there was Jane… we were always so close, yet always ended up so far away. There was most definitely a black fucking cloud following me, and its name was York Beach. Yup, a lot of things flooded my mind (her ball rolled really far).

By the time I returned to the court, I was cocked and fully loaded, and poor Anna was about to be my target.

"I just get sick of this whole place sometimes. That's right, this place that you think is so cool to grow up in. Let me tell you how this place *really* is. Do you get to meet a lot of people here? Yes you do, but they usually leave your life as fast as they came! If you're lucky, it's just a meaningless one night stand or just a trivial couple weeks of fun. But if you're like me, you end up giving a piece of your heart to people, only to have them take it and leave and fade the fuck away! Summer relationships around here always end the same—great time but bad timing. After a while you learn to accept that, but when your real, true friends fade… that fuckin' sucks! Maybe I should be emotionally unattached like Doug—no commitments, no strings, just pure fun."

Anna just stood there looking at me. Then it happened. Her lips slowly started to form a smile. Oh, it got worse. She actually had the nerve to walk over to me and say, "You're too depressing for me." And then she kissed me on my cheek, continued to smile, then walked away towards the playground.

My blood was still boiling from my rant, and I didn't appreciate her making light of my feelings. I'm not proud of what happened next, not by a long shot. For whatever reason, I was so offended and upset, that I made it my personal mission to break her down. There was no way someone could be that positive, and innocent, and sweet. If it's true that misery loves company, I was about to pull her into the dark side. Like I said, I wasn't proud of my twisted actions.

I marched into the playground, faced her on the swings, and then picked up where I left off.

"You come here like most people do, to get away from their

real life, their real problems. Whether it's for two weeks or two months, they get to relax, get a little wild, but in the end, they have their real homes to go back to. Most people only get to see this place as a full, happy beach. They never see it when it's cold, lonely and empty. Just the locals like me do. I don't expect you to understand. You live in a simple, small town where everyone knows everyone and nothing much ever changes. It's so much better that way. You definitely have it made, Anna."

"Don't even go there!" she said, slightly irritated.

It was about a three on the irritation scale. I knew I could do better. I just needed to find the right button to press.

"Seriously, Anna, you have no clue what it's like to deal with this place and its constant revolving door of friendships. Both our towns might be considered small, but I swear I would trade with you any day."

Apparently, I found the button. She went from a three to an eight on the irritation scale.

"That's bullshit!" she said as she stopped swinging. "The dark cloud thing was funny at first, but now it's just pathetic. You have a great life, a cool job, and some super-amazing friends. Have you ever actually taken the time to look around you? Like *really* look around? This place is absolutely gorgeous. Most people would kill to grow up here. I'm not sure if you're desensitized, or jaded, or are just plain spoiled."

I wanted to rebut, but I was kind of speechless. I had never seen her this upset.

"Personally," she continued, "I think everyone should appreciate where they're from, but that being said, don't even compare our towns. My town: population 721... one general store with one gas pump, two churches, and acres and acres of cornfields. If we didn't want to drive the 40 minutes to the movie theater, we would spend our nights getting drunk out on the old railroad tracks. And you're right, I only have a handful of friends, yet here I am, on vacation by myself. I've seen the same exact faces for 23 years... the exact same! Every summer you get the opportunity to meet so many people from so many different places, and I'm supposed to feel sorry for you because you lost contact with some of them? And boo hoo, one of your best friends slowly faded out of the picture. Do you know how I lost my best friend? Huh?"

Again, I was speechless, and I could only manage to shake my head no.

"I lost my best friend when I walked in on her screwing my boyfriend! And have you ever wondered why people like me pay big bucks to come here in the summer?" she said, rhetorically. "Because this place is so fucking beautiful, that's why!!"

That was the first and only time I'd ever heard her say fuck. With that, she jumped off the swing and exited the playground.

"What the hell did I just do?" I mumbled to myself.

If I was in my car right now, I would be beating the bejesus out of my steering wheel and chastising myself. She was right, I was a jaded, spoiled brat. Actually, I was worse than that, I was a jaded, spoiled asshole.

It was at that moment, I realized that in such a fucked up world, it was refreshing to know, that in her smile lay such a hopeful girl. I wasn't about to let my pessimism... or realism affect that.

I ran, not walked out of the playground, and when I finally caught up with her, she was walking on the beach. I had no idea what to say to her—sorry just seemed too cliché and dumb. I needed something that would bring back her sweet and innocent smile. As I stepped in front of her, I ended up taking a page from her book.

I simply smiled, kissed her cheek and said, "You're kinda too depressing for me."

She stopped walking and her eyes slowly made their way up to mine. I figured my copycat-comment could go one of two ways: She'd either crack a smile and accept my apology, or she would knee me in the nuts and walk off. Thankfully, my nuts lived to see another day.

It took 8.3 seconds, but a smile finally broke across her face. I gave her a hug and whispered in her ear, "I'm sorry." Cliché, yes, but still appropriate.

We continued to walk on the beach, but nothing was spoken for a few minutes. She finally broke the silence with an unnecessary apology.

"I'm sorry for making light of your feelings, and I'm sorry for calling you desensitized and jaded. I'm also sorry for saying the F word."

She would have continued apologizing, but I would have none of that.

"You were totally and completely right. About all of it," I said.

Again, nothing was spoken as we headed further up the beach. At that point, she grabbed my hand and said, "Can we go home?"

"Yea, sure. I'll take you home."

Her grip tightened as she clarified, "No, I was hoping I could spend the night with you tonight?"

"You want to spend the night with me? At my place? As in, *spend* the night? With *me*? Like in my *bed*?"

As you can tell, I was a little caught off guard. But the combination of her blushing and her flashing her crooked smile was enough to seal the deal for me.

I did mention her smile was crooked, right? Crookedly

beautiful for sure. And yes, Doug was not wrong when he said her ass was pretty God damn amazing too.

So, without overthinking or overanalyzing the situation, I took Anna back to my place to spend the night... in my bed... together. The overthinking would come later.

I'll leave what happened later that night to your imagination. I will say this: It wasn't as wild or loud as Doug's hotel-sex story, and as far as I recall, there was no jackhammering going on either. It wasn't one-night-stand-sex, but it also wasn't "making love". We had sex. Great fuckin' sex.

24

"LITTLE THINGS" – Matthew Ryan

Anna left my apartment bright and early the next morning. It wasn't because she couldn't wait to get out of there, not at all. I already told you—great fuckin' sex. The real reason she rushed out so early was to meet Adam, Mike, and Doug for her surfing lessons.

I stayed in bed a little while longer, but decided I should get up and head down to the beach. I figured Anna would appreciate it if I used her camera to capture her surfing moments on film.

She was in heaven, but not because she was riding killer waves, it was just because she was trying something new. I actually don't think she stood on the board for more than five seconds at a time. Wave after wave, she was knocked on her ass, but wave after wave, she kept pulling herself back up and trying again. No matter how hard she wiped out, the smile never left her face.

Then, after what seemed like forever, she did it. She caught a wave and rode it, kind of. It wasn't picture-perfect, but she actually stood on the board and rode for a solid ten seconds. I dare anyone to find me someone whose smile was bigger or brighter than Anna's was at that moment.

"Did you get that? Did you get that?" she excitedly said to me as they exited the water.

I held up her camera and gave her a big thumbs up. Adam and Mike gave her a high five.

"Not bad, Iowa girl," said Doug, offering her a fist bump.

"Yea, not bad," said Mike. "Despite the six shark sightings."

We all looked over at Doug.

"It never gets old," Doug smiled proudly.

Adam turned to Anna and said, "Now that you've popped your surfing cherry, you should swing by the shop and pick up some authentic surfing gear to commemorate the occasion."

"I would love that! Can we go right now?" she said, looking over at me.

I gave her a smile then looked over at Adam.

"Meet you back at your shop?" I said.

Mike ended up joining us, but Doug said he had some stuff to care of back at Hoohahs. Over the next hour or so, Anna must have thanked Adam a dozen times for taking her surfing.

While we were at Adam's shop, Anna bought a couple of classic Billabong shirts, some more postcards, and Adam sold her a surfing compilation DVD.

Between our late night (of having great sex) and waking up super early, we were both tired. And considering that Anna spent most of the morning getting rocked by waves, I think she was even more exhausted than me.

Not a lot was spoken on our ride back to York from

Oqunquit, which was probably a good thing. I had no idea what to say about last night, and more importantly, I had no idea what was going through her head either. I will say this, despite not talking on the ride back, it wasn't an uncomfortable silence.

The funny thing about life… is when you think you have it figured out, it gets complicated… and when you think it's complicated, it gets… well, more complicated. I was about to find that out.

I was truly having a great time with Anna this past week, and for the first time maybe ever, I wasn't thinking ahead. I was just enjoying the moment.

Was there a part of me that missed Jane? Sure, but I knew she was where she needed to be, and after our face to face last week, I felt a sense of closure. Even more impressive, I was finally seeing the Felicia thing for what it really was. It was just a little two week whirlwind romance that lacked serious substance. I think I clung onto Felicia because she was the first person I had strong feelings for after the Jane debacle.

Equally impressive, it had been days since I specifically checked my messages for Felicia's call. There's a big difference, however, telling yourself you're over someone and seeing them face to face again. When I saw Jane face to face, the old feelings came flooding back, but like I said, I knew she was where she needed to be, so that made it much easier to handle.

My next face to face with Felicia would be a bit more challenging. Like I said earlier, when you think life is complicated, it has a tendency to get more complicated.

When Anna and I returned to my apartment, I saw a familiar car parked in my driveway. Before I had a chance to process it, there she was—Felicia. She was sitting on my steps, waiting.

My heart lept... or did it sink? I honestly can't remember what my heart fucking did! All I know is it was one awkward situation. Although, it quickly became apparent that it was only awkward for me. Before words could form or fall out of my mouth, the girls had introduced themselves to each other and shook hands.

When I told Doug about this awkward situation later, the idiot asked me if a threesome had crossed my mind. Seriously, this is what I deal with when I tell Doug anything. The answer, by the way, was absolutely, positively NO! The thought of a threesome didn't enter my mind for a second. Well, not until Doug brought it up. But even then, it was a fleeting thought at best.

Anyway, back to my awkward situation. After the girls introduced themselves, Felicia asked if I wanted to hang out on the beach for a little bit. To make matters twice as worse, she even invited Anna to join us. Anna politely declined. Apparently, she already had plans with Taylor (more on that later).

After Anna left, Felicia and I grabbed a couple of chairs and headed down to the beach.

"I stopped by the bar to see if you were there, but Doug said you'd probably be at home," she said. "He still hates me, huh?"

"He doesn't hate you, he just—"

"Doesn't like me very much."

"Something like that," I smiled.

"I suppose I deserve it. I've been kind of shitty to you the past few months."

It was at that point, I knew the conversation was taking a turn and going down a strange road. A strange road that would force me to test my resolve. Telling yourself you're over someone and doing it while sitting face to face with them are two completely different beasts.

"So who was that Anna girl? Are you guys—"

"No. No at all. We're just friends," I pointed out.

I guess it was just a natural reflex, but I found myself almost downplaying my friendship with Anna. I'm not really sure why I needed to show Felicia that Anna and I were just friends, especially considering I still had no desire of getting back together with her. Honestly, I didn't.

The longer we chatted on the beach that day, the more she hinted at us getting back together. Ironically though, the more she talked and hinted, the more I realized she wasn't "the one". Doug was right, over the past few months, I had created an image of how I *wanted* our relationship to be, not how it *really* was.

Those great conversations and amazing moments we once shared, not only seemed like a lifetime ago, but they also seemed like just that... moments. There was really no substance to our little two week romance, or to our friendship for that matter. It really was all in my head.

I'm sure we all have ideas what the perfect relationship would be like; from the type of conversations you would have, to the type of dates you would go on, and even the different places you would go on vacation with them. I think it's a good thing to know the type of relationship you want as long as you realize you can't just plug anyone into that scenario. I guess love is like a puzzle, and no matter how badly you want to shove two pieces together, they have to fit... perfectly.

As we sat on the beach that day, Felicia did most of the talking. She talked a lot about the classes she was taking and her new job and new apartment. I was happy that her future was starting to take shape and that she was so focused, but that's where it ended. I had no desire to be part of that future. Still though, Felicia was pulling out all the tricks. She began reminiscing about our "time together".

Things like: *"Remember when we went to..."* or *"Remember when we did..."*

The way she talked, you would think we dated for months. This must totally be what I *sounded like to Doug this past year. At one point, she even said, "That was one of the best nights of my life."*

There was a part of me that was touched, flattered even. But there was also a part of me that began to laugh internally. Best night of her life? Come on now! It was a fun night and all, but it was obvious she was exaggerating for effect. I should know, I do it all the time.

Not only did Felicia continue to reminisce about our time together (our little two week time together), but she was making it even more blatant that she wanted to get back together. I remained quiet and just listened. I think she sensed my apprehension because at one point, she slowly removed her shirt, revealing her tight white bikini top. She arched back in her chair putting her girls on full display. Yup, this chick was playing hardball.

You are probably wondering, why would I spend the last six months trying to win her back only to waiver when I actually succeeded? I know I told you that I was a very competitive person, but this was not a case of *wanting what I can't have and then not wanting it once I got it.* I suppose there have been times in my life that I've done that, but this wasn't one of them.

As Felicia continued to talk, I started to zone out, realizing just how much I had overblown what we had together. Maybe it was as simple as being attracted to the newness of it all. The fact that we had so much in common musically, mixed with the fact that Felicia was my first sex after the Jane breakup, absolutely contributed to me twisting our relationship into something it wasn't.

And yes, Doug informed me of all of this months ago, but what can I say, sometimes you have to find out for yourself… the hard way… the six-month-hard way.

What finally snapped me out of my zone was when Felicia cut right to the chase and said, "You've always been there for me even when I didn't deserve it. I guess I just didn't know what I wanted… but I think I do now."

At that point, she reached over and put her hand on mine. For six LONG months, this is what I wanted to hear—exactly what I wanted to hear. I'm not going to lie, I started to waiver. What if this was the fresh start we needed? Maybe those relationship scenarios would come true after all. And yes, my mind also thought about having sex with her again. My resolve was shrinking. Other parts of me were growing, but my resolve was definitely shrinking.

In the movie *L.A. Story*, Steve Martin said, "We don't always recognize the moment when love begins, but we always know when it ends."

Now, I'm not saying I loved Felicia, because I didn't. Even my twisted mind knew it wasn't love, but the sentiment of that quote was about to ring true. I was about to have full closure in the Felicia chapter of my life.

"Look at that bum scrounging through the garbage over there," Felicia said, pointing over to old man Ugo.

"He's not a bum," I laughed.

"Well he looks like one, and look, he's got two little rugrats helping him."

I gave Ugo a wave, and before I could explain to Felicia who he was, his great grandkids rushed over towards us. Their little bodies were covered in sand as they stood directly in front of us with their hands behind their backs. Their smiles weren't directed at me, but at Felicia. They were wide-eyed and smiling ear to ear at her. It reminded me of how I once used to look at her.

The little boy moved his hand from behind his back. In his dirty, sand-covered hand, he offered Felicia a seashell. She hesitantly took it, and the kids giggled then scampered off. When they were out of sight, she tossed it on the ground and wiped her hands on her towel.

Felicia wasn't a bad person. She certainly wasn't a "fuckin' bitch" as Doug so eloquently put it, but she did have certain insensitivity issues that sort of come across as bitch-like. I immediately flashed back to Anna's reaction to the same situation. I remembered how touched and appreciative she was.

That was who I wanted to be with. Not Anna per say, but someone with those same sweet characteristics. We sometimes find closure in the strangest places. On that day, I found mine in a seashell.

So, as I walked off the beach, I felt pretty damn good, empowered even. This girl… woman, had just said everything I wanted her to say for six months, yet I stood my emotional ground. It wasn't that I thought she was being insincere, not at all actually. I truly think she meant what she was saying, but for whatever reason, her words just weren't resonating with me. In my heart, I knew she was not the type of person I wanted to be in a relationship with.

My friends and I joke all the time about women having superpowers over us. Whether it's their smiles, or cleavage, or ass, or simply their womanly womaness, they always seem to have these superpowers over us. But not on that day, my friends! For on that day, I found myself blocking and deflecting each and every one of her powers. On that day, my friends, I was not unlike a God damn superhero!

It didn't matter that Felicia had just said everything I had ever wanted her to say. It didn't matter that she was in a bikini top with her 34D's bulging out. It didn't matter that she was emitting the intoxicating smell of suntan lotion. And it sure as hell didn't matter that her nipples stood at attention, just waiting to seduce me. None of it mattered.

So, as I walked off the beach that day, I stood tall, chest out and head held high. It was a victory for all of mankind. Surely there would be a statue built for this momentous victory (if not a statue, a sand sculpture at least).

We said our goodbyes, and although she would call me multiple times to hang out over the next few weeks, she eventually caught on that I was indeed over her.

To be fair, if she would have suggested her place to hang out that day rather than the beach, I more than likely wouldn't have survived the temptations of close quarters. There would have been no victory, no statue, and certainly no closure.

Also, if I'm being honest, Anna had a lot to do with my realization. Her positive outlook and her sweet innocent nature made me realize the type of girl I wanted to be with, and even though she was leaving soon, I knew my future love interest needed to have way more Anna qualities than Felicia qualities.

Yup, Anna definitely had a hand in my victory that day, but make no doubt about it, I was still superhero-esque!

25

"FADE INTO YOU" – Mazzy Star

As soon as Felicia drove off, I got in my car and drove down to Hoohahs for a celebratory drink. It was a good thing I did, a big beer delivery just came and Doug was there by himself.

"Where are the tie dye twins?" I asked.

"One of the granola girls should be here any minute, and the other will join her and Taylor later on. I've got a hot date tonight."

"Really? With who?"

"Are you testing me to see if I actually remembered her name?"

"Um, no. I was just asking who she was."

"A cute redhead I met at the gym," he said.

"Ahhh, well that's cool. What's her name?"

Doug pondered a second then gave me a quick glare before uttering, "Shut up."

"You should really make name tags for them when you meet," I laughed.

Doug looked at me suspiciously then said, "Why are you in such a good mood?" Then it hit him. "Oh no. You saw Felicia this morning, didn't you? I can't believe she came here looking for you. Doesn't she know that I fuckin' hate her?"

"Oh, she knows," I said.

Even though Hillary was working with Doug, I decided to hang out for the afternoon and help him out. Really, I just wanted to stick around so I could fill him in on the Felicia situation. I told him word for word about our beach conversation.

I told him how she basically put it out there that she wanted me back, and I told him how I stood my ground. He wasn't as impressed as I thought he'd be, and he certainly didn't seem very appreciative of my superhero moment.

The only thing he said was, "I told you ALL of this six months ago."

Not surprisingly, what actually impressed Doug, and what he showed the most appreciation for was when I told him about Anna and I having sex.

After two high fives and three fist bumps, Doug said, "See, I told you, getting laid again would solve everything."

"What are you talking about?" I asked.

"I'll tell you what I'm talking about. While you've been a sad fuck for the last six months, I kept telling you the best way to get over Felicia, or any girl, is to get laid again! Never underestimate the power of a good fuck… or a bad one for that matter."

"Oh god," I said. "You're ridiculous."

"Am I? Or am I a genius? Because it seems to me that less than twelve hours after having sex with Anna, you anoint yourself superhero status for turning down Felicia's advances. Coincidence? I think not! The true superhero here is the masked man known as Captain Sex!"

In my heart, I knew my desire to not want to be with Felicia had nothing to do with Anna and I having sex. Zero, zip, nada. I will admit, hanging out with Anna this past week did make me realize that Felicia wasn't the type of girl I wanted or needed to be with. I guess I always knew that, but hanging out with Anna helped bring it to light even more.

Convincing Doug of this would be an impossible task. So impossible, in fact, I didn't even try. With Doug, you needed to choose your battles wisely, so I simply said nothing and went back to work. Around four o'clock, I wished him good luck on his date and then I headed home.

The once blue sky, now had a few dark gray rain clouds moving over the beach. Just as I made it back to my apartment, a warm summer rain began to fall. Once inside, I kicked off my shoes and moved straight for the couch. This was my first opportunity to sit by myself and examine my thoughts from the last twenty-four hours.

Overall, I was pretty damn content. I refused to overanalyze my night with Anna, but I couldn't help but wonder what she thought about all of this. We hadn't yet spoken a word about the previous night, and I wasn't sure if I should even bring it up.

It wasn't some cheap, meaningless one night stand, but we also knew she was leaving in a few days. I mean, two people can have sex once without it being meaningless, right? And it can still be special enough without it being *too* meaningful, right?

As I lounged on my couch, I decided not to say a word to her about last night. I would leave it up to her if she wanted to bring it up. Like I said, I was feeling pretty damn content.

From day one, I knew we only had two weeks, and from day one, I knew a future relationship with her was out of the question. It sucked that our time was almost up, but this time (unlike most times) I really, really had mentally prepared for it.

Before I knew it, I had dozed off on the couch. When I awoke, it was to a rapid knocking on my door. I got up and opened the door and found Anna standing there widely smiling in the rain.

"Come on in before you get soaked," I said, waving her in.

She declined my invitation, and instead, she offered out her hand and said, "Let's go down to the beach!"

"Say what? You do realize it's raining out?"

"There's got to be nothing better than running and dancing on a beach in a warm summers' rain."

"Sure there is. It's called lounging on a comfy couch in a warm, dry apartment."

"You're really not gonna go to the beach with me?" she said, almost pouting.

"I really am not, Anna," I replied.

"Fine, be a fuddy duddy. I'll go without you," she sneered, then bounded off towards the beach.

First of all, I couldn't believe I'd been called a fuddy duddy not once, but twice this summer! What in the crap is up with that?

Second of all, for a brief moment, I was tempted to join her, but then I saw how hard it was raining and how wet it looked. The brief moment passed, and I made my way back to my couch, but not before getting a pair of sweatpants, a tee shirt, and a towel and placing them on the table. I might have been a boring fuddy duddy, but I was a considerate one.

A solid fifteen minutes went by before my front door swung

open and a shivering, soaking wet Iowa girl appeared. I smiled and shook my head then pointed at the towel and clothes. She returned my smile and revealed her backpack in her left hand.

"I came prepared," she said. "But thanks anyway."

She changed in the bathroom then joined me on the couch.

"I really can't believe you didn't join me."

"Was that on your bucket list? Dancing on a beach in the rain?"

"No, but it should have been. It was so fun!"

"I'll take your word for it."

After she was settled in on the couch, she asked, "How was your day? How'd it go with Felicia? She seemed nice."

Rather than go into detail like I did with Doug, I chose to simply play it off.

"It was okay. We were only at the beach for an hour or so. I ended up working with Doug most of the day."

"I heard he's got a hot date tonight," she said.

"That's what I hear," I said. "I'm sure we'll hear all about it tomorrow."

Anna laughed and said, "Yea, Doug is pretty open about offering up details."

"Ya think?" I laughed. "So, what's on the agenda for us tonight? Preferably something that doesn't revolve around getting wet in the rain."

"Pfft, you really don't know what you're missing. I can't believe you've never danced around in the rain."

"Oh, I have. When I was like five."

Anna whipped a couch cushion at me then said, "We should order pizza and have a movie night."

"Really? You only have a few days left. What happened to doing and seeing as many things as possible? Things you can't do in Iowa?"

"I am. I'm eating pizza and watching a movie with you. I can't do that in Iowa, now can I?"

"I suppose not," I said. "What do you wanna watch?"

She thought for a second then she focused her eyes on the back wall. I looked over and saw it was my *Field of Dreams* poster.

"Yes!" I exclaimed.

I'm not sure what triggered it, but while we were waiting for the pizza to arrive, my thoughts turned to something Anna said at the courts the previous night; about how her boyfriend cheated on her with her best friend. The last twenty-four hours had been such a whirlwind, so I didn't have a chance to comment on it yet.

"Hey, I'm sorry about your best friend and your boyfriend. That must have been really hard on you."

She nodded then said, "Thanks. It was very hard. More so losing my best friend. We were friends since kindergarten."

I couldn't image if Doug or Pete ever cheated with one of my girlfriends. Hell, I would be furious if they were with a girl that I *liked,* never mind was dating.

"Never in a million years would I have expected her to do that to me," she said. "Neil, on the other hand... let's just say it wasn't the first... or second time he had cheated on me."

She must have sensed the words forming on my lips because she sighed and said, "I have no idea why I put up with it all those years. Like I said, I come from a very small town, so my boyfriend options were somewhat limited. I guess back then, I was more scared of being alone than being treated like crap. And I know this is going to sound like a stupid justification, but despite him cheating on me or treating me like crap, we really did have some nice moments together."

I was about to scoff at this, or at the very least, roll my eyes at her, but… but I would have been a big, fat hypocrite. I've been just as guilty for thinking a few *nice* moments can outweigh the dozens of shitty ones.

"And every time I was on the verge of breaking up with him for good, like for good for good…"

I knew exactly what she was about to say.

"… he'd always find a way to convince me that he was going to change and be a better person and a better boyfriend, and I was the idiot who believed it. I know, I know, you're thinking that I'm just some typical poor white trash from corn country. Someone you'd expect to see on Jerry Springer."

The Springer comment made me laugh, but the other stuff struck a chord.

"I don't think that at all," I said. "I see a sweet, innocent girl who fell into a trap that we all have fallen into. We sometimes wish and believe so hard in what we *want* to be true, that we sometimes don't know the difference when it's not."

Without making too much eye contact, Anna offered up a smile that told me she appreciated my understanding.

The gravity of the conversation immediately lightened when the pizza man came a knocking. Pizza, Mountain Dew, and watching *Field of Dreams* with a cool chick—not a bad way to spend a rainy summer night, or any night for that matter.

Just to prove that there was indeed a black cloud following me, our movie night was eventually interrupted by a phone call. It was Taylor asking for my help. Apparently, Steph called out sick, and Hillary came in for a little bit before claiming to also not feel well.

This little tie-dyed-conspiracy left Taylor all by herself at the bar, and with no way of getting a hold of Doug, she called me. As relaxed and comfortable as I was there with Anna, I knew I couldn't let Taylor down.

Anna said she would come down to the bar with me, but I told her to stay and relax. I was hoping I wouldn't be too long. It was Wednesday, and a few of the other local bars were doing Ladies Night, so I was hoping we would be slow enough so I didn't have to be there all night. I did make Anna promise not to watch the rest of the movie until I got back. I paused it at the part just before Shoeless Joe Jackson made his appearance on the field.

Unfortunately for me, Hoohahs was busy enough where I couldn't really bail early on Taylor. I didn't get back to my apartment until just after midnight. I was certain Anna would have long since gone home, so I was surprised to see her car still there. I was even more surprised when I entered my newly cleaned apartment. It wasn't a disaster when I left, but there were quite a few dishes in the sink and random clothes and shit strewn about.

While I was gone, Anna washed and dried the dishes, picked up my clothes, and it looked like she vacuumed too. I didn't even remember owning a vacuum.

The lights were off with three candles burning, and Anna was sound asleep on the couch with Mazzy Star's – "Fade into You" playing in the background. It reminded me of when Jane used to live with me for that short period of time. I would sometimes come home and find her the same way; sound asleep with candles burning and music on. It was a great picture to come home to.

Anna looked so comfortable and peaceful. I didn't want to disturb her, so I grabbed a blanket and covered her up. I left the music playing, but I blew out the candles and quietly went to my bedroom and crashed.

26

"FARE THEE WELL" – Indigo Girls

It was mid-afternoon when I entered Hoohahs. Dawn was behind the bar waiting on a customer, and Taylor was at the other end of the bar talking to Anna. As I moved closer, they both looked up with smiles on their faces.

"Uh oh. What are you two conspiring about?"

They continued to smile as they shrugged.

"You better be talking about Doug and not me."

Again, they shrugged.

"Speaking of which, where is Doug?"

"Pete and Michelle had some house stuff to take care of, so Doug is babysitting Kayla," said Taylor.

"Did Pete's parents die?" I asked dumbfounded."

"Nope. Doug actually volunteered."

Just then, Dawn called over, "Hey, Taylor, delivery for you."

We all looked over and saw a delivery girl standing there holding a dozen red roses. Taylor walked over and took the flowers then proceeded to casually toss them onto the counter.

"Those aren't from that douchebag are they?" I asked.

Taylor nodded and Anna said, "I thought you dumped him?"

"Oh I did, but he's been calling me nonstop."

"A dozen red roses? The jerk must really like you, huh?" I said.

"Pfft, the jerk is trying to make up for his major fuck up," Taylor said. "I was just looking for the whole friends with benefits type thing, but he started getting too clingy and shit."

"I hate that," said Anna.

"Being clingy is bad enough," said Taylor, "but I draw the line being called the wrong name during sex."

"He did that?" I asked.

"Not once but three times!" exclaimed Taylor as she picked the bouquet back up. "The idiot can't even get original with the flowers either. An apology with red roses? Could he be more cliché?"

With that, she tossed them in the garbage and began waiting on the next customer.

I turned to Anna and whispered, "Maybe Doug is right about red roses being the triple kiss of death."

"I didn't even get that when Neil cheated on me." Anna pondered then said, "Actually, I've never gotten flowers sent to me."

"Really? Never?"

"Nope. But if I did, I certainly wouldn't want roses."

Anna went on to tell me all of her favorite flowers, including her most favorite – the stargazer.

After her flower talk, I went behind the bar and grabbed

myself a beer.

"We still on for dinner tonight?" I asked.

"We are," she said. "But on one condition."

"Oh yea, what's that?"

"I pick the place, and it's my treat! Unnegotiable!"

I looked at her long and hard and finally said, "You drive a hard bargain, but it's a deal."

***

Anna chose the York Harbor Inn for our final dinner in town. We spent a good portion of dinner reminiscing about the last two weeks. The more we talked about it, the more I realized just how much we had done and seen in such a short period of time. It definitely felt like I had known her for more than just two weeks.

After dinner, we took our final stroll up to the Cliff Walk, and as expected, Anna took dozens of pictures. Later on that night, once it got dark, Anna convinced me to take her up to the lighthouse. Without question, I had been up to the Nubble more times the past couple of weeks than the last two years combined. Every time we went, Anna made it abundantly clear just how much she loved it there.

Whenever we would go there, I was content either sitting in the car or sitting on one of the benches overlooking the lighthouse. Not Anna. She could never sit still. She would bounce around from rock to rock to rock, with her smile never leaving her face the whole time. Sometimes I felt like a parent watching their child bounce about.

"Careful... the rocks are slippery down there... careful... oh, careful," I said, cringing.

When her pace finally slowed, she gravitated to a large rock, which was just out of reach from the spray of the crashing waves.

"This is my new favorite place to stand," she smiled.

"You have favorite places to stand?"

"Don't be silly, of course I do. There's this old, rundown barn at the end of my road, and it has a little ledge out the top window. You can see for miles there. It's a great standing place. Also, when I was little, there was this big branch that held my tire swing. I remember climbing up and standing on the branch and feeling like I was on top of the world. In retrospect, I was probably only fifteen feet off the ground."

Anna gazed out at the ocean, then to the lighthouse, and then back to the rock. She nodded at me and said, "Yup, definitely my new favorite standing place."

Satisfied with her proclamation, she continued to smile and watch the waves crash below her.

"Don't you ever get tired of watching the ocean?" I asked.

"Heck no!" she said as if that was crazy talk. "Whether it's calm or harsh, or blue, green, or black, it's always so beautiful. And then the salt air hits your nose and you can't help but feel alive."

She always seemed to get excited over the littlest and simplest of things.

It was as if she read my thoughts because the next words out of her mouth were, "Personally, I think it's the little things that matter most in the end. Am I right or am I right?"

I was happily mesmerized as her crooked smile made another appearance.

She noticed me staring at her and said, "What? What are you staring at?"

"Just staring at that smile of yours," I said.

Anna rolled her green eyes at me then made her way over

and sat on the bench. I followed and sat next to her.

"So," Anna began, "I've been doing some thinking about your black cloud issues."

"Oh God. I thought we covered this?" I said.

"Just hear me out. I really think you need get rid of the timetable you created for yourself. Having goals and aspirations are one thing, but creating a detailed timetable is borderline insane."

"It wasn't that detailed," I mumbled.

"Uh huh," she said. "From the outside looking in, I think you're doing pretty okay with your life."

"Ha. Thanks, Anna."

"I've also been doing some thinking about your revolving doors."

"My what?" I asked.

"You know, all the people who come in and out of your life here at the beach."

"Oh, those revolving doors."

"Just because people leave or fade away from your life, it doesn't mean they were never meant to enter it. Do you wanna hear my theory?" she asked.

"A theory?" I laughed. "You've been hanging around Doug too much."

"Do you wanna hear my theory or what?"

"And just like with Doug, I don't have a choice, do I?"

"Nope," she smiled then began her theory. "I think every person that enters your life brings new experiences, and even if they're only there for a short time they leave memories behind."

"Ummm, that's your theory?"

"No, I'm not done. I just think the more memories you have, the happier you'll be as you grow older. I've always looked at it like this: every time there's a good memory, it creates a new star in my sky, and one day, when I'm old and gray, I want to be able to look up and see my sky full of stars... and not just a dark, blank sky." She gave an innocent shrug then said, "Anyway, that's my theory."

Once again, I was struck by the innocence and beauty she possessed, and once again, I found myself just staring at her.

"What? You think I'm full of crap, don't you?" she said.

"Not at all. I'm just amazed at how you make the simplest things seem so... so meaningful. Personally, I don't know how the fuck you do it."

She pondered for a moment, as if actually thinking how she did it. She shrugged her shoulders, and as her smile grew ever-wide, she looked up at me.

"It's probably just the way I smile," she said, then stood up and made her way to my car.

I was in no position to argue with that, nor did I want to. I joined her in my car and drove her home.

What happened next was a microcosm of what always seems to happen to me. I go from having an amazing moment to watching it all fall apart and go to shit just like that.

The ironic thing is, Anna was about to say what I wanted every "summer relationship" to say. Yet... it still went to shit.

"Can I ask you a question," she said as we pulled into her driveway.

"Sure."

"Do you regret us sleeping together?"

"What?" I said, slightly taken off guard. "Not at all."

"I just know how you feel about getting involved in the summer-girl thing."

"It's just..." I tried to mentally organize my thoughts. "It's just that I didn't want to complicate things… for either one of us. Especially with you leaving soon."

This is where I was really thrown for loop.

"But what if I didn't have to leave?"

"What?"

"What if I go home and maybe decide to move here? I've been talking it over with Taylor, and she said her roommate just moved out and she offered me to—"

"Whoa, whoa, whoa," I interrupted. My head was spinning. "What about your new job?"

"I can get a nursing job anywhere," she said. "And Taylor said there are tons of hospitals in the area."

"Is this because of the other night? Us having sex?"

"No. It's just that ever since I've been here, I've fallen in love with this place. It's like, I have this weird connection to this place… and to you."

As her words hung in the air, it was as if I hit the pause button and time stood still, allowing me to analyze this whole crazy conversation. I'm a lot of things: impulsive, impatient, an over-thinker, etc, etc. but right then and there, I became perfectly clear-headed. A voice of reason, if you will.

"Anna, I think you've fallen in love with the *thought* of this place. It's not the same thing. It's not real. It's just an escape. No one should make a life changing decision while on vacation. I really feel you should think this through more."

I can't believe those words fell out of my mouth. I absolutely wanted Anna to stay. Absolutely. The hell with Taylor's place, Anna could stay with me! It would be amazing… but eventually reality would hit.

"I have thought it through," she snapped. "It's all I've been thinking about! Don't you want me to stay?"

Of course I want you to stay! I fucking love being with you!

That's what my heart wanted to say, but I didn't. I was honestly trying to do what was best for Anna. I honestly was. She didn't see it that way.

"Is this because of Felicia?" she quietly asked.

I gave her a curious look.

"I'm sure you still have some sort of feelings for her, but you did tell me that you had no desire to ever get back together with her, right?"

Anna was correct. I positively had no desire to get back together or even hang out with Felicia again. Just then, I had a split-screen flashback of Anna and Felicia's opposite reactions to receiving the shells from the little kids. Yup, I had zero desire to get back with Felicia. Ever.

Unfortunately, my flashback caused me to pause, and Anna saw my pause as something different. She became expressionless. It was like the hope was sucked out of her.

She hung her head in embarrassment and softly said, "Oh, I get it."

She then had her own pause, which I should have used to correct her false assumptions of me and Felicia. But I didn't. The King of Babble was 100% speechless.

"I feel so stupid now," she said, opening the car door. "I'm sorry. Forget everything I just said."

She got out of my car and hastily headed towards her cottage.

"Anna, wait," I shouted through the open window. "Let me explain."

"You don't owe me an explanation, really. I'll see you later."

I watched as she opened then closed her cottage door. I sat there, still, with a million thoughts running through my head. I knew I needed to clarify my feelings and my reasoning to Anna, but I also knew that now wasn't the right time. I didn't want this to turn into a Josh babbling session, so I decided to head home and sort through my emotions and come up with the perfect words to explain to her where I was coming from.

27

"WAVE OF MUTILATION" – The Pixies

Ok, so I didn't actually go straight home that night, but I did attempt to sort through my emotions. I just decided to do it with the help of my two best friends. I went by the bar and told Doug I had a code red and needed a walkabout. We then swung by Pete's and dragged him away from watching *Sportscenter*.

Doug raided Pete's fridge and snatched a six pack for the walk. We loaded one in each of our shorts' pockets then headed out. My mind was still running a mile a minute, but I gave them the gist of what happened earlier.

"So, you don't want to get back with Felicia, right?" asked Pete.

"No. Not at all!" I said, convincingly.

"Why did you let Anna think that you did?" asked Pete.

"I don't know. When Anna asked if I wanted to get back

with Felicia, I just kinda froze. And when I paused for just a second, she must have assumed my pause meant I wanted to be with Felicia, and... I didn't get a chance to tell her the truth."

"Which is?" asked Doug.

"Which is, I would love for Anna to stay here, of course I would, but I don't think she thought it through enough. She's on vacation for Christ sake! The first real vacation that she's ever taken, I might add. Of course this place is new and exciting, especially when you've never been outside of corn country. It's like I told Anna, no one should make a life changing decision while on vacation. Remember all those spring breaks we spent in Florida? The perfect weather, the warm ocean water, the hot girls, the wild club scene... it was like heaven."

Pete and Doug both smiled and nodded.

"But you lived there for the last four years, Pete. Right in that same area. Is it still like heaven?"

Pete slowly shook his head no and said, "We actually couldn't wait to get out of there."

"Exactly my point. Vacationing somewhere and living there are two different things. The decision should come from her head not her heart. What happens when the excitement wears off? Anna told me that she's very close with her mom. What happens if she gets homesick? What if she doesn't land a nursing job right away? And what if she regrets not taking the Iowa job? Being a nurse is her passion. I'd hate to see her have to take some stupid waitressing job while she waited for something to open up. This is just like the Jane thing all over again."

There was no way I could stand having another girl turn down a big job opportunity just to live in this stupid little town with me. And I certainly couldn't stand her eventually regretting her decision and holding it against me.

Doug cracked open his second beer and said, "She's not Jane. All of that stuff you just mentioned might not happen."

"But it might," I said. "I know you guys are gonna give me shit for this, but I can't bear letting her become a huge part of my life only for her to get bored of this place… or of me. I just can't take another person fading out of my life."

I braced myself for what was sure to be the *make fun of Josh* section of the walkabout. To my surprise, it never came.

Pete spoke first. "We get it, bro. We really do. If some chick I just met wanted to drop her whole life and move 1500 miles to be with me, I would probably be nervous just like you. I also agree with you that she should probably go back to Iowa to think about this. It's definitely not a decision to make in the midst of a vacation."

"That being said," interrupted Doug, "you should have told Iowa girl what you just told us. You shouldn't have hinted you didn't want her here because you wanted to get back with Felicia."

I opened my second beer and nodded in agreement.

"I know. I plan on explaining everything to her tomorrow. I think as soon as she gets back home and starts her career the way she originally planned to, she'll realize that she was just caught up in the moment."

I knew I was doing the right thing by not encouraging her to drop everything and move here. I knew I was, but sometimes doing the right thing still can leave you as empty as doing the wrong thing.

28

"A FEW HOURS AFTER THIS" – The Cure

Late the next morning, I got in my car and headed towards Anna's cottage. I didn't really have a speech planned. I figured I'd just wing it. Well, maybe I had vague outline of a speech planned (basically just bullet points).

I knew if I told her about what happened with me and Jane that she would totally understand where I was coming from. I was even confident that we could still head into Boston that morning and end her trip on a high note as planned.

On my first drive-by, her rental car wasn't there. I then drove the entire loop of the beach and did drive-by number two. When her car still wasn't there, I assumed she was hitting the beach for the day. It was the perfect beach day; eighty degrees and a bright blue sky. I checked out the two spots where she liked to lay out. One was at Short Sands just to the right of the Fun Floats, and the other was directly behind the bath house at Long Sands.

When those searches came up empty, I did a third and final drive-by of her cottage. This whole drive-by thing probably would have gone on for a while, but when I drove through Short Sands a second time, I noticed Taylor's car in front of Hoohahs. The bar wasn't open yet, but I swung in to see if Taylor knew where Anna might be.

"Hey, what are you doing here so early?" I asked as I entered the bar.

Before Taylor answered me, she gave me this weird sort of stare-down.

"The air-conditioning guy is coming and Doug had plans, so I told him I would unlock the place."

"Gotcha," I said. "What big plans did Doug have?"

"I didn't ask," she said, almost annoyed. She then continued her stare-down at me.

"What?"

"Oh, I think you know what," she huffed.

"Um, no, I don't."

"Nice job running Anna out of town," she said, accusingly.

"What do you mean out of town?"

"She left already. She's going to stay in Boston tonight and do some sightseeing there until her flight tomorrow afternoon."

"You saw her?"

"I met her out for coffee this morning before she left."

"Fuck. She didn't even say goodbye to me."

"Why the hell would she? Especially after what you said to her last night. She's embarrassed. She opened up to you and you go and tell her that you want to get back together with Felicia?"

"I didn't say that!" I said, defensively. "All I did was pause a second. I was just trying to gather my thoughts. She just read it wrong, that's all."

"And you didn't bother to set her straight?"

I was used to getting grilled by Doug or Pete, but by Taylor? This was bullshit! I tried to turn the tables on Taylor.

"And what are you doing telling her she can move in with you? And telling her she could *easily* get a nursing job around here? She has a job already! And a place to live!"

Taylor shook her head in disgust and replied, "You're a real piece of work, aren't you?"

I was too upset and pissed off to respond. I simply turned and left. I couldn't believe she went to Boston without me. I couldn't believe she left town without saying goodbye.

I suppose if this was a romantic comedy I would have hopped into my car and driven to Boston. I would have searched the entire city for her, and just when I was about to give up, our eyes would meet across a crowded Boston Commons. I would give her a long, heartfelt (babbling at times) speech on how I screwed up, and how different she was from most girls, and how I loved her crooked smile and her deep, sea-green eyes.

I would tell her there was nothing in the world I wanted more than for her to move to Maine and be with me. We would then embrace and kiss deeply, all the while everyone in the park would clap for us. Oh, and don't forget the happily ever after ending.

Spoiler alert: None of that would happen. The logistics alone would have made this nearly impossible. Boston is a big city. The chances of randomly running into someone within a day were slim to none.

You also have to remember this was the summer of '99, so

cell phones were few and far between. It's not like I could text Anna to find out where she was. Neither of us had cell phones yet. Actually, I think Pete was the only one who had one at that time.

You also have to remember, social media was still years away, so it wasn't like I could stalk Anna by checking out the location of her latest Facebook post. Nope, none of that Hollywood ending shit would be happening. I was left to my own devices. In other words, left sitting alone under a black fucking cloud in York Beach with yet another person disappearing from my life. Sadly, this one was all my doing.

29

"PERFECT MEMORY (I'LL REMEMBER YOU)" – Remy Zero

Before Anna left town, she did exchange home phone numbers with Taylor, and although I was tempted to call her a couple days later, I didn't.

I missed Anna, of course I did, but I was convinced I did the right thing by deterring her. That being said, I still felt like total shit for how it all went down. I knew I still needed to explain everything to her on why I thought she was rushing into things. I knew if I told her about my Jane debacle, she would be more understanding to my initial reaction.

Up to that point, I was known for overthinking, not having patience, and for always rushing into things, and yet, there I was trying to be the voice of reason. The irony wasn't lost on me.

I really wanted to tell Anna just how much I loved hanging out with her and getting to know her while she was here. I had a list of a bunch of other things I wanted to tell her (yes, an actual list), but I wasn't ready for that phone call yet. I knew she was probably still hurt and embarrassed of how it all went down... and maybe a little upset at me as well.

Besides, if I called her right away, I would have spared my friends and co-workers the experience of me wallowing around like a sad fuck. Pete and Doug were well-versed in my wallowing, but they were also well-worn out with dealing with it. Their support and sympathy only lasted four days. After that, they stopped trying to cheer me up.

There was no more offering to go to a Sox game, or go to the batting cages, or go out drinking for the night. And after day four, there was no more suggesting that we needed a guys' camping trip up Maine. The only thing Doug continuously suggested was for us to hit the local strip joint, *The Tens Club*. I think we both knew that was less about cheering me up and more about him getting lap dances by strippers, who he thought he had an actual chance with.

I eventually apologized to Taylor for snapping at her and being a jerk. I did my best to tell her where I was coming from, and although she understood, she still thought I needed to explain it all to Anna.

Luckily for me, I was able to stay busy following Anna's departure. Hillary and Steph left on their tree-hugging pot-fest, so I ended up working a ton of hours. And to be fair, I wasn't really a wallowing, sad fuck all the time. I was pensive and quieter, and not overly social, but I definitely wasn't grumpy or mean to anyone.

On a positive note, Felicia called me multiple times to go out, and each time I turned her down politely with different excuses. After the third time, I think she got the message that I was finally over her. There would be no fourth call. As a matter of fact, I didn't hear or see her again for almost a year after that. Ironically, the more I thought about it, I shared and felt more things with Anna in our two weeks than I ever did with Felicia. Not even close actually.

At the ten day mark of Anna's departure, I casually asked Taylor if she had talked to her since she returned to Iowa. She said she hadn't. Hmmm, ten days ago they were going to be best-buddy roommates, and yet they haven't talked once since she left. This is exactly what I was talking about! Out of sight, out of mind.

It's so easy to put York Beach in the rear view mirror once you're back in your familiar surroundings, and it was obviously just as easy for Taylor to put Anna in her rear view mirror as well. I was going to point this out to Taylor, but I decided against it.

I imagined Anna was already back in the swing of things; hanging out with her friends, her mom, and she probably already started her new job at the hospital. I hoped she wasn't stupid or desperate enough to get back with her loser ex-boyfriend. I missed her like crazy, but I knew I did the right thing.

I was tempted to call her every day; to apologize, to explain, to just to see how she was doing. Basically, I really just wanted to hear her voice. I wasn't sure what the proper waiting period was for this.

I was never really good at that whole "proper waiting period" to call someone. Scott would say wait three days. Pete would say wait a week before you call a girl. Doug would always say, "If she is really interested then she will call you."

I was usually more on the impatient side. If a girl gave me her number at 11 PM and told me to call her tomorrow, there was a very good chance you would find me dialing her up around 1AM. Technically, 1AM was tomorrow, right? Unfortunately, most girls didn't really care about technically. If you haven't already, check out the movie *Swingers* with Jon Favreau and Vince Vaughn. The *answering machine scene* was me through and through.

The fact that I was going on two weeks without calling Anna was pretty impressive for me. I wasn't feeling very impressed however. I guess part of me was hoping Doug's theory was right; that if she really missed me and wanted to talk to me then she would call. It wasn't looking good though.

It was the end of a slow Wednesday when Doug approached me. I was in the office finishing up some paperwork for him.

"Hey, we're all going out to Bickford's after work. You in?" he asked.

I half shrugged and said, "Thanks, but I think I'm just gonna head home."

"Alright, suit yourself," he said, shutting the door behind him.

Less than ten seconds later, the door reopened.

"You know what, Josh, it's not alright. For years I've watched you wallow over girl after girl, and don't get me started on the last six months of this Felicia bullshit! You mope around while the rest of us tip-toe around your feelings, but not this time. Quit feeling sorry for yourself! I get it, you were probably right, Anna was probably rushing into things, and I'm sure by now she realizes that. So just fucking call her and talk! You know you want to."

I thought this was a good time to throw Doug's advice back at him.

"What ever happened to your theory that if she really

wanted to talk then she would call me?"

"Who the hell actually listens to my theories? Half the time I'm just talking out my ass," he said. "Look, call her or don't call her, I don't really give a flying fuck. What I do know, is I'm not gonna watch you be a sad sack of shit for the rest of the summer."

With that, Doug turned and left, slamming the door behind him. *What the fuck crawled up his ass? Is this because I didn't want to go out to eat tonight? And how dare he call me a sad sack of shit.* I tossed my pen down, leaned back in my chair, and slowly let Doug's speech sink in.

When I finally exited the office, Doug and Taylor were finishing closing up.

"I'm gonna do it! I'm gonna call her!" I said proudly.

"Who? Anna?" asked Taylor.

"About fuckin' time," smiled Doug.

"Can I have her number?" I asked Taylor.

"You're going to call her now?" she asked.

I looked up at the clock and then over to Doug. He thought a second then slowly shook his head no. I was tempted to blurt out that "technically" it was only 12:45 AM in Iowa, but then I remembered how far "technically" usually got me. I relented and informed them I'd wait and call her first thing tomorrow morning.

Doug read my mind and pointed out that 6 AM should NOT "technically" be considered first thing in the morning. Of course, Taylor agreed with him and we settled on 10 AM our time as the proper call time.

I hadn't even made the call yet, but I was already feeling relieved… nervous, but relieved. So much so, that I went out to eat with Doug and Taylor that night. And not only did I pig-out, but I offered to pay for all three of us, and I did it without Taylor accentuating her cleavage. So there! Josh was back!

30

"FLY AWAY" – Poe

I tossed and turned all night trying to come up with the right words to say to Anna. In my heart, I knew even if I came up with the perfect speech, I would probably just stray from it anyway and start babbling. I finally dozed off around four in the morning, but was up and ready to go by eight.

I grabbed a coffee next door and proceeded to watch the clock, and although I had the phone in my hand at 9:59 AM, I didn't actually dial until ten o'clock on the dot.

With each ring, my heart raced. To my disappointment, on the fifth ring the answering machine came on. Even though it was just a recording, my heart beat faster and happier just listening to Anna's voice.

"Hi, we're not here right now so leave your message at the beep."

In the split second I had before the beep, I told myself to

be BRIEF and CONCISE.

"Hi Anna, this is Josh… from the beach… York Beach… in Maine. Feels like forever since we talked… I kinda miss that. Anyway, I hope you're doing okay. If you want, you can give me a call or whatever. My number is 207 555 1342. I should be home most of the day today… but feel free to call me anytime… even if it's super late at night… I'm a night owl. Anyway, I hope to hear from you soon. Bye."

I hung up the phone and proudly leaned back on my couch, feeling like one brief and concise mofo!

Even though I didn't actually talk to her yet, I once again felt a relieved feeling of satisfaction. As you might have guessed, I made sure to stay close by my phone for as long as I could that day. As you might also have guessed, as the day moved on, so did my neuroses.

By 5 PM, I was bouncing off the walls with doubts.

Why hasn't she called me back yet? Did Taylor give me the right number? That was Anna's voice, wasn't it? Wait! Did I leave my number?? If so, maybe I suffered temporary dyslexia and gave her the wrong digits. Maybe she's still not ready to talk to me. Or maybe she doesn't want to talk to me again.

By 9 PM, I had calmed down a bit, and my thoughts became more rational.

She probably started her job already and is working 12 hour shifts. By the time she came home, she was probably too tired to even check the answering machine. I'm sure she'll call me tomorrow. Yea, she'll definitely call tomorrow.

The more I think about it now, it really would have been great to have cell phones back then. I still would have anticipated her call all day, but at least I could have left the house once. This stay-by-the-phone-at-home thing was very exhausting… and non-productive.

By the time I had to go to work the next day, I still hadn't heard from her. My whole shift I kept wondering if she called yet. If there was indeed a message from her when I got home, I planned on calling her back ASAP... no matter what fucking time it was at night.

I didn't get a chance to test that theory out because around eight o'clock I broke down and called her again from the bar. I figured worst case scenario, even if I got the answering machine again, I could leave her the bar's number as well. I figured that would ease my mind a bit.

It was early enough in the night that we weren't that busy yet, so I told Doug I needed to make a call in his office. I didn't tell him to who, but he knew exactly who I was calling.

I picked up the cordless phone and dialed her number, which I had committed to memory the day before. What else was I supposed to do stuck in my house yesterday, huh?

I paced around the office as her phone rang. By the third ring, I prepared myself for another brief and concise message on her machine. On the fourth ring, however, a woman's voice, who I assumed was her mother, answered.

"Hello?" she softly said.

"Hi. Mrs. Jensen?"

"Yes?"

"Hi, this is Josh... Josh Wentworth... from Maine. I met Anna this summer while she was here. I'm not sure if you guys got it or not, but I left a message on your machine yesterday. I left my home number, but I was also gonna give her my work number too... unless she's home right now?"

I didn't give her a chance to respond as I continued my nervous babbling.

"Although, she's probably at work now, huh? How's her new job going anyway? I bet she loves it, and I bet she's great at it too."

I knew I needed to let this poor woman get a word in edge-wise, so I cut to the chase.

"Ummm, is Anna there, by any chance?"

There was a long pause, and for a second, I thought she might have grown tired of my babbling and hung up on me.

"Hello?" I said.

"I'm sorry, Josh… Anna was in a horrible car accident a couple nights ago… she's gone…"

My pacing stopped. My heart stopped. As the words *she's gone* still hung in the air, I fell onto the couch. I had no idea what to do… or what to say. Through the phone, I could hear her crying.

Overwrought with emotion, her voice finally broke, "I'm sorry, Josh… I'm sorry…"

With that, she hung up. I sat there holding the phone in my hand for what seemed like an eternity; emotionless, speechless, numb. At one point, I tried to stand up, but my legs were too shaky to support myself, and I fell back onto the couch.

I felt sick to my stomach and my heart felt as empty as I've ever felt in my life. My body continued to tremble, but for whatever reason, there were no tears forming in my eyes. I don't know how long I remained in the office, but it was long enough for Doug to come looking for me. He knew immediately that something was wrong.

31

"OCEAN VIEW" – The Push Stars

The next couple of weeks blurred together. I walked around in a haze of sadness and alcohol—lots of alcohol. And by walked around, I mean within my apartment. The only time I left was to wander next door into the Oceanside Store for food and more alcohol.

After a week of family and friends "checking in" on me and offering their support and pep-talks, they finally got the hint. They knew I needed some space to try and process everything. But seriously, how the fuck do you process something like this?

It seemed like just yesterday we were watching *Field of Dreams*... we were taking long late night drives... we were watching the sunrise over the Nubble. It also felt like just yesterday I was sitting in my car telling Anna that besides Mr. Murphy, I had never really experienced someone close to me dying.

By week two, I still felt empty, and numb, and as sad as I've ever felt, but thankfully my urge to constantly drink had subsided. Although, you wouldn't know it by looking at my apartment. There were bottles of various alcohol scattered everywhere.

To his credit, Doug made it a point to stop in and check on me at least once a day. At first, he tried to give me his best pep talk, but he eventually gave up on that. By week two, he was popping in with food and would hang around with me for a little bit. Sometimes he wouldn't even say a word to me, he would just sit and listen to whatever sad fucking song was playing on my stereo system.

My drinking pace had slowed, but I still felt empty and numb. I also found myself feeling angry and short-tempered, even when there was no one around but me. The passing days blurred together, and because my shades were permanently pulled, the time of day blurred together as well.

That being said, I had no idea what time it was as I dozed off on the couch. With a pillow over my face, I had The Smiths' *Louder than Bombs* album cranked on. Just as the song "Unloveable" was fading out, there was a knock at my door. As usual, I didn't respond.

A second later, the door creaked open. Considering that Doug rarely knocked, I knew it wasn't him. At that point, I had zero patience for another visitor, especially one who was interrupting The Smiths' classic album. Luckily for them, they weren't interrupting The Cure's *Disintegration* album. There would have been some serious F bombs and bottles thrown.

"Unless you brought some food, I'm not really in the mood for a pep talk!" I said, underneath my pillow.

Just then, I felt something hit my chest. I peered out from the pillow and saw a box of Chicken in a Biskit. I removed the pillow and turned to thank who I assumed was Doug or Pete, but to my surprise, it wasn't them. It was Scott.

"What are you doing here?" I asked, more curious than sarcastic.

"I was just in the neighborhood," he said, more sarcastic than serious.

I watched as he looked around at the disaster that was my apartment. There were old pizza boxes, chip bags, and beer cans strewn about. He cleared some space on the chair and sat down.

"I ran into Doug at the grocery store the other day, and he told me what happened. I'm sorry, Josh. I can't imagine what you're going through."

For whatever reason, the anger and resentment I'd been harboring for Scott seemed to dissipate, but I still had no clue what to say to him. I sat up and ripped open the box of Chicken in a Biskit. I offered Scott some and he continued to speak.

"Doug said she was a pretty great girl. She must have been. Doug rarely approves of any of your girl choices."

A slight smile fell on my face as I nodded in agreement.

Scott looked around the apartment and said, "You shouldn't do this to yourself, man."

"Do what?" I said, knowingly.

"Come on, Josh, I know you too well. You're gonna sit here in the dark, drink cheap beer, and listen to depressing music."

As much as I wanted to, it was hard to argue with him; not with the crushed cans of Natty Light laying all over the floor. And considering the Smiths' ultra-sad song "Asleep" was now playing, I certainly didn't have a leg to stand on.

"You really should get out of the house, bro."

It was right then and there that my resentment and anger

started to bubble up again.

"Whoa, whoa, whoa! Who the hell are you to give advice? I haven't seen you around in years, and now you're gonna tell me how to feel? Save your fucking voice, *bro!*"

"You're right. I've been a lousy friend the last few years, and you can blame me all you want for neglecting our friendship. I take full blame for that, but don't go and shut everyone out and blame yourself for what happened to her. It's not your fault."

Between friends and relatives, I had been hearing the same shit for two weeks. Shit like, *"You can't blame yourself,"* or *"You really need to get out of this apartment and get on with your life."*

The last thing I needed was to hear this same thing from someone who bailed on our friendship years ago. With the pillow over my head, I rolled on my side away from Scott.

He just sat there for a minute or two before finally saying, "Whatever. It was stupid of me to come here anyway."

Somewhere between Scott getting off the chair and him reaching my front door, I removed the pillow from my head. I was tired of hearing everyone's cliché pep talks, and advice, and overall sympathies, but I was even more tired of being tired. I was sick of my darkened apartment, and I was even sick to death of listening to my stupid Depression Sessions.

I don't remember the exact words that came out of my mouth, but I think it was something like, "I thought I was doing the right thing. She wanted to drop everything to move here. I swear I thought I was doing the right thing."

Scott removed his hand from the door knob and came back in and sat down. I wasn't sure how much or what exactly Doug filled him in on, so I spent the next hour going over the events of my two weeks with Anna. In doing so, I also ended up covering what went on with Jane and I in the last couple of years. I even briefly covered the Felicia period of my life. Mostly, though, I focused on Anna.

"I just keep thinking about our last conversation. If only I—"

"Don't go there, Josh. The world is full of *if onlys* and *what ifs*, but nobody ever wins that game. Seriously, man, none of this is your fault."

Deep down, I knew I wasn't the direct cause of what happened. I knew that. But I still couldn't help but wonder what would have happened if I embraced her big idea of moving here. Maybe we would be sitting next to each other on the beach right now. Or maybe we would be driving around listening to music and talking about anything and everything.

Or maybe by now, she would have come to her senses and decided York, Maine wasn't the place for her. Scott was right, nothing good comes from playing the *if only*/*what if* game.

"It's this fucking beach, ya know?" I said. "Hellos always come so easy… and goodbyes too fucking fast."

Scott got up and walked over to the fridge. He grabbed a couple bottles of water and tossed me one.

"Maybe we should just be happy that hellos come at all?" he said.

I opened the water and took a long swig, and for the first time in two weeks, my thoughts focused on something other than Anna. Right at that moment, I felt an overwhelming appreciation of my friends and family who had been there for me. The fact that Scott and I hadn't hung out or spoken in the last few years was insignificant. What counted was him sitting in front of me right then and there. And just like that, my guilt went from Anna to Scott.

"I'm sorry for not going to your wedding," I said.

"Forget about it," he said, sitting back down.

"You're one of my oldest and best friends. I should have gone."

"I didn't provide much of a wedding invitation. I was actually surprised Doug showed up. Although, it was an open bar," he smirked.

"Well there you have it," I laughed.

I think that was the first time I laughed since... since the phone call.

"How are things with you and Lauren? Married life good?"

"Married life is good. A little getting used to, but good. Speaking of married life, I heard that Pete and Michelle are moving back?"

"Yup. And a second kid on the way too."

This game of small talk probably could have gone on for a while, but I decided to cut to the heart of the matter. The elephant in the room, so to speak.

"What happened with you? With all of us? You just... kinda faded away."

Scott paused a moment then softly said, "I know. I'm sorry."

"Did we do something wrong, or—"

"No. It was nothing like that. I guess it just felt like things were changing. With Pete leaving town and getting married, and with me and Lauren starting to get serious... I guess I just wasn't into hanging out at bars anymore."

"Scott, I think our friendship was more than hanging out at bars."

"I know. That's not really what I meant. I was just trying to concentrate on building a future with Lauren. From the moment I met her, I knew she was the one. And no, I'm not saying I chose her over you guys. In the beginning I was just trying to spend as much time as possible getting to know her, and I figured spending a little time apart from you guys would just be a temporary thing."

I sat on the couch and listened as Scott continued his explanation.

"Then, right after Pete's wedding, I lost my job. I've lost jobs before, but for whatever reason, it hit me hard. I think it was because it forced me to think about my future. I knew I wanted to be with Lauren, but I had no fucking idea what I wanted to do with my life. I guess the more I blew you guys off, the easier it was to keep doing it. I know that sounds horrible, and it probably doesn't make any sense."

It actually made perfect sense to me. It reminded me of a lyric from a Cure song called "Fear of Ghosts" – "*The further I get from the things I care about, the less I care about how much further away I get*".

Scott was right, sometimes the more you distance yourself from people, the easier it is to keep them at a distance. He had slowly done it over the past few years just like I was doing it over the past few weeks. It had become easier telling people I was fine and to leave me alone rather than admit that I wasn't.

I didn't want to be in this fucking apartment anymore. I didn't want to be depressed anymore. I truly wanted to dig myself out of this deep, dark hole I had put myself in.

As I sat there reconnecting with one of my oldest and dearest friends, I knew he was there offering me a rope to pull myself out of my hole.

"Why don't you take a shower and throw some shorts and sneakers on," he said.

"What for?"

"Well, a shower because it's obvious you haven't had one in a long, long time… and shorts and sneakers because we have a four o'clock challenge at the courts."

"A challenge?"

"Yea, Doug and Pete threw down a 2 on 2 challenge against us. It's been a few years since I've picked up a ball, so you might have to carry us. And maybe afterwards we can go grab a drink at this bar I've been hearing so much about. What's it called again?"

"Here Hey Hoohahs," I said.

"Ah yes," he said. "What the fuck does that even mean anyway?"

I shrugged and said, "I'm not even sure Doug really knows."

"That might be the weirdest bar name I've ever heard," he laughed.

"Yea, but I have to admit, it's kind of growing on me," I said.

Scott looked at me like I was crazy then pointed to the clock and said, "Chop, chop, dude. It's almost game time."

I smiled, grabbed the rope, and began pulling myself out.

32

"LIKE SHADOWS" – Bill Janovitz

My heart was still heavy, but it felt good to be out and about again, especially with my closest friends. For the record, Doug and Pete gave us a beat down. Neither Scott nor I could ever get into a rhythm, and despite what Doug claimed, it was less about him being an animal on defense and more about us just being rusty.

After the game, Michelle and Kayla made their way over from the playground. It was the first time Scott met Pete's daughter. It was a pretty cool moment for me, so I knew it must have been even better for Pete. Before the girls left, Michelle made it a point to give me a big, supportive hug. It was very much appreciated.

Afterwards, the four of us guys headed over to Hoohahs for a few drinks. It was a little strange being in there, especially after not showing my face in there for weeks. I could tell everyone was unsure what to say to me. Before they walked on egg shells too long, I made sure to let them know I was doing okay.

Taylor was the first to give me a huge embrace. I even got hugs from the tie-dye twins, which left me smelling like patchouli for the rest of the night.

As proud as Pete was showing off his daughter to Scott, I think Doug was just as proud showing off his new bar to him. All and all, it was a great night, and the fact that we topped it off with a mini-walkabout made it the perfect night.

Our walkabout route took us through Short Sands and up through the side streets of the Nubble area. It had been a long time since our last walkabout, so we had a lot of stuff to catch up on... a lot of important stuff.

"So, who's this Shannon girl you were all over tonight?" I asked Doug.

"Just a chick I've kinda been seeing for the last week or so," he said, playing it off with a shrug.

"No shit?" I said. "I've been out of commission for a few weeks and Dougy goes and gets himself a girlfriend."

"She's not my girlfriend," he quickly pointed out.

"They've gone on real dates and everything," joked Pete.

"Wow," I said as I gave Doug a slap on the back. "And she's of age?"

"Twenty-five," boasted Doug. "And yes, I confirmed it this time."

"Owning a bar is the perfect business for you," said Scott. "You get to card your patrons and future hookups all at the same time."

"Looks like our Dougy is all grown up," I laughed.

"You guys are assholes," Doug said.

"No, we're being serious," I said. "Not only is she of age, but she actually seems like she's pretty nice too."

"Pretty nice rack too," added Pete.

"Hey! That's my girlfriend you're talking about," smiled Doug.

"I didn't think you were a big boob kinda guy?" asked Scott.

"Yea, he's a fried egg guy," I clarified.

Pete and Scott looked curiously at each other.

"It's not that I don't like big boobs," said Doug, "I just prefer smaller ones. That being said, Shannon's melons are pretty fun. They're like two firm cantaloupes."

"Well, there ya go," laughed Scott. "You've got a fruit salad to go with your eggs."

"Hey, Scott," I said, "did Doug tell you that he might be semi-gay?"

We proceeded to fill Scott in on Doug's experience with the crossdresser earlier in the summer.

That particular walkabout wasn't the funniest one ever, and it certainly wasn't our longest one either, but for me, it might have been my most favorite. It was definitely my most needed.

33

"TREASURE" – The Cure

A couple of days after our walkabout, I started working back at the bar. It was strange and uneasy at first, but it proved to be just what I needed. I'm not sure you ever really get over a tragedy like that, but there are definitely moments along the way that make it easier to cope and move on. Being back at work with my friends was one of those moments. Another one of those moments happened a few days after I started back.

It was mid-morning, and I was still in bed when the phone rang. My heart went into my throat when I saw the number on the caller ID. It was Anna's house in Iowa. My phone rang four times before I had the nerve to answer it.

"Hello?" I hesitantly said.

"Is this Josh?" a woman's voice asked.

"Um, yes."

"This is Mrs. Jensen. Anna's mother."

There was a brief moment of silence before she continued.

"I just wanted to call and apologize for being so short with you before. I—"

"You really don't need to apologize, Mrs. Jensen."

"No, I do. My mind was so numb… I was still trying to process everything… in some ways I still am."

Again, there was a moment of silence.

"I just wanted to call you and tell you thank you."

"Thank me? For what?"

"Anna never stopped talking about her trip to Maine. She also never stopped showing me picture after beautiful picture of her trip. I can't stop kicking myself for not going on vacation with her. I should have taken time off of my job… hell, I should have quit my stupid job to go with her."

It seemed I wasn't the only one playing the *if only/what if* game. My heart felt for Mrs. Jensen. I knew my pain wasn't even in the same stratosphere as hers. The loss and heartache she must have felt was inconceivable to me.

"It was quite obvious that my daughter had fallen in love with your state, and I think you had a lot to do with that. I know you did, actually. So thank you for showing my baby the time of her life."

As her voice began to break, I quietly said, "I appreciate that, ma'am, but… but it was only two weeks. I only knew her for two weeks."

Mrs. Jensen let out a slight chuckle and said, "You should know better, Josh… to Anna, two weeks was a lifetime. She always lived in the moment."

I sadly smiled, knowing she was 100% correct. Anna absolutely loved and appreciated the little things more than anyone I had ever met.

"Your daughter was amazing," I said, without hesitation.

"Her grandmother used to say that Anna's smile and spirit

could outshine the brightest of stars. She called her an old soul."

My mind immediately went back to that night at the fortune teller. I just remembered how excited she was to get our fortunes told. I felt embarrassed and ashamed at how much of a downer I was that day. My silly problems... my complaints... my pessimism... my stupid fuckin' black cloud analogies. I was a fuckin' idiot.

"Last night, I finally gathered the strength to go into Anna's bedroom for the first time since..." She paused, gathered herself and continued, "On her desk I found an envelope she had addressed to you."

My heart sank and the phone nearly slipped out of my sweaty hand.

"I hope you don't mind, but... I opened it up and read it. I wasn't being nosey, I swear. I was just trying to feel close to her again."

My heart was now racing with curiosity.

"What did it say?" I asked.

"I mailed it to you this morning," she said. "Just know this, Josh, the letter confirmed just how much Anna loved her trip out there. Thank you for being a large part of it."

When the phone call ended, I sat there emotionless. Actually, it was more like the opposite. I was full of emotions. It wasn't like the last time I got off the phone with Mrs. Jensen. Even though I was still certainly saddened, I also felt a small sense of happiness, appreciativeness, and maybe even a bit of closure. What I really was feeling was anxious; anxious to get my hands on Anna's letter.

I could have stayed in bed all day and let my imagination get the better of me, but I decided to change my typical habit, and I chose a better way to cope with my anticipation. I volunteered to work doubles at work for the next few days. I knew it wouldn't completely take my mind off the letter, but it would be a pretty good distraction.

I ended up telling Doug and Taylor about the phone call and the forthcoming letter, and they did their best to take my mind off things. In Doug's case, he took my mind off by lamenting the end of his relationship with Shannon. Personally, I think it was a simple case of Shannon realizing Doug wasn't *the one,* so she ended it before it got too serious. I wish I could have been that smart in my past.

Surprisingly, Doug took the breakup hard. It would be nearly three weeks before he completely got over Shannon. And by get over, yes, I mean get laid again. And yes, it would be a young blonde with a slamming ass and little fried eggs.

During my three open-to-close shifts, I did my best to play armchair shrink and offer Doug some possible reasons why Shannon might have broken up with him. As expected, he wanted nothing to do with my astute reasoning. He claimed (even to this day) that the breakup was simply due to "the curse of big melons."

The age-old theory of melons vs. fried eggs dominated our conversations for all three of my long shifts.
Nothing could have completely taken my mind off of the incoming letter, but Doug's theories came pretty damn close.

34

"PICTURES OF YOU" – The Cure

As I've probably mentioned before, Labor Day weekend pretty much marked the end of summer, and considering it was the last hurrah for most people, it was always an extremely busy weekend. The week leading up to Labor Day, however, was usually slow. College kids were already back in class, and even some of the grade schools had already started back.

My third double-shift in a row fell on the Wednesday before Labor Day. It was so slow that we ended up closing a couple hours earlier than normal. Doug wanted to go into Portsmouth for a bite to eat, and although I was starving, I was way too exhausted to go with him. Chicken-flavored Ramen noodles would have to do for me. All I wanted to do was go home, stretch out on the couch, and catch the end of the Sox game.

I pulled in my driveway, exited my car, and started to make

my way to my front door. About halfway there, I stopped and decided to check my mail. I assumed coming from Iowa, Anna's letter was still a day or two out, but I checked anyway.

Fully expecting a pile of bills and junk mail, I was surprised to find a 6 x 9 yellow envelope addressed from Iowa. I was excited and happy, yet there was this sick feeling in the pit of my stomach.

Hesitantly, I took the envelope out of the mailbox. It had some heft to it, which piqued my curiosity even more. I rushed inside and sat on my couch. Needless to say, Ramen noodles and the Sox game would have to wait.

I'm not quite sure, but I think a good five minutes passed by where I just sat staring at the envelope. Finally, I opened it. Upon quick inspection, there were two letters and a stack of photos. I decided on the letters first.

The first letter I read was from Mrs. Jensen. It was more like a short note than a letter. It read:

Josh,

Enclosed is the letter that Anna intended to send you. I also enclosed a bunch of pictures she treasured from her trip. I would have sent you all of them, but some "just spoke to me" and I needed to hold onto them.

Thanks again for showing my daughter such a wonderful time.

Mrs. Jensen

I set her note aside, took a deep breath then carefully opened Anna's letter.

Josh,

I figured a letter would be better than me stumbling over my words on the phone, and I wanted to take the time and say everything I needed to say. First of all, I need to apologize for leaving like I did. I feel horrible for that! I guess I just felt embarrassed about putting you on the spot with my big idea of moving there. It wasn't really fair to you for me to spring it on you like that. I'm sorry.

I guess looking back on it, you were right when you said people shouldn't make life-changing decisions while on vacation, and maybe I was rushing into things.

I'm not really sure if you still have strong feelings for Felicia or not. My heart tells me you don't, and that you were just caught off guard by my big idea. Either way, I completely understand. If you wanted to drop your whole life and move to Iowa, I'd probably be freaked out too.

But whatever the reasons were, PLEASE don't have any regrets about us – because I don't. Not at ALL. Those might have been the best two weeks of my life. Besides actually saying goodbye to you in person, I wouldn't change a thing.

I know how bitter and depressed you get when you give a piece of your heart to someone, only to see them "fade away." But please, Josh, don't get depressed about us - because the piece you gave me, I'll treasure forever! And I know this might sound cheesy, but I've never felt closer to someone in such a short time.

Also, you'll be happy to know that I rented and watched Field of Dreams the other night. It was really, really good! I'm still not sure I would drive half way across the country just to see the field though. Haha.

I truly hope we see each other again one day, but I do promise that I will call you soon. Like I said, I just needed my explanation to be in letter form first.

Take care and say hi to everyone for me.

Anna

PS: I really, really think you should sit down and write your screenplay again! Personally, I think the regret of NOT writing it will far outweigh the thought of writing it but not ever seeing it get made into a movie. And if it's too hard get it made into a movie, then maybe you can write it as a book. I would definitely read it!

PPS: Most of all, Josh, thank you for adding stars to my sky!!

I really can't explain it, and I know it doesn't really make sense, but my heart felt so empty, yet so full at the same time. The letter itself was emotional enough, but when I looked through the dozens of enclosed pictures, it took emotional to a whole new level. It was like I was looking at a complete montage of our two weeks together; from the first day I played tour guide, right through our amazing lighthouse trip up the coast of Maine.

Between continuously gazing at the pictures, and rereading her letter, I had no idea how long I sat on my couch that night. When I finally decided to go to bed, I carefully started to put the letter and the pictures back into the envelope. It was at that point, I noticed there was something else in the envelope. I reached my hand in and pulled out two shells. They were the same ones that old man Ugo's grandkids had given to Anna.

35

"HE DIDN'T" – The 6ths

For all intents and purposes, Labor Day weekend marked the end of the season for Hoohahs. Officially, though, we didn't close up for good that year until Columbus Day. That final month was pretty much relegated to just Fridays and Saturdays.

The tie dye twins had ended their tenure and were both back to school up at UVM. Dawn ended up getting a job at a daycare center, and Taylor landed another bartending job over at the Gaslight in Portsmouth. This left Doug and I to handle things on our own, which was fine, considering how slow it got at the beach.

In the future, Doug would build up a really good local following and would be able to stay open all year round, but as far as 1999 was concerned, we officially closed on October 10th.

During that final month, Pete and Michelle sightings were

few and far between. Not only were they still getting settled in their new house, but Pete had started back at his job full time. Between new house stuff, and his commute to Portland every day, and him doing the family thing, we rarely saw him.

Seeing as the crop of summer chicks had long since gone back to their real homes and lives, Doug was left with just the local, familiar York women to flirt with. So in other words, Doug was in the midst of a sexual drought. This forced him to up his daily "masturbatory sessions." His words not mine. One can only assume, without sex, he had set his sights on the "shot glass" challenge.

Overall, though, Doug's comments and behavior were pretty tame during that final month—normal even. As a matter of fact, there were times when he could be frighteningly normal… and profound… and dare I say, sweet? Our final night of the season was a prime example.

It was an extremely slow night and was only 11 PM when the final straggler left. Doug locked the door behind him and put up a *Closed for the Season* sign. By the time he made his way back to me, I had two celebratory beers sitting on the bar for us.

He killed most of the lights with the exception of the ones behind the bar. I turned the music down slightly and joined him up at the bar. It wasn't an upbeat mix, nor was it one of my Depression Sessions. It was "A Mellow Mix"… yes, there is a difference, slightly.

I raised my beer and said, "A toast – to the first full season of Here Hey Hoohahs! Congratulations, man."

He proudly smiled as we clinked beers.

"Thanks," he said. "So, what do ya think? Successful first summer?"

"Hell ya," I said. "Why, what do you think?"

Doug paused a moment then his smiled grew and he said, "I think we fuckin' killed it!"

With that, we toasted again. Doug slowly looked around at his bar… at his long-time dream. I could tell he was extremely proud and satisfied, and why wouldn't he be, he was living his passion.

"Hey, you do know I couldn't have done this without you?" he said, turning back to me.

I modestly brushed off his comment.

"No, I'm serious, Josh. I very much appreciate everything you've done, and I'm not gonna keep badgering you about it, but you do know there's always a place for you here. As a co-owner, I mean."

"I know. Thanks. I appreciate that. Maybe one day I'll take you up on it."

We spent the next few minutes drinking our beers in silence. As the song "He Didn't" by the 6ths came on, my thoughts turned to Anna. As the song played, my mind created a montage of our short, but wonderful time together; from our first encounter at this very bar, to the two amazing weeks that followed. There's a line in that song that says:

"And you'll dance with me – in the rain maybe
But we won't really mind & in the end we'll find
It was just a dance & our little romance
It'll fall to dust – but only just…
If you dance with me."

My thoughts went directly to the afternoon that Anna begged me to go run and dance in the rain with her. Fuck! Why couldn't I have just gone with her? Fuck!

My thoughts also turned to our final, regretful conversation in my car. Rather than take the time to say exactly what was on my mind with her, and rather than take the time to clear everything up right then and there, I chose to wait for a tomorrow that would never come.

Doug knew exactly where my thoughts were, and as the song faded out, he said, "I'm sorry. I know it was a hard summer for you."

I didn't reply. I slowly just nodded my head.

"She was a great girl. I'm glad you guys spent so much time together. It was nice to see you in a good mood for a change," he joked. "I'm just kidding. But she was good for you though."

Again, I nodded. He was right, she always had a way of turning my grey sky blue, even when I didn't want it to be. I was glad we spent all that time together as well, but as I sat there in the darkened bar, all I could think about was our last night.

"I never even got the chance to say goodbye to her," I said. "If I would have known that was gonna be our final conversation, I woulda told her how I really felt about her."

Out of his shirt pocket, Doug pulled out two cigars. He handed one to me, and without saying a word, he lit them both up. We took a few puffs, and as the smoke filled the air, Doug fixated on his beer bottle then slowly spoke.

"Do you remember when my grandfather passed away awhile back?"

I nodded.

"The doctors told us well in advance that his weeks and days were numbered. He only lived an hour away, but up until then, I only visited him a few times a year, tops. But the last couple months of his life, I went down and saw him every weekend."

"Yea, I remember," I said, quietly.

"I always started and ended every visit with 'I love you, Grampa.' As a matter of fact, the day he died, I had just told him I loved him less than two hours earlier. No regrets, right?"

Doug paused long enough to finish off his beer.

"After he passed away, I found myself lying awake at nights, and all I could think about were all the times I *didn't* say I love you... or all the times I *didn't* visit him for months on end."

At that point, Doug turned his attention directly to me.

"It doesn't matter what your last words are to someone... it's not the end that counts. It's everything in between. And in my opinion, you and Anna had a wonderful in between."

With that, Doug stood up and put out his cigar.

"I just wish she knew how I really felt about her," I said.

Doug grabbed our empties and proceeded to throw them away. He then walked over to me, put his hand on my shoulder and said, "If this dumbass saw how much you cared about her, I'm sure she did too."

Appropriately, those were the last words spoken that night.

36

A few days after we closed for the season, I woke up bright and early. Although, seeing as the sun was still an hour away from showing itself, I suppose it was more like dark and early. I climbed out of bed, got dressed, and then I headed outside to my car. If I wasn't fully awake already, the cold October air made sure I was. After I climbed into my car, I made my way up to the Nubble.

I was the only one up at the lighthouse, and due to the frigid early morning temperatures, I left my car and heat cranked on. As I sat there watching the Nubble's red light make its way around and around, I had the music turned down low (Depression Session #7).

When I was fully entranced by the Nubble's monotonous pattern and glow, my mind began to open up and thoughts just seemed to spill out. It had been nearly two months since

Anna's death, and although I still hadn't completely come to terms with it, I was in a better place. I was finally able to look back on our time together and smile.

Ever since I received Anna's letter, a day hadn't gone by without me rereading it at least once. It was ironic, the letter was born out of a regretful situation, yet it was one of the best letters I had ever received.

I thought a lot about the two weeks we had together—two measly weeks. I was reminded of something I said to Scott when he came to my apartment last month; about how it always seems that hellos come so easy and goodbyes too fast. I also thought about Scott's response, which was, "Maybe we should just be happy the hellos come at all."

The more I thought about his comment, the more it resonated with me. It went well beyond my short time with Anna. It was about everyone who had ever come in and out of my life. I needed to be done lamenting those who had left my life or simply faded away. I needed to embrace the fact that they entered in the first place. More importantly, I needed to embrace and appreciate what and who I had in the here and now.

It was at that point, my focus moved from the rotating red light of the Nubble, to the yellowish orange glow of the sunrise over the horizon. Maybe Anna was right, maybe this is the most beautiful place in the world. Anna was definitely right when she accused me of taking this all for granted. I think her exact words were *"desensitized, jaded, and just plain spoiled."*

True, true, and true!

I really am lucky to grow up in a place like this, and even more lucky to have such great friends. When I think about all the people who have passed through this beach and have passed through my life, I can't help but be overwhelmed with all the amazing memories.

Yes, there were a lot of sad and depressing memories as well, but the good far and away outnumbered them. I was *only* thirty years old, yet my sky was full of stars.

There's a line in *Field of Dreams* which states: "We just don't recognize the most significant moments of our lives while they're happening..."

Whether it's not recognizing significant moments or simply just taking them for granted, God knows I've been guilty of that myself... more than most maybe, but because of Anna Jensen, I try to recognize and appreciate them a lot more now.

It's also because of Anna that I (pretty much) got rid of that silly timetable in my head (the whole career, girlfriend, marriage, kids' timetable). I also tried to tone down my dramatic black cloud analogy. Shit like that should be reserved for people who actually have it bad in life.

It would take some time, but I knew my half-empty glass would one day fill up again, but no matter what my future holds, and no matter how many people come in and out of my life, there will always be a piece of Anna with me.

As far as my friends are concerned, it's inevitable that as time passes, we'll all lose contact a bit, but for now, I'm glad we're all so close. Unfortunately, Scott's reconnection was short-lived. He slowly faded out of our lives again. This time, however, it didn't bother me as much. I knew it wasn't personal. I guess his future path just didn't involve us, and while that kind of sucked, it was okay. I was just thankful that our paths had crossed for as long as they had.

As you can tell by reading this book, I took Anna's advice and started writing again. It had been eleven years since my first disastrous attempt at writing my screenplay. It had also been eleven years since I lit the piece of shit on fire.

Back then, all I knew was I wanted to write a movie about me and my friends growing up in York Beach. When I originally attempted to write this all those years ago, it lacked substance and direction, which is why I quit and lit the fucking thing on fire.

Back then, I chalked it up to – I sucked as a writer, and if I ever wanted to be a real writer, I couldn't just pick up a pen and write, I needed to go to school for that shit.

Looking back at it now, none of that was true. The real reasons my original story lacked substance and direction were simple: I was only nineteen fucking years old!

Note to self: if you want to write a story about you and your friends growing up, then maybe you should grow up first!

I didn't suck as a writer, and I didn't need to go to school for writing... I just needed some real life experiences first.

Anyway, I spent the winter of 1999 writing the screenplay, and when I finished, I read it. To my surprise, it didn't suck. Not at all. Since then, it has gone through many incarnations, and sadly, it also has gone through many failed attempts at getting financed and made for the big screen.

When all seemed lost, and just when I figured it would be collecting dust for the rest of my life, I remembered something else Anna had mentioned. She once said that even if it didn't get made into a movie, I could always turn it into a book.

Long story short, that screenplay I had started (and torched) way back in 1989, eventually became the novel you just read. Kind of cool how things work out, huh?

After I watched the sunrise that morning, I knew there was one more thing I needed to do. I reached in my back seat and grabbed a bouquet of flowers I had bought the day before. It contained all of Anna's favorite flowers, featuring the stargazer as its centerpiece.

I exited my car and slowly made my way down onto the rocks, and as the waves crashed below me, I carefully placed the flowers on a large rock; the large rock which Anna proclaimed as "her new favorite standing place."

Sometimes, it's not until you realize that nothing ever lasts for long, that you truly appreciate the fact that it ever existed at all.

The End... for now.

About The Author

Jody grew up in the Kittery/York area of southern Maine. He originally started out as a screenwriter. As of now, he has written nine feature-length screenplays ranging from dramas, to dramedies, to comedies. Not only did Jody grow up in Maine, but he makes it a point to utilize and represent his state as much as possible. From Maine's scenic rocky coast, to its remotely pristine backwoods, to its eclectic characters; all serve as backdrops and pay homage to his beloved state. His ultimate goal is not to just sell his scripts, but to have them filmed right here in the great state of Maine.

Unfortunately, searching for the proper financing has been a long, tiring, and at times, disheartening process. Feeling helpless in the whole "funding" process, Jody decided to reverse the typical Hollywood blueprint. That blueprint being: It's almost ALWAYS a novel that gets turned into a screenplay and not a screenplay which gets turned into a novel. Jody's thought process was simple: It's much easier to self-publish a book rather than self-finance a movie, and who knows, maybe, just maybe, this will be a screenplay that gets turned into a book only to eventually get turned back into a movie! But even if this wild idea never comes to fruition, at least by turning it into a novel, the *stories* themselves will be able to be enjoyed by the public. Whether it's two or two million people who buy his books, Jody is just happy that they are no longer collecting dust in a desk drawer.

Other books by Jody Clark

"The Empty Beach"
The Soundtrack to My Life Trilogy-Book One

"The Wild Irish Rose"

"Livin' on a Prayer – The Untold Tommy & Gina Story"

Available at

www.vacationlandbooks.com

I do most of my posting & promoting via my
Facebook profile

Feel free to friend me!!!

Jody Clark(vacationlandbooks)